TALES OF THE
FAR 遠西 WEST

TALES OF THE FAR WEST

遠
西

Tales of the Far West

Copyright © 2011 by Adamant Entertainment

Cover by: Rick Hershey and Gareth-Michael Skarka

ISBN-13: 978-1-937936-01-3

www.intothefarwest.com
www.adamantentertainment.com

Printed in U.S.A

TABLE OF CONTENTS

Introduction 7

He Built The Wall To Knock It Down 11
by Scott Lynch

In Stillness, Music 57
by Aaron Rosenberg

Riding The Thunderbird 73
by Chuck Wendig

Purity of Purpose 79
by Gareth-Michael Skarka

Paper Lotus 85
by Tessa Gratton

In The Name of the Empire 93
by Eddy Webb

Errant Eagles 115
by Will Hindmarch

Railroad Spikes 143
by Ari Marmell

The Fury Pact 159
by Matt Forbeck

Seven Holes 169
by T.S. Luikart

Local Legend 179
by Jason L. Blair

Crippled Avengers 193
by Dave Gross

INTRODUCTION
by Gareth-Michael Skarka

It was a long war, and hard-fought. The August Throne was in no hurry, however. The Secession Wars ended with the inevitability of a coming winter.

The new world was created. Peace and prosperity for all. For those who had lost everything in the war, there was no place for them. They headed West, to start new lives. For warriors, even those who had fought on the winning side, there was no place for them, either. Steeped in too much blood, and possessed of a skill and trade that was no longer desired, they also headed West.

Beyond the Periphery lies the Frontier. Settlements began to blossom. Yet even here the flower of civilization asked too much tending, and so men and women pushed further West.

Beyond the Frontier. Into the Far West.

The road to the Far West began five years ago, in May of 2007. That's when the idea settled in my head, and development began. The inspirations for Far West were, like many things, seemingly separate events which suddenly coalesced.

In the introduction added to the more recent printings of his Dark Tower series, Stephen King wrote something which really resonated for me:

> *"....I saw a film directed by Sergio Leone. It was called The Good, the Bad, and the Ugly, and before the film was even half over, I realized that what I wanted to write was a novel that contained Tolkien's sense of quest and magic, but set against Leone's almost absurdly majestic Western backdrop."*

That planted the seed. Fantasy, but instead of elves and dwarves in a mythic amalgam of Western European culture and history, one which was based upon the American myth — the West.

The seed grew. I've been an afficianado of the wuxia genre

for quite some time, and I've always been struck by the similarities between it and the American Western. Both are heroic genres, set in an mythologized idealization of a culture's past. At the core of both genres, in fact, lies a similar theme – a theme once spelled out for me in a delightful drunken evening at a convention hotel bar by friend and author. Kenneth Hite, who said that all of the best westerns can be summed up as follows:

Civilization must be protected from the Barbarians, and to do that, somebody has to pick up The Gun. However, if you pick up The Gun, you become a Barbarian.

The same theme is echoed in the tales of the wuxia. The wandering heroes were outsiders, who do not follow the rules of conventional Chinese society because of their focus on individuality and the use of force to resolve conflict. Their wandering lifestyle, and rootless existence was seen as a rejection of family and traditional values, and yet the virtues that the wandering heroes espoused (traditionally these eight: altruism, justice, individuality, loyalty, courage, truth, disregard for wealth and desire for glory) contained most of the values considered by the Chinese to be the signs of a superior person. So the heroes in wuxia are heroic, protecting civilization, but outside of it.

From there it was a short leap to combining the two. Not only were the themes similar, but the trappings were also often repeated in both genres: the wandering hero, the frontier location, the evil landowner, the downtrodden peasants, etc. I had my genre: The Wuxia Western Fantasy.

I decided to add elements of steampunk for one reason only: It's cool.

OK, OK, there's more to it than that. I wanted some element of the fantastic — the wuxia tales feature high-flying kung fu, but only a minority of the tales involve "magic", as fantasy fans would define it. The majority of 'magical' elements in wuxia stories are secret knowledge — alchemy, hidden techniques, etc. Far-fetched, to be sure, but within the realm of "science", as it was understood. Given the 19th-century vibe of the western, the best analog to that would be steampunk. Far-fetched, but within the realm of "science", rather than the truly magical, and in keeping with my personal belief that steampunk works best as a seasoning, rather than a main dish.

So I had my basic elements — the ingredients for my genre mash-up.

Over the next five years, the concept went through a number of iterations. It started as a tabletop role-playing game (RPG) — the pen-paper-and-dice variety, like *Dungeons & Dragons* — but I wanted more. Short stories were written... novels begun. But there was more that I wanted to include. A webseries was outlined; online video that could eventually be compiled and sold as a DVD. All the while, there was a dissatisfaction in having to nail down the epic setting and concept into just one thing.

Then I discovered the concept of transmedia storytelling. Simply put, transmedia is storytelling across multiple forms of media in order to have a wide array of entry points by which consumers can interact with a particular property, each of which add additional layers to the overall narrative, yet also stand alone.

...and that's when everything clicked. I would create the world of Far West and then provide a wide array of methods to explore that world. I assembled a development team and we set to work, and launched the Far West website (**http://www.intothefarwest.com**) in June of 2011, featuring fiction vignettes, development articles, art and discussion forums. After a record-setting crowdfunding campaign via Kickstarter, we prepared to release our first commercial efforts: The Far West Adventure Game (a tabletop RPG), and the fiction line -- which kicks off with this collection of short stories. Other expressions are currently in development, including mobile applications, music and more.

The authors featured herein are stalwarts of the science fiction, fantasy, horror and adventure genres; best-sellers and award winners. More importantly, they are friends and colleagues, and I thank them for jumping into our sandbox to play.

Welcome to our place. Keep your boots off the table and your weapons holstered, if ya please. We run a respectable joint.

Gareth-Michael Skarka
Lawrence, Kansas
Lunar New Year 2012
Year of the Water Dragon

HE BUILT THE WALL TO KNOCK IT DOWN
by Scott Lynch

1

He called himself False Note. It wasn't his real name. Hell, it wasn't even his real fake name.

He was old but unbent and his sins hung on him like bark on a tree. That was my impression the first time I ever saw him, keeping his own company in the darkest corner of Tychus Sload's Lucky Sky Diamond Diversion Parlor. He looked like a man waiting for a funeral to break out, or a man who'd make one if it didn't get there in good time.

I knew the dust on his boots wasn't working-day dust or wasting-time dust like mine. That dust he trailed was old bad news stretching back across leagues, years, and lives.

At a glance, my eyes saw clear. Trouble was, I was twenty-two, and those eyes weren't fastened to anything worth writing home about. If I'd had brains enough to fill a rattlesnakes's ball-sack I'd have spun on my heel and gone anywhere else that night, anywhere a man like that wasn't waiting for something.

But I was twenty-two, invincible in my own stupidity, and I was at the frayed end of a bad employment situation in a nowhere-town that had never seen any good ones. Ain't That Something, they called it, because the gods need places to point at and laugh.

Ain't That Something had been hitched to a silver mine but the vein was thinner than a whore's rouge, and when it ran dry the crowds and money waiting past the eastern horizon elected to stay over the horizon. Ten days' ride north of the Bloodiron, up into the shadow of the Eagles' Claws, Ain't That Something was a dry misfire of a town and I got a hell of big surprise when I showed up aiming to make my fortune.

Sload's Lucky Sky Diamond had the same problem. Lavishly built in expectation of great things, what it got instead was us, night after night, the dregs too damned stubborn to give it up or too short-sighted to save our gambling money for the long haul back to anywhere.

We crept from sober to drunk under the yellow light of oil lamps hanging from brass sculptures of tigers and dragons. Their haunches were spread to receive copper wire that would never be laid; their mouths gaped for glass bulbs that would never be shipped within a hundred leagues of that place. We drank Sload's worst until the images on the cards swam like hot desert air, then we went to our beds on all fours. You could have gathered up the sum total of our wit and good fellowship in a thimble.

There were six of us worth mentioning that night. Tychus Sload was a given, a snuffed candle of a man, a Seccesh war veteran who'd saved thirty years to build his dream then sunk it by building where he did. At the table with me was Jozan Shung, swollen like a toad, who carried a sawed-down coach gun and called himself Scattergun. When he got tight he acted like the rest of us did, too.

Hot Molly had what you might call a rugged natural geography and a limited acquaintance with bathing. Her temper named her. There was no place in the civilized east for a blacksmith, even a skilled one, who'd put a client's head between hammer and anvil for late payment. Now she hunted work town by town on the frontier, where murder was less disqualifying in most trades.

Next to Molly was Timepiece, formerly the discount sort of bad man who'd thumped indentured workers for one Chartered House or another until he'd been aged and beaten out of the game. His left arm was ten years gone. He had a colorful story about some admirably-endowed bandit queen with a hatchet, but when Timepiece moved just right I could spot the scars of grep fangs on his shoulder and collarbone. His replacement arm was rusty steam-cobbler piecework, hacked up from old farm tools and busted Drudges. He loved the name Timepiece, and thought it was because he set the pace for the sad circle of bummers around him. Actually it was because his godsdamned arm made more noise than a box full of wind-up clocks.

So there was Jozan, Hot Molly, Timepiece, and your dutiful scrivener, all sitting at a table just past midnight, while Tychus Sload listlessly polished glasses that had never been used and that stranger, that waiting stranger, drank his tea in an island of shadow between the jaundice-colored lights.

"Heavens," said Timepiece, his voice as grit-clogged as the gears of his arm. "Why heavens, just look at this hand. I swear if these cards had tits I'd marry 'em."

He set his cards down paint up, and the rest of us were done in. As he'd promised, it was a marriageable spread. His fourth or fifth in an hour. Still, he laughed like he'd done something clever and his arm went *whirr-click, whirr-scree, whirr-click* as it swept the little pile of clipped silvers toward him.

So went the game, most nights. Timepiece had two nested machines bolted into that godsdamned arm, and one was a pointlessly complex channel-fed card-sorting mechanism that was noisier than the rest of the affair put together. He was hellfire proud of it, even spent hours fussing over it with oil and jeweler's tongs. If he'd loved the rest of his arm half as much it would have been a museum piece. Anyhow, it was no secret that when he used that thing to deal a hand it tended to miraculously come out in his favor. We pretended not to notice. He'd cheat us, we'd cheat back in turn, and when stumbling-off time came we'd all be back to equilibrium, losers together, less the price of our drinks.

That was most nights. The night I met False Note, I got wound up and sent the game right off a cliff.

I'd love to blame it on that quiet stranger, waiting for whatever wind he thought was going to blow, but that's not even a near-truth. I was drunk in the deadliest way, deep enough to be prickly but not deep enough to be numb and slow. I was in a bad humor, too, dwelling on the idiocy of my situation, grudging Timepiece those precious silver bits he scraped up even though I knew I'd probably chisel them back just as soon as he quit dealing.

"Hell, Timepiece, you're already married to the secret of your success." I took a long slow swallow of whatever Sload was passing off on us that night (lead sugar, vinegar, grep piss— gods knew) and it didn't make me any smarter. "After all, ain't like that arm of yours can get up and walk away whenever it wants to."

That opened a hole in the conversation. Timepiece had gathered the cards and now he slotted them into his arm mechanism in groups of five or six, slowly and deliberately like a man feeding shells to a carbine. The ominous silence stretched and his bloodshot eyes were on me all the while.

"You got any inclination to clarify that remark?" he said at last, too softly.

"If you're gonna keep that thing rigged up to four-flush us, don't you think you ought to have the courtesy to vary the miracle every now and then? Maiden's Tits, it's more regular than the sun and the moons!"

With that, I broke the magic for good. When you're sitting at a table like that, you can call one another scoundrels, murderers, grep thieves, ingrates, and fancy dancers of the cheapest persuasion. You can joke about being crooked as a general and constant state of affairs. But what you can't do, what you can't *ever* do, is accuse someone of cheating right then and there. Not unless you're ready to play for blood.

Click. Timepiece shoved the last bunch of cards into his dealing mechanism. *Sha-chock.* The arm primed itself for the next deal. Timepiece still hadn't taken his eyes off me. Hot Molly and Jozan

Shung were giving me the stink-eye, too. They weren't real tight with Timepiece, but they were sure tighter with him than with me. Somewhere behind the booze and bitterness my better judgment was waking up. Too late.

"Why, I do believe that touches on my honor, you skinny little serpent-tongued son of a bitch," said Timepiece. Now he sounded downright jovial, but there was no mistaking what burned behind his eyes.

He reached out with his metal arm and took my just-emptied glass in its misshapen hand. Gears ground, pistons popped, and tinkling fragments rained on the table.

"How's that for a new trick?" He got up slowly, like some range beast rearing up to make a show in front of its den, which I suppose is exactly what he was. His smile was wide and full of piss-yellow teeth. "You wanna see some fresh miracles out of this arm, you just step right outside and I'll accommodate your godsdamned curiosity."

"Well, uh, maybe I was a little hasty, Timepiece." A little! Maybe water was a little wet and the sun was a little in the sky. My bad weeks in Ain't That Something had made me careless. I'd fancied myself hard and ready for the world, but I had no arts for hurting folks, not even to stack up against cast-offs like Timepiece, Molly, and Jozan, and that realization was coming on awfully fast.

"Yeah, take it easy, Timepiece," said Sload. I don't know if it was the threat to my tender young self or the busted glass that got his attention. Probably the glass.

"He called me a cheat!" said Timepiece.

"He did not," said the stranger.

It was like the shadows had decided to talk, or one of the sculptures. I mean, I'd guessed the stranger must have a voice of some sort. Hard to explain the tea otherwise. But he'd been wordless for so long, watching us, that he'd faded into the background for me. Timepiece seemed equally surprised at the man's decision to quit making like wallpaper.

"Now that's a *novel* interpretation of recent events." Timepiece turned his back on me to address the mystery man. I should've been insulted, but it was a pretty fair assessment of the threat I posed.

"Cheating's a marginal sin," said the stranger, rising casually to his feet. All my first impressions of him came rushing back as he stepped into the light. That brown face had seen some weather, all right. That long hair was the color of a raven that had flown through falling ash. "He accused you of being artless. And that's. . . much worse."

"Mister, this ain't your game, but you just dealt yourself in." Timepiece lost his feigned joviality. Now his voice and his body matched what I'd seen in his eyes.

I mentioned that Timepiece had a second device nested in his arm, beside the card-game-ruining mechanism. This was a spring-loaded compartment clutch for a short-barreled revolver with cracked ivory grips. A whore's gun, basically, but nothing bigger could hide in his forearm. Automata squealed and spat that gun into Timepiece's flesh-and-blood hand. He held it up to catch the sickly yellow light.

"Oh, come on now, Timepiece," said Sload. "There's no need for that!"

"Shut it." Timepiece twirled his sad little shooter languorously and didn't take his eyes off the stranger. "See, someone makes noise about my honor, I'll make noise of my own. But I'll go all the way. *All the way,* get it?"

"If you had any notion of honor," said the stranger, his voice cold, "you'd carry a good piece, and you wouldn't keep it in a metal purse, and you wouldn't pull it just to make yourself forget how small you are."

Almighty gods. I thought I'd had everyone's attention when I mouthed off to Timepiece. Jozan and Molly were clutching the table, they were so excited. Tychus Sload had a look on his face like he was about to shit twenty pounds of hot bricks.

"Show us your iron, you clown!" shouted Timepiece.

The stranger flicked the lapels of his wind-worn duster open just enough to show what he was carrying— a plain leather belt above his slim-hipped jeans. Not a holster in sight.

"I think you're gonna be awfully surprised if you figure you can hide behind that fact that you ain't running heeled," said Timepiece.

"I think your opinions are as worthless as your honor," said the stranger.

Timepiece's gun came up. It was dead center on the stranger's chest from six feet away.

"Mister, you ain't drunk and you're provoking me awful fierce. So I tell you now, I swear to the gods, you find a gun or you borrow one, or I'll put you down like a dog right here on Sload's floor!"

"You are provoked," said the stranger. "I invite you to do something about it."

"Mister, arm your damn self *right now*." Timepiece was steady, I'll give him that. He moved his thumb, and two pregnant sounds echoed across the diversion parlor. Half cock. Full cock. "I AIN'T KIDDING!"

"I don't need any other weapon." The stranger hooked his thumbs in his duster pockets and rolled his shoulders, making a soft crackling noise. "The one you're holding will be entirely sufficient."

Three seconds went by like three years. Timepiece's gun hand was still steady, but I could see the rest of him, and he was heaving. Disbelieving. One angry breath. Two angry breaths.

Three. There was a sound like rope snapping taut, then the room shook to the thunder-crash of that little gun.

If nobody's ever let off a shot nearby while you're under a roof, let me assure you, your ears will ring like they've been boxed. My jaw went wide open with the pain of it, and it took me a moment or two to piece together what I'd seen.

The encounter had not concluded to Timepiece's advantage.

That snapping sound had been his right wrist. When his brain had told his finger to pull the trigger, he'd been looking down the barrel at the stranger's chest. By the time his finger got the message, the stranger had somehow moved and forcibly reversed Timepiece's gun hand. One hundred and eighty degrees, honorable reader, then thunderclap. Right in the heart.

Timepiece spun as he fell backward. His metal arm slammed down hard, scattering clipped silver pieces, and anchored him there grotesquely as though he'd been frozen in the act of crawling up onto the table. As the smell of gunsmoke wafted past me, Timepiece's arm went into death-jitters and started spitting up cards.

Snick, snick, snick, snick, snick went the dead man's last deal, into the stunned silence. The stranger stood there holding Timepiece's ivory-handled gun, almost disdainfully, while *snick snick, snick*, the cards shot out into a meaningless pile in front of me.

Molly made the first move after that. Her temper, I guess. She had a belt-buckle gun that weighed half a pound and was chambered to heave real metal, a pair of coin-sized shells. She'd shown it off once or twice, and it had scared me then. It scared me even worse now that she tore it out and banged off a shot at the stranger.

Again, double-thunderclaps, double flashes like lightning. I heard the sharp bangs and then a strange underwater sort of echo. My ears weren't pleased at all.

Molly and the stranger had fired at one another across a space of seven feet. There was hardly any way to miss, and yet Molly hadn't quite hit.

There in front of me, rolling around and smoking atop the pile of cards, was a little gray object like two metal mushrooms slammed together. Two bullets tip to tip.

Molly hadn't quite hit. The stranger definitely hadn't missed.

That right there would have been enough for most folks. Enough to know they were up against some hard old kung fu straight off the Dust Road. Mysteries that ordinary folk ought to step aside for, if not take to their heels outright. Yet by the same token, this stranger was an opportunity. For deadbeats like Timepiece and Molly and Jozan, when they hunker down in a place like Ain't That Something it means they're as far from glory as the living can get. But if you could throw down with someone who had the real art, if you could win a wild fight, well, maybe you could crawl back on the path to making your name a Name.

That's why Molly saw the evidence and unloaded her second shot anyway.

Flash-and-thunder, flash-and-thunder. Something hot stung the top of my hand and at last the petrification of my wits came to an end. I flinched away from the table, staring down at the red welt where the second lump of fused bullets had landed just behind my right knuckles.

The stranger must have figured he'd made his point. His next shot knocked Molly out of her chair with a dark red hole above her left breast.

That brought Jozan to his feet, as fast as Jozan had ever moved in the time I'd known him. While I scrambled for the nearest wall, he drunkenly swung up that hand-me-down carriage gun of his.

"I'd love to see you try and knock down a cloud of buckshot, old man!" Jozan hollered. I could make out the words, but everything sounded flat and wrong, with a steady ringing behind it.

"That's exactly why I won't," said the stranger.

"They call me Scattergun Shung!"

"Nobody calls you that," said the stranger, gently, "except when you're alone in front of a mirror."

Jozan opened his mouth to say something else and the stranger fired from the hip. Jozan's would-be retort was transmuted to a scream, and when he held up his right hand I saw that the stranger had taken off his trigger finger, right down to the bottom knuckle. Neat as any sawbones and a fair sight faster.

The stranger folded his arms and waited.

Jozan shuddered, sobbed, and then awkwardly shifted his carriage gun, cradling it with his blood-streaming right hand while he reached for the triggers with his left.

"You can lead a horse to water," sighed the stranger. His final shot gave Jozan the dubious honor of a third eye, directly between the other two. A heavy heap of surprised dead man hit Tychus Sload's formerly clean floor.

The air smelled like whiskey, blood, and brimstone. Clouds of gray smoke drifted up over the card table and got lost in the dark corners of the room. The stranger tossed Timepiece's empty pistol down beside its owner, then turned toward the door.

"Hells and ancestors," I whispered. I was still drunk, and I was struck pretty dumb by what had just happened. Again, I'd like to blame what came next on all that, and on the stranger. But I did what I did for the same reason Molly and Jozan had thrown their lives away. That stranger and his mysteries were the only ticket out of Ain't That Something the gods seemed likely to punch.

"Take me with you," I hissed.

The stranger stopped, and without turning around he said: "The hell would I do that for?"

"Teach me."

"Walk east long enough and I'm sure you'll find an Imperial grammar academy."

"Sir, I've got nothing holding me here," I said. "I've got nothing holding me anywhere. I don't know how to fight and I don't know how to shoot, but you saved my life and I'll follow you anywhere you want me to."

Now he turned. His eyes were like the holes in the night sky where there aren't any stars. I felt about ten years old and three feet high.

"What arts do you have?" he said.

"Well, I'm, uh. . . a scrivener, of sorts. When there was supposed to be a silver mine here, that meant business offices and contracts and mail—"

His soft laughter shut me up.

"There's no contracts and no mail on the Dust Road, boy."

"Then I guess I'll quit being a scrivener. Teach me."

He stared at me. I felt steel-plated fear gathering in my guts. The last three people who'd annoyed him hadn't even been dead for three minutes.

"Timepiece," he said, pointing at the previous owner of that name. His finger tracked across the bodies. "Hot Molly. One-Finger Shung. You got a toy name I ought to know about?"

"Uh, no sir. I'm. . . Andus Cadwallader. I never did anything to, uh, get a more colorful one. And I didn't use my real name much. . . I mean, who's gonna respect an Andus Cadwallader in a place like this?"

"If no one respects Andus Cadwallader," he said, "it's because *you* don't respect Andus Cadwallader."

I didn't know what to say to that. I bowed my head like a damned little kid.

"If you're coming with me," he said after a long silence, "I'll call you Stray. You'll be Stray until you grow into something else. . . maybe even Andus Cadwallader."

"What do I. . . what do I call you, master?"

I let that word out without thinking about it, and he didn't correct me.

"If you have to call me anything, you might as well call me False Note."

A fresh metallic sound echoed across the main room of the Lucky Sky Diamond. Tychus Sload was still behind the bar, but he was fixing to rejoin the conversation, this time over the barrels of his own shotgun. Both hammers were cocked.

"Now you just hold it there," he said. All the blood had gone right out of his face. "Maybe that was self-defense, mister. Maybe you ain't done nothing wrong. But there's. . . there's gonna be questions. We gotta get the sheriff in here. And you gotta stay."

The sheriff! Sure, Ain't That Something had a fellow with a badge and a gun. The gun was hung on a wall, the badge was pinned to three hundred pounds of pickled lard. If the sheriff kept his usual habits, he'd be awake to ask questions around the middle of the next afternoon.

"Conversation with your sheriff is no enticement," said False Note. "And neither is your tea, I'm afraid."

"Then you'll just have to be enticed by my shotgun."

False Note didn't have to say anything. The look on his face conveyed the profoundest sort of disappointment.

"Don't get cute," said Sload. "That was fancy work with them drunks at kissing distance. I'm thirty feet away and you ain't armed."

"That's true," said False Note. "I'm not armed. At the moment."

I saw the workings of Sload's throat bulge and bob as he tried to dry-swallow his fear. The gun wavered.

"Last call, barkeep." False Note again hooked his thumbs into the pockets of his duster, again rolled his shoulders. "Someone's getting paid to dig three graves tomorrow. Work's so thin around here, you think they'd miss you if I made it four?"

The gun went down, and then it went back beneath the counter, and that's why Tychus Sload lived long enough to leave this story on his own terms.

False Note nodded, then turned back to me. "I've got someone on my backtrail, Stray. Maybe coming faster now if they get wind of this. You still want to come with?"

"I said I'd follow you anywhere, Master False Note."

"You don't know a godsdamned thing," he said. It was next to a whisper. But he didn't tell me to go away.

"Should I maybe gather up these guns, master?" I said. "You might want to be armed if you've got. . . well, trouble following."

"Oh, I've got a gun. Packed away. I'm not quite ready to wear it yet." He smiled. "As for these unworthy things, leave them. If the need arises, I'll find someone else to take one from."

Master False Note turned and went out into the night. Those were his last words for some time. I followed, unsteady on my feet. It took three days for that ringing in my ears to go away.

2

The gods sent rain to chase us out of Ain't That Something, gray tumbling lines of it that might have been cold when they left the high country but came down warm as horse lather.

False Note, as indifferent to weather as he was to shots fired in anger, rode out on a fine horse accustomed to his voice and habits. I had Hot Molly's four-legged disaster. I named her Hand-Me-Down, but she answered just as well to long strings of random blasphemies. We headed south, keeping our distance from the hacked-out wagon road but moving parallel to it.

Now, I was no stranger to riding moderately hard and sleeping rough. I'd been away from the comforts of actual civilization long enough to grow some calluses on my delicacy. Still, my elation at escaping from my exile was soon as damp and saddle-sore as the rest of me, and False Note, while cordial in his cool fashion, was in no hurry to unravel the mysteries of his history, plans, or destination.

"Were you a Ranger?" I asked one night as we made our camp during a pause in the rain. After a long silence, I added: "It's just that... the things I hear they do with guns, well, one might assume—"

"Stray," he said, "are you ready to take some instruction?"

"Oh, I. . . well, of course!"

"Make a fire."

We'd been out for four or five nights, and it was the first time he'd permitted light after sunset. After much prayer and furious fussing, I eventually conjured a weak, flickering smoker. From his gear, False Note brought forth a lacquered wooden box, secured on three sides with brass clasps.

When he opened it, I saw that half the padded interior was lined with cylinders and the other half with an assortment of paper envelopes. "Cartridges," he said, one finger hovering over the cylinders. He moved it to the other side of the box and said, "Tea."

I nodded.

"On the trail you might be wet. Your clothes might be wet. Horses might be wet. Water might be falling so heavy it's leaking through your eyeballs and filling your skull. But *these* you keep dry." He shut the box again and snapped all of its clasps tight. "If you can't keep the cartridges dry, you won't live. And if you can't keep the tea dry, why would you *want* to?"

He stowed the box, and when he returned he said: "Now, we'll discuss how to boil water properly."

My tutelage had begun. In the preparation of tea.

Four more days we headed south. The rains passed and each night we camped beneath the silver light of Wolf and Rabbit. Each night I discovered just how much consideration one man could give to the subject of leaves steeped in boiling water.

"This is Jononzal Resplendent Thorn," said Master False Note, waving one of his paper packets at me. "Smell that faintest hint of dragon cactus? When you smell that, Stray, you'll know you must dash it in cool water and let it sit for at least a quarter of an hour before you place it in the—"

"Master False Note," I snapped at last, "begging your pardon, I like tea as much as the next man, and you do make a fine cup, but this is all it's been for night after night now. Tea. Sifting, boiling, serving. Smelling, tasting. Over and over again! How can I be of *use* to you like this?"

"I'm a scant fraction of a man when tea and I don't keep our usual appointments."

"That wasn't tea you were serving in the Lucky Sky Diamond!"

"Ah." False Note returned the Jononzal Resplendent Thorn to his box and I swear I felt his disappointment like a physical weight. "You look at kung fu and you only see results."

"Results? What else am I meant to see?"

He said nothing, and by the way he said it I deduced that I was expected to fill the silence.

"I see results like me not being dead at Timepiece's hand!"

"That bravo with the ridiculous arm wasn't defeated a week ago," said False Note. "He was beaten before you were born, Stray. Nor was he defeated by the way I handle a weapon. He was beaten by the way I select tea. By the way I brew it. The way I wake up and go to sleep. The way I choose a horse and sit its back. The way I look at the sky."

"But—"

"I'm speaking of the pursuit of excellence in all things. *All things!* Presence of mind and devotion to craft. A great artist has these. A great chef. A great master of tea. There's powerful kung fu in a well-built house or an eloquent letter, but the limit of your imagination is bones breaking and bullets flying. Why do you believe I interfered with that business in Sload's parlor?"

I hemmed and hawed and made nervous circles in the dirt with my bootheels. At last shame, which I possessed in more abundance than sense, drove me to swallow my modesty and reply. How could I follow this man into the middle of nowhere, relying on him for all things, if I wasn't willing to be honest with him?

"I assumed," I said, "that I'd done something brave."

"I thought as much." False Note smiled thinly. "Bravery is cheap. Bravery is common. Bravery is what's put just about every man or woman I've ever killed in the way of my guns.

"Timepiece offended you, Stray. But it wasn't merely because he was cheating you. That would have been an animal reaction, howling senselessly because something had taken your food. For that I would have sat quietly and let you die. Instead, you were offended because your opponent was *boring*. Now, that was a human reaction. A perceptive reaction. Only the perceptive student can be taught anything meaningful."

He handed me his box of tea and cartridges. "Count six shells and pass them over," he said. By the time I'd done so, he'd rummaged in his gear and produced a clean, sturdy-looking revolver. He flipped the loading gate, and the motions of his fingers were almost hypnotically smooth as he rotated the cylinder and slid the cartridges home. When finished he thumbed the hammer back and held the weapon out to me, barrel downward.

I took it gingerly, keeping my fingers well away from the trigger. I hadn't often handled guns, but I resolved not to flinch.

"Now," said False Note. "Point it directly at me. Place your finger on the trigger. Apply the required pressure."

I gulped. So much for resolving not to flinch!

"Master," I said, "Before I do that, I just want you to assure me that—"

"Your life is in immediate danger," he said, the same way most folks would mention the weather. "I'm counting to a certain number in my head. If I reach it before you pull that trigger, I'll be leaving this place alone and I'll sell that barely adequate horse of yours in the next town."

Even by invitation, even under such a threat, even knowing that he had all his arts and an obvious lesson up his godsdamned sleeves, honorable reader, I assure you that pulling the trigger was the hardest thing I've ever done, drunk or sober.

But I believed him. I pulled.

The hammer fell with a snap-click that echoed across our little camp. That, and nothing more. I stared at the gun like an idiot.

False Note held up a single cartridge. I groaned.

"You watched me load, but you didn't see me load five," he said. "I handed you a hammer over an empty chamber, but you didn't even check." The gun vanished from my hand; it felt like a breeze blowing past my wrist, and between blinks the revolver was his again. "Presence of mind. Do you begin to see what I mean? How can you expect *results* if you can't demand excellence from yourself in all the simpler matters?"

"I'm sorry, Master False Note."

"Why are you apologizing to me?" He unloaded the gun. "You're the one living his life half-awake."

False Note finished unloading, and while he stowed the pistol back in his gear, I carefully re-seated the shells inside the wooden box. Neither of us spoke for a few minutes. I sulked while staring into the fire, and he was gracious enough to let me.

"I'll do better," I said at last. "And it isn't like the horse is my fault, master."

"Get some sleep, Stray." I think one corner of his mouth might have crept upward just a fraction of a hair's width. "We'll resume your instruction tomorrow evening. With Jononzal Resplendent Thorn."

3

The gods had other plans.

All memory of rain was banished by the next afternoon. A sun hotter than spent brass ruled a cloudless sky from horizon to horizon. We negotiated a tricky slope or two and threaded our way down into a long canyon, running north-south, that False Note said would open up again within shouting distance of the Bloodiron River.

I first spotted the stranger at about half a mile, through gently rippling whorls of heated air and dust. All I saw at first was a large dark mass, but as our mounts slow-trotted down the canyon the shape gradually resolved into a man lounging on a rock in front of a horse.

I licked my chapped lips nervously. Without the distraction of a gun in my hand my wits were sharp again, and this fellow fairly glowed with the self-confidence of someone used to handing out more trouble than he received. His presence in False Note's direct path was not auspicious.

He was a Castalan, born brown and weathered browner, not quite as dark as your dutiful narrator but at that moment much better dressed. He was a dandy, yet there seemed nothing impractical about his elegance. His open coat flared in the back but was cut well clear of the holsters at his belt. His conical bamboo hat trailed expensive black silk ribbons, but the chin strap was cinched tight for action rather than comfort. Sunlight flashed on his boots, shod heel and toe with silver, and on his pistols, which had polished grips of the same.

"Hail, strangers!" He spoke with good cheer, and as we neared I could see that he was doing something to a length of rope coiled beside him. "You fixed for the Bloodiron?"

"That's the idea," said False Note.

"Well, this might not be the right canyon for it."

I was close enough now to see that the stranger was deftly tying a row of fat round knots into one end of his rope, cinched tight together like the segments of a rattlesnake's tail.

"Unless the gods moved the Bloodiron while my back was turned," said False Note, "I must respectfully disagree."

"Oh, the river's there. This canyon just might not be the one to bring you to it." The stranger, finished with his knots, stood up. "I suppose it depends. You wouldn't by any chance be a... music lover, now would you?"

A hot breeze stirred the dust between the stranger and False Note, who reined in his horse and peered down at the man from a distance of ten yards.

"I don't think you'd appreciate the sort of tune I play," said False Note.

"Hell, I'm broad-minded." The stranger spun his coil of rope lazily in one hand. "I dance to anything, and I dance with all comers. Silverheels, they call me."

I whistled softly. My readers will no doubt recognize the name of the bounty tracker who allegedly followed the Ghost Heart Brotherhood from Desilvair to the Dreaming Desert, and as a matter of record correctly deduced, in one night, which of the five hundred prize greps of General Ten Fists' herd had swallowed the general's signet ring. To have such a one chasing us! But of course I was as inconsequential to him as a spare handkerchief in False Note's pocket.

"I happened to ride into Ain't That Something two days after a peculiar and memorable event," said Silverheels. "However, I didn't expect to overtake the very architect of that affair north of the river. Frankly, that kid's horse has slowed you up."

I ground my teeth together and jerked Hand-Me-Down to a halt behind False Note's horse.

"You do know who's coming after you?" said Silverheels.

"I do," said False Note. "Though I would be very surprised if she sent you."

"Of course she didn't." Silverheels' grin showed just about all of his teeth. "Her interest in you is what you might call deeply... philosophical. Mine's strictly financial."

"You mean to sell me to her," said False Note.

"She was ready to hire me to help track you. I figure she'll pay a hell of a lot more when I have actual possession."

"When?" said False Note.

"Oh, indeed. When." Silverheels grinned again. "After all, I ain't no diversion parlor deadbeat."

He clicked his heels together, bowed slightly, then shook a lasso loop out of his rope and began twirling it, politely waiting for False Note to get down from his horse. My master did this with a sigh. Dirt crunched under his boots, and there Silverheels' forbearance ended.

The lasso flicked out faster than a scorpion's tail. False Note bent like a reed, faster still, and the lariat cracked against empty air. The other horses took this as a matter of course, but Hand-Me-Down whinnied and bucked, and it was all I could do to stay in the saddle.

Silverheels pressed False Note, his rope hissing and snapping like a bullwhip, one hand working the lasso and one hand working the heavily-knotted tail. This exploded out, again and again, blasting clouds of dust into the air as False Note leapt and whirled, staying untouched.

I could tell False Note was impressed by the fact that he made a play for his saddlebags, where his weapons were stowed. Silverheels let the knotted end of his rope pendulum toward himself, then kicked it straight and hard into False Note's horse's rump. The horse bolted and galloped off, and False Note had to tuck and roll as those menacing rope ends once again swooped and howled around him like the blades of an out-of-control windmill.

I got Hand-Me-Down settled, then realized that I ought to do something other than gape. Armed only with this vague sense of obligation, I started to swing myself out of the saddle. All this achieved was to remind Silverheels that I existed. The knotted end of his rope shot out again, but this time it smacked into Hand-Me-Down's head with a noise like a mallet hitting a flour sack. My damned horse turned into several hundred pounds of taffy under me. Then, just as suddenly, I was in the air.

Silverheels' lasso had me, tight as an iron band, pinning my arms to my side. The world became a roaring, rushing blur— I had disjointed impressions of bright sky, brown rock, and a fluid dark shape that had to be False Note. Whooping and laughing, Silverheels used me as a weighted flail in his efforts to knock my master senseless. The only person going senseless was me, however. With each whirl an invisible hand squeezed the insides of my head tighter and tighter, and red-black shadows blotted out the corners of my vision.

The earth came out of nowhere and landed directly on my face. Then darkness, then silence.

Then dust up my nose.

I came to coughing and sputtering, sitting in a me-shaped furrow in the dirt. I hadn't been out for long; Silverheels' lasso was still cinched tight around me but the line was slack. My master had taken the rope at a point between myself and the bounty hunter, and now something like a tug-of-war was going on. Twelve feet of rope, straight and hard as an iron bar, linked the two fighters as they shuffled and strained for leverage. Silverheels smiled through it all, plainly exhilarated, while False Note glared sternly, as though the Castalan was just another student failing to grasp his lessons.

Arm-length by arm-length, step by step, the men closed the distance between them. Eight feet, six feet, four feet. At last, with a noise like an old tree cracking in half, the rope snapped. A fountain of dust exploded. False Note and Silverheels rebounded apart, flung like sling stones.

Even the bounty hunter's horse took that as a sign to back off. I stumbled up and lurched out of the way as it pounded through the spot where I'd been sitting.

"Here, kid," said Silverheels, who was back on his feet. "See the Dust Road up close." One boot flashed in a silver arc. From the forward point of his kick a cloud of dust rose like a man-sized wave and rushed toward me. It hit with a curiously liquid but irresistible pressure, and once again I was down on my backside, coughing and stunned.

"Let me sketch a few pictures in the dirt for you too, old man," said Silverheels. "Lean Wolf! Sated Wolf! Rushing Rabbit!"

As he spoke he kicked the canyon floor. From the first kick the dust rose in a sharp crescent, like a new moon. From the second it rose in an enveloping globe, a full moon. From the third it became a smaller, tighter-knit sphere. Each of these dust constructs bore down on False Note with the speed of a charging horse.

My master swept his wide-brimmed hat from his head and wielded it as though swishing away flies. With three blindingly fast swats he knocked the dirt constructs apart. While the dust was still settling harmlessly in front of him, he plucked a heavy stone from the ground, dropped it into his upturned hat, then let it fly toward Silverheels like a discus.

"If astronomy's your pleasure," said False Note, "let me show you some stars."

The whirling hat struck the bounty hunter just above his left ear, cutting the strap of his conical hat and knocking it away. Silverheels took a tumble. No longer grinning, he sat up and frantically fumbled for his pistols with hands that had temporarily lost their cleverness. Alas for him, by the time he found his holsters they were empty. False Note stood over him calmly, the former contents of those holsters in his hands.

"Looks as though I submit," said Silverheels, spreading the fingers of his empty hands. A dark red line trickled down the side of his face.

"Stray, you all right?" said False Note. He thumbed back the hammer on one of the pistols, and Silverheels winced.

"I suppose I'm honored just to have a role in the proceedings this time around, master." I finally loosened the lasso and shrugged myself out of it. Dust puffed from the creases of my clothes, and I sneezed.

"The boy's fine," said Silverheels. "I wouldn't have hurt him none. Not permanent."

"That's right," said False Note. "Now, where was she, last you heard?"

"Her? Closer than you might think," said Silverheels. "She knew you were in Abuldane not a month gone. She figured that mess at the lantern festival had to be your doing. Got a right posse working for her, too. Scouts spread far and wide, some names you might recognize. The Brass Halves, for instance. You do have yourself some enemies."

"I made some enemies," said False Note.

"There's truth." The bounty hunter put a finger to his bleeding head and puckered his lips. "In Abuldane she was fixing to hire an airship to get herself an eye in the sky. Maybe use it as a base to run her search. That's the last I know. That was three weeks ago. Now, you got the bulge on me fair and clear. I don't suppose you could find it in your heart to let me go, on account of bringing you all this information?"

"All you brought me was a pair of guns," said False Note.

One shot echoed through the canyon.

False Note stared at the body for a moment, then knelt and removed Silverheels' holster belt. This he buckled around his own hips before sliding the gleaming silver-handled pistols into it.

"Are you certain you're well?" said False Note.

I nodded. I was scraped and bruised, but the worst damage had been confined to my pride, and as you've seen by now it's nothing if not elastic.

"No tea lessons tonight." False Note collected his hat, shook the rock out of it, and put it back on. "No fire. We cross the river as soon as we can. Fetch your horse."

I took a few steps toward Hand-Me-Down, who was struggling to get back to her feet. Suddenly there was another loud bang from behind me. I jumped, and Hand-Me-Down toppled, a dark hole in her forehead.

"That's not your horse any more," said False Note. "Take the bounty hunter's."

I salvaged my gear from Hand-Me-Down's corpse, then stumbled dumbly past the body of Silverheels.

"We just... leaving him like this?" I said.

"I light pyres when they're available." False Note ran a hand soothingly through his horse's mane, then gracefully regained the saddle. "But I don't chop wood when they're not. Mount up."

4

We crossed the Bloodiron the next day, after detouring east until we reached the steam ferry at Last Chance Landing, which billed itself as the final "regular and civilized" crossing this side of the Last Horizon. The rains had swollen the river, and False Note claimed it would have been unwise to use any of the nearby fords. He bartered our way onto the ferry with shells and assorted junk from Silverheels' saddle bags.

The ferry hissed and chugged across the phlegm-colored water like an asthmatic dragon, breathing intermittent gouts of black smoke as sunburnt mechanics pounded the engines with hammers, fists, and harsh language. Nobody bothered us. In fact, I was fairly certain that several people had spotted the distinctive pistols False Note wore, and kept a nervous distance because of them.

For several days after that we rode past dusk and roused before dawn. Our path was due south, toward a dark line of rolling hills that grew slowly on the horizon. Beyond them lay the Rolling Steppes.

Once we reached the hills, False Note slowed our pace and resumed what I can only describe as my drills. By night we discussed tea and the scrivener's arts; he began requiring me to transcribe his lessons in the dirt with sharpened sticks. By day he quizzed me verbally, playing call-and-response games with words, sums, and historical dates.

At first I simply tolerated this. After a while I remembered my vow, and I began to apply myself to the exercises, to the "simpler matters" he was so adamant about. False Note's satisfaction was expressed only in nods and grunts, but I fancied that these were, for him, effusive praise.

He was a disquieting master whose manner has already been encompassed in my brief narrative; he lived a life of wary reserve punctuated by rare passionate outbursts of violence or philosophy. Under his spell as I was, a prey animal somehow adopted by a predator, I was sharply sensitive to each slip of his mask, each half-contemplated smile, each genuinely friendly nod.

This barely perceptible untightening of his demeanor was what sustained me through hot days and cold camps, through slim rations and saddle burns. There were no more booby-trap questions, no more games of chicken with pistols loaded or otherwise. For reasons of his own, False Note had decided he liked me.

I let that thought warm me because I didn't yet know what those reasons really were.

5

For a week we crossed the steppes. Then one morning a dust cloud rose behind us, thin and brown and very persistent. False Note made no effort to step up our pace, and as the sun crawled across the sky the cloud grew larger.

"Master," I said, "forgive me for intruding on your business, but you've got a real peculiar notion of what constitutes running from these people."

"We're not running, Stray. I mean to be followed, but on my own terms." He reined in and squinted at our pursuit. "I think it's time to leave another bread crumb on the trail."

Our ambush was a simple bait-and-switch operation. My readers will not be surprised to discover that for this little drama I was chosen to essay the role of "bait." We let our pursuer (for it had become clear that only one rider was at hand) close within a few hundred yards, then we bolted and ducked behind a small hillock. False Note leapt from his saddle and rolled into cover while I kept going with both horses, making noise and raising dust of my own. Before our would-be interloper rounded the hillock and copped to the rather simple deception, the crack of one gunshot echoed flatly across the steppes.

When I brought the horses back, False Note was standing over the sprawled body of a woman. Her black hair and brown duster both fluttered faintly in the dry breeze, and her horse paced nervously about fifty feet from where she'd toppled. False Note was reading a piece of paper.

"Unbelievable," he muttered, then folded the paper and slipped it into his pocket. "This even describes my eye color. And gets it wrong."

"Who was she?" I said.

"Someone born to be a footnote."

"Want me to get her horse?"

"Leave it. The people behind this will be along shortly by airship."

"How do you—"

"There are colored smoke rockets hanging from her horse's saddle. She didn't want a fight. She just wanted to identify us and fire off those signals. The ship must be relatively close."

35

He ignored the rest of the dead tracker's gear and weapons. The wind rose around us as I held his horse steady and he re-mounted. That wind blew out of the north, as though the gods had decided to give False Note's destiny a push toward him. The sun was as merciless as ever, but suddenly I felt cold.

"Master, what do we do now?"

"Now we ride," he said, "and look for a place."

"A place to do what?"

"A place to meet these people like they deserve. The right place. Excellence in all things, Stray. Excellence in every last detail. And for some of us this will be *the* last detail."

He rode south then, and I followed, and we spoke no more all day.

6

They called it Ghost Lantern, a speck of a town in the middle of all that dry rolling nowhere. We rode in at twilight, when the light had thinned to a line of molten copper under the press of gunsteel blue. That north wind shook the shutters of the town's few buildings. It fluttered the canvas of its tents and busted wagons, and streamed the coats and dresses of its few inhabitants in front of them as they shuffled nervously away from us with their hats pressed to their heads.

Ghost Lantern was another would-be mine, planted near steep-walled canyons full of rusted works and debris. As the darkness came down I saw the phenomena that had given the town its name, spectral green lights that flickered and flared around the abandoned shaft entrances. I shivered. Whether those lights were natural or unnatural, I could understand why the miners had lost their taste for venturing into the tunnels once the things had started appearing nightly.

This sad history of Ghost Lantern we learned from Jasilan Anjhou, proprietor of the Thirst-Vanquishing Pavilion of Auspicious Repose, a combination tavern, stable, signal station and hotel. It had no civilized plumbing and more words in its name than rooms to let, but we were the only guests.

Ghost Lantern was closer to death than Ain't That Something but crawling much more slowly to the grave. Ain't That Something was unraveling for lack of purpose; Ghost Lantern at least was seated above a small aquifer and its wells could provide sweet water for airships and caravans. A four-story airship anchor pole was sunk into the center of a courtyard just behind the Pavilion, where it creaked and swayed and added its rusty music to the sounds of the night.

Nobody came that evening. Nothing swooped down on us from out of the open sky, but I swore that I could feel it like a weird pressure over the horizon, a sensation of being watched. False Note was as content as I was nervous— evidently this was his "right place." We sat together on Anjhou's porch, drinking tea while the proprietor fussed over setting out paper lanterns. False Note accepted the man's cups, water, and pot, but insisted on using his own leaves.

I drank his Jononzal Resplendent Thorn. My master rolled cigarettes and smoked them slowly, all the while deflecting my questions about our business, and we waited.

Eventually I slept, and slept badly, though I needn't have troubled myself. When I crawled groggily out of bed in the morning False Note's pursuers still hadn't appeared. Nor were they seen by noon, or by supper. Anjhou clearly ached to discover what we were waiting for, but False Note had given him a generous surety of unclipped silver coins to keep his curiosity mostly strangled.

Celestial Wolf was rising in a darkening sky when a black shape finally crept over the northern horizon. It came on silently toward us, framed by the rising moon like a speck in a magnifying lens.

"Who's on that airship, master?" I asked, losing my patience after we'd watched it approach for about a quarter of an hour.

"It's a cargo of wagon tongues bound for Big Sky."

"A cargo of-- what? How can you know?"

I squinted at the incoming ship, and then at False Note. There was that faint twitch of his mouth, as though a shadow had shifted on a marble statue. By the proverbial tits of the Maiden, he'd actually cracked a joke!

"The gods wouldn't rebuke me with such an anticlimax," he said softly. "Not after all this time. There are others with her, I'm sure, but the woman most anxious to meet with me is called Winter Sky."

Sagacious reader, that name will no doubt ring like a temple bell in your memory. Winter Sky! A woman barely older than myself. I'd heard so many stories, some even from my drunken card partners in Sload's diversion parlor. She'd put a hundred capable foes in the ground. She had never been touched by bullet or blade. She came and went as she pleased, grinding any hindrance under her heels, on a ruthless years-long hunt for some private mystery.

That mystery, it seemed, sat across from me at the table on Jasilan Anjhou's porch.

"How do you intend to meet her, master?"

"Standing in the middle of the high street." He gestured wryly at the dusty one-wagon lane before us. "Such as it is."

"What if she has a rifle and a scope? She might just—"

"This thing between us, Stray... it isn't about who can get the drop on the other from two hundred yards."

"Look here," said Anjhou, who'd been hovering at a minimally polite distance until he'd heard the word 'rifle,' "do you gentlemen mean to say you're bringing some kind of trouble down on us?"

"Yes," said False Note.

"Well, but—" Anjhou sputtered on a bit, obviously surprised by such a plain answer. He seemed to think of a great many things to say, but his eyes kept returning to the guns at False Note's belt. "Well, should we... should I get the folks indoors?"

"Wild bullets have no particular respect for locked doors." False Note stood, rolled his shoulders, and cracked his knuckles. "If you want to do your townsfolk a favor, clear them all out. Back off a few hundred yards and find good cover."

"When should we come back?"

"You'll know when. Go now if you're going at all."

The thrumming hiss of the airship's engine could be heard, powering down as the craft came lower and lower near the northern edge of the town. Its irregular net-bound gasbag, limned by the sinking sun and rising moon, loomed over the town like a dark cloud. Horses and mules stamped nervously. Men and women, roused by Jasilan Anjhou, scattered into the hills to the east, well away from the abandoned mines. False Note, hands casually hooked into his gunbelt, strolled down the porch steps and onto what he'd called, with great generosity, the high street.

"Master!" I cried, "what should I do?"

"Go to my saddle bag," he shouted. "Bring my box of shells and the leather satchel under it. Put them on the table."

I ran to do as he asked. The airship settled over the town in a rush of dust and artificial wind, and I could see dark shapes moving about the gondola deck beneath the bag. I nearly jumped out of my shoes as what sounded like cannon-fire boomed out from the ship; for an instant I thought False Note's pursuers had decisively discarded all notions of fairness. Then gouts of dust fountained from the high street, and I saw that the noise had come from earth-piercing grapnels, fired straight down with lines attached. The ship was now anchored at three points, perhaps sixty feet up, rocking gently on the wind.

I placed the requested satchel and the wooden box on the table where we'd been sitting. False Note remained in the street, calm as a monk. I can admit, honorable reader, that the thought of scampering for cover seemed barely resistible. Those curious chains of guilt and duty and shame, which were really the same chain, kept me standing there

"And now?" I swallowed; the alkaline grit of Ghost Lantern was in my throat. "What else shall I do, Master False Note?"

"Just stay," he said. "If this goes as it should, I'll need you."

"I'm… honored," I said, coughing out the second word before I could slip and say 'terrified.'

"Keep your hands visible," he said. "Stand right where you are, and don't move. It'll make things easier for both of us."

There was activity above. Shapes came rasping and fluttering down the anchor ropes— a trio of men and women in long dark dusters, much like the one worn by the woman False Note had put down the day before. They slid down on the friction of heavy leather gauntlets and boots, then landed lightly and spread out, unslinging rifles and shotguns.

Another man and woman came down the bow anchor rope, side by side, with acrobatic slowness and grace. They were lightly dressed in black silk only a few shades darker than their skin, and their clothing was cut to fully reveal their wondrous accoutrements, gleaming redly in the dying light. The man's arms and the woman's legs had been replaced with elegant brass and iron machinery, well-armored false limbs ten orders of genius removed from the crude joke Timepiece had worn.

I knew at once that False Note faced Genon and Gaunan, the Brass Halves, the legendary brother and sister mercenaries of Sedoa. Surely their exploits are as worthy of illumination as any of the personages that have graced this narrative, but for brevity's sake I will content myself with just one striking anecdote (astute readers will find a hundred others readily available in any tavern). I have it on unimpeachable authority that when Genon and Gaunan first came to the city, they were without funds and without metal limbs. Those wondrous mechanisms were financed by years of escort and assassination services as provided by an armless boy and a legless girl.

I felt small, honorable reader. So very, very small.

"Mercenaries?" said False Note. "I'm not sure if I should be disappointed or insulted."

"It was all hands-off for us until Abuldane," said Gaunan, the female Brass Half. She had the rich voice of a singer. "We were just along to track you. Then we heard you killed a friend of ours. At the festival."

"Ah. Him. Some would say I killed him," said False Note. "Others might suggest that a mouth as big as his was bound to attract a bullet sooner or later."

"Can't deny he was a man with a rich supply of character defects," said Gaunan. "He was still a friend."

"And so I made it personal," said False Note. "I seem to have talents in that direction."

"Oh, we got a whole ship of grievances," said Genon. His voice was like dry velvet. "Delivered to you air freight, you might say. We spun coins to see who'd go when."

One of the duster coats, a woman, stepped forward and pointedly racked a cartridge in the rifle held across her waist.

"We got you first, you son of a bitch," she said.

"I'm sorry to hear that," said False Note. "Friends of another unhappy festival-goer?"

"A woman you left cold just a ways north of here."

"Ahhhh. So you're the Restless Eye Trail Agency. The *rest* of the Restless Eye Trail Agency, that is. 'Flat-country tracking a specialty. Reasonable Rates.'"

"That's us," said the woman.

"Your rates ought to be reasonable if you can't even get my eye color right," said False Note.

"We'll get it right in the obituaries," said the woman. She brought her gun up in a flash, and by unspoken signal her two companions did likewise.

I know False Note's hands moved. There were *results*, so they must have moved, though I never saw them. Fire blazed before his chest and a trio of shots rang out, compressed into the span of a single finger-snap. Smoke curled up from the silver-handled pistols, already returned to their holsters, before the first of the three Restless Eye trackers toppled. One of them went with his finger curled around the trigger of his shotgun and it barked impotently, spraying buckshot into dirt. Neither of the Brass Halves even twitched.

"Hells, that'll save the boss lady a fair bit of silver," said Genon. "Though I had thought they'd do better than that."

"I didn't," said False Note.

"What's the boy's story?" said Genon, pointing a metal finger at me.

"Not armed and not involved," said False Note.

"No promises if things get hectic." Genon's arms spun fully in their sockets like fast-turning wheels. The joints and gears were silent, and the pop of the pistons was the faintest menacing hiss, like the voice of a snake. "But if you're distracted by keeping an eye on him, so much the better."

Then the Brass Halves moved. Fire split the air between them and False Note. The silver pistols roared, and sparks flew like fireworks. Gaunan and Genon, whirling like airship propellers, deflected the cascade of bullets with their metal limbs, until False Note's guns were empty and they were upon him, one to each side. Brass arm and brass leg flashed; the Halves struck a mighty blow meant to close on False Note like snapping scissors.

The sound of their limbs meeting was like hammer ringing on anvil, but False Note wasn't there. Twirling his pistols, he leaned against one of the wooden columns of Anjhou's porch, not deigning to reload.

"Stay *precisely* where you are," he said to me. I nodded, mouth open in fright, and then the Brass Halves came on again.

Gaunan's legs moved like molten arcs, and poor Master Anjhou's porch steps exploded into kindling beneath them. She caught the shattered fragments of planking with further kicks, and a half-dozen arm-length shards of hardwood hit False Note's post like spears. But again my master contrived not to be standing where they hit; reversing the pistols in his hands, he moved inside the woman's guard and beat a gun-butt tattoo against her arms and chest. Stunned, she fell back, but Genon was there in an instant to shield her. False Note's blows rained without effect on metal arms.

42

Genon appeared to slip; he threw a haymaker right that False Note ducked, caught, and turned into a throw. The male Brass Half landed behind my master, so that they were back to back, and his mechanical arms instantly reversed in their sockets. They struck directly backward with their full strength and leverage.

For the first time in my travels with him, I believe I saw False Note taken by surprise. He flew through Jasilan Anjohu's largest glass porch window, and the crash of his landing inside sounded painful (and expensive to Master Anjhou). While fragments of glass and paper lanterns were still raining on the porch, Gaunan recovered herself and went in through the door. Genon dove through the broken window.

I obeyed my master's strict injunction to hold my tiny patch of humble earth, but I couldn't resist craning my head to follow the chaos that erupted inside the Pavilion of Auspicious Repose. Crockery broke, glass broke, and blurred shapes bounded back and forth. I heard shouts, curses, even laughter. Metal slammed against metal, gunshots rang out, tea-pots and broken chairs came flying out the windows and doors. Then the very walls of the building shuddered; dust puffed out from every crack in the walls and weathered roof-slats rained around me.

Genon flew out the porch door, headfirst, wrapped in a cheap red wall tapestry I recognized as a decoration from Anjhou's modest bar. His metal arms flashed up and cradled his head just before he landed hard. I was alarmed to see a pair of silver pistols clutched in his sculpted fists.

A moment later I heard crashing, whinnying, and clattering hooves from the direction of the stable. Several horses raced around the corner of the building. False Note stood atop his like a circus rider, reins in one hand, while Gaunan battled past the other animals toward him.

All the horses save False Note's cantered to safety, fifty or sixty yards away, while his wheeled and faced the female Brass Half. False Note barked a command, and the horse reared, lashing out at Gaunan with its forelegs. Iron-shod hoof rang on brass leg, and the woman stumbled back. She circled, wary of the animal's strength, dodging another kick, and then another. At last she scowled, spun, and matched a scream of exertion to a blindingly fast kick of her own.

Her brass leg punched clean through the horse's neck. I believe that caught everyone by surprise. The horse died instantly, fountaining blood. False Note was thrown. Gaunan was tugged down with the horse as it fell, and she required several moments to extricate herself from the mess.

Meanwhile, Genon stumbled up and won his fight with the red tapestry. Snarling, he tossed the empty pistols away, snatched a rifle from one of the dead trackers, and bent it in his arms until it snapped in half. Shells tumbled out of the busted cylindrical magazine. Genon caught these easily, then flicked one into his right hand. He held it up as one might hold a cigarette, pointed at False Note, and his metal thumb snapped down like a hammer.

False Note somersaulted toward me, and the bullet cut the air where he'd been standing. Roaring, Genon 'fired' cartridge after cartridge from his fingers, and False Note danced desperately as gouts of dirt were kicked up by near-misses. False Note leapt at me, arms and legs outstretched like a frog, and after landing on me with his hands on my shoulders, he pushed me down so hard the air was knocked out of my lungs when my posterior hit the dirt. An angry breeze ripped past the top of my hat, and I realized one of Genon's bullets had nearly punched my celestial ticket. The male Brass Half put up his hands in an apologetic shrug.

My master let the momentum of his leap carry him back onto the porch, and from there he dashed inside again. When he emerged from the doorway a few seconds later, he was juggling four or five glass bottles taken from Anjhou's liquor collection.

"My apologies," he said. "This is thirsty work. Let me offer you some beer."

He hurled a small dark bottle at Gaunan. Her blood-drenched metal foot met it in mid-air and it shattered, spraying her with a very mediocre lager but doing no real damage.

"And some rice wine, and some cactus brandy." Bottle after bottle flew from his hands; she swatted them all to shards and spray.

"Not to your taste? Try the Orinost Whiskey," said False Note, letting fly with the last and largest bottle. It, too, exploded at the point of a kick, and Gaunan didn't seem to care that the sharp-smelling contents splashed all over her.

"Well, surely you won't mind if I smoke," said False Note. He flipped one of his cigarettes into his mouth, struck a long match against his boot, and brought it up in one smooth arc.

Then he flicked it straight at Gaunan, a little wheel of wood and sulphur fire sparking in the twilight. She kicked it away with a contemptuous expression. I assure you her expression changed when the whiskey caught with a *whoosh* of blue and orange flame. Suddenly, she was half-enveloped in alcohol fire, screaming and flailing, her mechanical legs stamping as they burned.

"No," screamed Genon, "separate! Separate and roll!"

There was a sound of spring-loaded mechanisms firing. Gaunan disengaged from her legs, which remained upright and blazing like torches. The rest of her toppled into the dirt, where she heaved herself around wildly trying to smother the flames.

Genon, madder than a bull in a red cape factory, rushed False Note. "BRASS TIGER," he yelled, curling his impeccably sculpted hands into brutal claws.

My master played hard-to-get and those metal fingers shredded railings and planks all around him. The two of them moved through a storm of wood splinters, the repair bill for Anjhou's pavilion rising with every flash of brass.

"Paper lantern," my master said, seizing one of the unlit globes that had managed to survive the assorted onslaughts. He ducked one more sweep of Genon's deadly arms, then popped back up and slammed the paper globe down on top of Genon's head. Temporarily blinded, the man clawed at the lantern, and False Note unleashed a flurry of punches with the rhythm of a galloping horse. He pummeled Genon, chin and chest and stomach, until the lantern-headed man was teetering like a lost drunk.

"Music of the spheres," said False Note mildly. Then he gave Genon a mighty kick between the legs. The man sailed off the porch and landed on the high street a few yards from his sister, where he flopped around moaning. No doubt he wished that certain other portions of his anatomy had been replaced with unfeeling brass.

His sister, badly burned and gasping for breath, had managed to beat the live flames down. Her metal legs flickered with fading tongues of fire, but she didn't look eager to reclaim them. As False Note strolled toward her, she raised her hands meekly, then let herself fall back to the ground, coughing.

My master seemed satisfied. He recovered the silver pistols, re-loaded, and holstered them. Then he took a long drag on his cigarette and looked up at the airship.

"You spun *coins* with these people?" he yelled.

"And I made sure they won." The voice was a woman's, and it might have been beautiful if it hadn't been so hard. "Knew if they could get the bulge on you I had the wrong man."

"It's been fifteen years, I think." False Note took a last drag then flicked the dying cigarette at Gaunan, who flinched away from it in horror. "But I'm the right man."

The woman plunged from the airship, straw-colored hair and black silk coat fluttering like wings. She didn't bother using the anchor ropes to slow her descent. She simply landed, full of calm arrogance, as though the laws of gravity were quaint customs she chose not to observe.

The green fires of the abandoned mines were just starting to flicker in the distance as Winter Sky faced my master on the high street.

7

"Those aren't your guns," she said.

She was heartbreakingly beautiful, but the heartbreak was all for things lost. There was nothing gentle in her, nothing giving. She looked even younger than me, but she was a blade that had never even been fitted for a scabbard. Pale scars furrowed her left cheek and funeral pyres smoldered behind her eyes.

"They were recently donated to my cause." False Note rested his hands on the butts of the pistols. "They'll do for starters. I suppose you're implacable in this business?"

Winter Sky reached under her coat and drew out a lever-action rifle with the stock and barrel both sharply cut down, what some folks call a 'Mare's Leg.'

"I tell you, old man," she said. "as I tell the earth and the sky and the gods, that tonight I put you down in the dust. If anyone lights a pyre for you when I'm done, they'll be strangers to you, and if anyone prays, they'll be prayers for torment, and if anyone remembers your name it'll be when they're scraping something off the bottom of their boots."

"You're going at this in the right spirit," said False Note. "Stray!"

"Stay where I am and don't move an inch?" I said.

"Precisely."

They faced each other at twenty paces in the shadow of the airship, and the light fell on them like gemstones— pale jade from the haunted mines, translucent diamond from the moon, and rich bloody red from the dying sun. Then they moved, and thunder tore the twilight, and they painted constellations of fire in the air between them.

I can't describe it in any other way. Neither of them ducked, dodged, or flinched. Hands blurred, hammers fell, spent brass sailed into the night, and bullet met bullet, without fail, without exception. They reloaded calmly, as impossibly fast as they shot, and then they resumed. Dirt spattered between them as shot after shot was swatted down.

They were shrouded in the sparks of perfect negation, fusillade after fusillade. They fired faster and faster with each round, until the torrent of gun-blasts roared like a beast and smoke swirled around them like fresh-born whirlwinds.

At last it stopped. My ears rang from the noise and my mind whirled. False Note and Winter Sky staggered out of the smoke, and at first I thought they were hit. Then I saw the bent barrels of the silver pistols, and the Mare's Leg broken nearly in half. In their last furious rain of lead they'd managed only to disarm one another.

False Note tossed his guns aside and stepped toward her, palms up, clearly offering open-handed combat rather than conciliation. She threw her own broken weapon down and shook her head.

"Fire and smoke," she said. "You go the way you've lived. Or I do."

"There's a game," said False Note, "maybe more of a ritual, for people like us. You might have heard of it. Four hands, one chance."

"Feet on the floor and one beneath the hammer," said Winter Sky. "Get your real gun, old man."

"You've earned it," he said. He turned and walked past me, toward the teetering wreckage of Anjhou's porch. Winter Sky followed him like a baleful ghost. Something passed between them that even my fear-whetted senses couldn't grasp at. In his place I never could have turned away from her, but somehow he accepted that getting back-shot was an impossibility. An *aesthetic* impossibility. It was art to them, an art more important than life.

The table we'd been using sat in the only corner of the porch that hadn't been demolished. Each of them stood behind a chair, and False Note took up the satchel I'd fetched. He unbuckled it, reached inside, and drew out a long-barreled revolver.

Then I had some answers.

The gun was fashioned from dark metal, and its surface *crawled*— the whorls and designs there, almost like reptile skin, led my eyes around in disquieting patterns. It wasn't engraving. I would almost describe it as mottling, from some chemical action or sinister internal quality.

I had heard of that weapon. I had heard that there was one and only one like it in all the west, and no doubt, honorable reader, you have at some time heard the same. It has no past, no known origin, no chain of stories and owners. It came from darkness and wrought darkness in one pair of hands.

Man and gun had been called by the same name.

"Mourning Song," whispered the woman.

False Note had vanished. With each step up to the porch, with the act of drawing forth that dread piece of iron, he'd cast off a lie and made himself whole again. That gun belonged in that hand, and seeing it there was akin to realizing that I'd been traveling with a demon all the while, and hadn't known it until he'd unfurled the wings from his back and spread them to the sky. He was Mourning Song.

My eyes stung from building tears. "Oh, *gods*," I whispered.

"Yeah," said Winter Sky.

Hope Breakers, they'd been called. The enforcers of the Steam Barons. Never formally hired. Never acknowledged. East of Sedoa, it's dangerous to even say the name. They're still out there, still flying no flags, but everyone knows who lines their pockets and who calls them down.

Calls them down on villages that won't surrender choice parcels of land to the railroads. Calls them down on men and women who refuse to drive another iron spike for starvation wages. Calls them down on desperate agitators trying to break the chains of company towns.

There were and are Hope Breakers, and above them all, casting his shadow over a thousand shallow graves, rode Mourning Song. For twenty years he'd spread misery, for fifteen he'd vanished into legend. Now it seemed that someone he'd wronged had finally grown old and powerful and interesting enough to draw him out of the shadows.

"Where?" I said, looking directly at Winter Sky.

"Two Moon Springs," she said. "I doubt you've heard of it. There's no town there any more."

"I've heard of… that sort of place," I said.

"Railroad baron wanted our wells. Wanted the townfolk to sell them for an insult. You could get more silver by smelling a coin purse. Promised they'd 'administer' them fairly, which meant they'd suck the wells dry for steamer engines and sell us our own dreg-water back at jackpot prices. So my folk told the railroad to go kiss a mule's ass. Next sunrise, Mourning Song and all his hard cases were lined up at the edge of town. Like the railroad had expected that answer. I was seven years old."

Mourning Song nodded. He broke his long dark pistol open, but let Winter Sky continue.

"Some of the folk thought they could fight, but they were wrong. Mourning Song had everybody caught and lined up, and his thugs smashed some buildings for wood. Then they started building a gibbet.

"All the women in Two Moon Springs had beautiful long hair, and all the men had the same, or beards. Mourning Song told them they would cut it all off themselves, and from it they'd weave the nooses with which they'd be hung while the children watched. If a single noose broke, the children would die too, but if the people wove well, the children would be spared."

"And the people of Two Moon Springs," said Mourning Song, as he opened his wooden box and selected a single cartridge, "even the ones that were not parents, loved those children very much. So they wept, and cut their hair, and they wove. But one of them didn't mind his work closely enough."

"So Mourning Song shot him when his noose snapped," said Winter Sky. "Then he and his men turned their guns on us, while our mothers and fathers were still kicking. While they could still see."

"My orders were to close that town down and put a righteous fear into the heart of anyone who'd try to follow its example." Mourning Song slipped the cartridge into his gun. "All my life, I pursued excellence in all things. Excellence in every last detail."

"That morning you failed," said Winter Sky.

"That I did," said Mourning Song. "I was sure I'd kept my word and killed every last one of you."

"Forehead crease," said Winter Sky, raising a hand and tracing a line across her hairline. "Knocked me cold. You know how they bleed like mad, too. I must have looked deader than ten ghosts. And then when I woke up and I was the only living soul in the whole town, I swore I'd master any art I needed to hunt you down and send you to hell, even if it took a hundred years. Turns out I needed fifteen."

"Last word's not written yet, girl." Mourning Song set his pistol down in the middle of the table, gently, and thumbed the hammer back. "Four hands."

Winter Sky shrugged her coat off and rolled up her shirt sleeves. Mourning Song did the same. Then they sat down facing one another and put their hands on the table, palms down.

"One chance," said Winter Sky.

"Feet on the floor," said Mourning Song, narrowing his eyes.

"And one beneath the hammer," said the woman.

As she breathed the last word, each of them grabbed for the pistol. Yet they adhered firmly to the rules of the duel— their boots were planted firmly on the planks of Anjhou's porch. Their bodies were steady, their heads were level, and their arms and hands were blurs snapping, punching, blocking, and rebounding around the pistol.

I watched in profound awe and disquiet as they fought, feeling like an intruder to some secret temple ritual or supernatural event. They made and deflected more attacks between each breath I took than some pugilists throw in a complete fight. Their neck muscles stood out like cords. Their jaws were clenched, and the sweat on their brows beaded and ran in the eerie confluence of sky lights and mine lights. Blood spattered; it ran from their palms, their knuckles, their wrists, and still they strove to reach the pistol.

How long it lasted, the gods know. My head swam and my heart pounded. I had seen False Note... Mourning Song... toy with opponents before, but this was *all* of him, everything he had, all the stuff of his life and spirit burning in a desperate flare, skill outside any lines my imagination could draw. Winter Sky met that skill. She matched it. And then she exceeded it.

Orange fire flashed above the table, and the sound of that gun was like heaven's thunder. Mourning Song toppled backward, taking his chair with him.

8

"Stray," he croaked.

I walked up onto the porch slowly, balancing on debris. Winter Sky was still in her chair, the pistol lowered, and her eyes were unfocused; whatever she was seeing at that moment was for her and her alone. Mourning Song has been hit low, below the sternum, and a dark stain grew on his shirt as I watched. He held his hand out, and I didn't take it.

"What the hell did you ever need me for, anyway?" I said.

"I can't undo what I did," he wheezed. He could still speak plainly enough, but it was obvious that blood and air alike were going places they weren't meant to go inside him. "And I can't pretend I repent it. But when I found out Winter Sky was after me... when I found out why, I knew I could get one last thing right. I knew I could end the story properly."

"You *let* her kill you?"

"No! Wouldn't have meant anything... if I'd just given it to her. Wouldn't have meant anything to *her*! She had to be able to take it. Had to be able to face me down and best me. Either I would fix my mistake, or that mistake would fix me."

"I still don't see where I fit," I said.

"I took her family from her," said Mourning Song. "I took everyone she loved. So it couldn't be right... if she killed me when all I had to lose was my life. If she killed me when I didn't have anyone I cared about, even a little."

"Gods and ancestors!" I shouted. "So I'm just... a pet! Just a brush stroke on your damned canvas!"

"The world's the canvas," said Mourning Song. The color was running out of him, now, and shadows were pooling around his eyes. Winter Sky stood up at last, reloaded the dark pistol, and snapped it closed.

"You got anything else you want to say to him?" she said, gently.

"Yes." A thin line of blood trickled from his lips, and he strained to raise his head. "Stray, I—"

Winter Sky shot him, punching a hole in his right lung. I was so numb I didn't even flinch from the noise. Mourning Song the gun roared again, and Mourning Song the man was knocked prone, his heart smashed, his words stolen right out of his throat.

She'd frustrated his final desire; taken from him the very last thing he'd ever wanted to do. I reckon she got that part right. Though one could argue that in besting him thus she'd finished his design as perfectly as he could have wished. I don't know, honorable reader. I can't wrap my head around it. Versions of the truth chase each other around the question like moons and sun across the sky.

It was excellence in the very last detail, for someone. The gods can say who.

Winter Sky faced me then, the gun still smoking in her hand.

"If we wanted to get down to the fine print," she said, "it would have been a more perfect symmetry if I'd killed you while he was still alive to watch."

I said nothing and I pleaded for nothing. Was I brave? Was I tired? Sometimes they bring you to the same place.

"What's your name?" she said at last.

"Str... Andus," I said. "Andus Cadwallader."

"Get water." She slid Mourning Song into the holster formerly occupied by her Mare's Leg. "Then get a horse. Pick a direction and never let me see you again."

I stumbled past the corpse of Mourning Song's horse, past the now-unconscious Brass Halves, past the bodies of the trackers who'd never get paid. I calmed Silverheels' horse down and filled water bags from the town's smaller well. Then I rode north, without any real plan except burying Ghost Lantern under the horizon behind me.

Winter Sky was still standing on the porch as I rode out, staring down at Mourning Song's body, lost in her thoughts. Her airship swayed and weaved in the moonlight, and the spectral fire of the mines glowed at her back. I saw this, then I turned my eyes north and never looked back.

I rode across the steppes for two days before a cargo airship swung low and hailed me, its captain curious as to what an obviously unarmed and half-witted young man might be doing in the middle of bugger-all nowhere. I happily bartered my horse for passage to their next destination, Sedoa, where I remained thereafter and where I now ink my brush for the last few words of my tale.

I realized almost immediately how naïve I'd been. The exercises in concentration that I'd assumed were some sort of precursor to being judged worthy of instruction in Mourning Song's battle arts were actually his way of re-sharpening my awareness of the only truly useful skills I possess. I've wielded them well in earning my modest living here— my script is more pleasing to the eye, my figures more accurate, my tutelage in facts and dates more vigorous. Sedoa is a rough city, but a busy one, and a capable scribe needn't go hungry.

Here I am and here I stay, Andus Cadwallader of the Street of the Ox and Anvil. Of the others mentioned in my tale, you may now know more than I, honorable reader. The Brass Halves are out there somewhere, recovered from their injuries and perhaps wiser. Winter

Sky has vanished on her own business. I heard a rumor that there was a mask waiting for her in the Empire, but whether she has gone east to accept it, I cannot say.

Peace and luck to you, honorable reader, and good fortune under moons and sun. I have found my place in which to live and be small, and small I intend to remain. For I have lived with greatness, and stood among those who cast shadows on the world like storms before the sun, and knew how to make artful gestures of everything including their own deaths.

Gods save me from artful gestures! Let me keep my ragged edges, and scribe well enough to live and have a few comforts despite them. Let that be my excellence in the last detail.

Scott Lynch is the author of the Gentleman Bastard sequence of fantasy novels. He lives in Wisconsin, where he serves as a volunteer firefighter. He is outranked by one cat and one girlfriend, acclaimed SF/F writer Elizabeth Bear.

IN STILLNESS, MUSIC
by Aaron Rosenberg

He paused many times, the fire's light flickering across his solemn features, the silk fluttering between his fingertips. The weight of those fetters was far beyond their thin skeins, and he could feel it bearing down upon him, quenching the music and laughter of his soul. Yet, after each moment of reflection, he resumed his task, winding them about with precise care. The night was already grown full, and he had much yet to do. The decision had been made, the die cast, and he would see it through, no matter how it tumbled his fate. Such was his choice.

The silk called, its soft rustle like the fluttering of many tiny wings, and he smiled sadly at the irony, but his fingers did not pause again in their steady work, and at last he was done.

Now, to begin.

He gave no salutation or obeisance when escorted in, for such was not his clan's way, and he had seen the scowl tighten the broad features of the man he faced, throwing every line into sharp relief. Glints of jade shone from ear and brow, nose and lip, and clattered as fingers tapped upon the handsomely carved table.

"You have a message?" the man demanded, arrogance in every syllable, unquestioned authority couched in his posture, in the way he sat back in the ornate high-backed chair as if at ease yet remained coiled, ready to pounce.

Melodious Flight inclined his head, as much to acknowledge the question as to honor the man, though he knew such a person would take it for the latter. That was of no consequence, and if it eased his mission, it was a happy coincidence he would gladly accept.

"Do I address the Jade-Encrusted Noble?" he asked from beneath his peaked straw hat. The question was a mere formality, the man's grunt as much answer as he'd expected, yet the forms must be observed.

"Where is it?" came the demand, a second later. "Out with it, man!" This from one of the Noble's men, the same who had led him into this sumptuous chamber, a rough-hewn man whose fine vest and well-oiled hair did little to disguise his brutish nature. "Hand it over!"

Melodious Flight did not answer with words. Instead he raised his walking staff, politely ignoring the gasps as those around him drew back. Only the smallest smile touched his lips as he raised the long rod to his lips, his fingers finding the indentations with the ease of much practice, his mouth pursing slightly.

And then he played.

His fingers danced about, the butterflies tattooed upon them fluttering with each note, and for a brief, joyous instant Melodious Flight lost himself in the music. But this message was brief, and required only a single refrain—as soon as it was done he raised his head and spoke, his words mingling with the lingering song:

bridges fire consumed   *a path now devoured*
time hurries apace   *money runs on hooves*

"What? Damn!" The Jade-Encrusted Noble's fist slammed down on the table, cracking its delicate lacquer, his face flushed with anger. A map hung upon the wall behind him, and he rose with a powerful thrust of thick legs, the gem-studded hems of his long silk robes swirling at his silk-slippered feet as he turned to study it, every muscle taut. One hand rose, as if the jade upon it carried it aloft, and a finger stabbed at the scroll where an image of this very ranch had been daubed.

"Without that bridge, it'll take an extra week or more to get to market," he mused, tracing the route his cattle would need to take. "I'll lose money with every day!"

"Can't we take some other route, boss?" the rough man inquired, the words bursting from his heavy lips like futile cannonballs, to crash into the tension of the air and scatter across the fine wood of the floor.

"There is nothing faster, you idiot!" his master snarled, not bothering to turn. "Unless—" Now he did whirl about, but his gaze snared not the rough man but Melodious Flight instead. "You!"

Melodious Flight bowed in response. He had not yet lowered his staff, and it rested in the crooks of his arms as he raised both hands before his face, the butterflies there settling as if at rest.

"How did you get here so quickly, if the bridge is gone?"

In reply he fitted the instrument to his lips once more, his butterflies stirring to flight as he played and quieting when he sang:

where water once ran   families take root
only paths remain   clear to sharpened eyes

"The old riverbed? Hmm." Jade flashed along that snaking path, following it from the point closest to the ranch, down and down and around, to just beside the cattle town where Melodious Flight had received this commission. "Yes. That would work nicely." Now the man's cold eyes, the same pale green as his ornaments, sought his henchman. "Tsang, tell the men to ready the cattle. We leave at first light."

The man called Tsang shifted, his booted feet betraying concerns his face would not reveal. "We're taking the riverbed? Boss, there's a whole village there, clear across it, just around the bend. Ain't no way the herd'll fit past."

"Then we will go through." The oil lamps that lit the room reflected in the cattle baron's eyes, full of avarice and impatience and little else.

It was another man, this one short and reed-thin, his narrow eyes as quick as the slender fingers dancing upon the handles of his pistol and his braided whip, who raised the objection: "My lord, the cattle will hurt themselves smashing through those houses. We could lose hundreds or more, and if enough are injured they'll clutter the path, slowing the whole drive."

It was clear to Melodious Flight that the man's master started to snap at this unwanted reminder, but bit back the attack with an effort. At last he nodded, though the jerkiness in even that simple motion betrayed the rage roaring beneath his skin. "Yes, thank you, Nimble. You are correct. We cannot risk the cattle."

For an instant, the tightness Melodious Flight had not realized encircled his heart relaxed, and air seeped once more into his lungs where he had been withholding it. *This is none of my concern,* he reminded himself sharply, his butterflies shifting in protest as his fingers tightened around his staff where it now stood beside him, its hollow metal tip resting firmly upon the ground. *I have delivered my message. My task is done. I can do no more.*

Yet still he stood there, listening, his body at rest but his mind awhirl. And his stomach clenched anew when the lord declared, "Then we must sweep those ramshackle huts from our path. Burn them out, Tsang. Tonight. I want the riverbed clear by dawn."

Tsang nodded, bowed, his yellow eyes already alight with the promise of fire to come, and turned to go. As he did he nearly bumped Melodious Flight, those same eyes widening at the sight of the Wandering Star clansman still standing there patiently, and then flicked back to his master in mute question.

The Jade-Encrusted Noble did not miss this exchange. "Yes, yes, here," he snapped, and tossed a coin across the room. Its worn metal caught the light as it twirled, and Melodious Flight snatched it from the air, butterflies closing about it and quenching its cool reflection.

He dipped his head again, then turned on his heel and strode from the room, his staff tapping the floor beside him in counterpoint to his footsteps.

All the way out of the sprawling manor house, across the wide yard, and even through the handsomely carved prayer gates, Melodious Flight tapped. His thoughts still danced and his heart still fluttered, unsure of the way to go. If he were wise, he knew, he would simply continue walking. There were other towns, other villages, other self-styled lords, all in need of messengers. The Wandering Stars were famous for the sanctity of their assignments, and for never interfering with the world around them. They traveled, and they carried, and they appreciated beauty in its many forms, even adding to it from time to time, but they did not get involved in the everyday affairs of other men. They could not—the world expected, even demanded their indifference, paid for their neutrality.

Yet he had passed through that village on his way here. He had seen its children at play, its men and women at work. He had listened to the rhythm of hands and feet and voices raised in harmony, eking out a meager existence there where water had once roared and fish had once sported, raising beans and soy and wheat in the mud that had been left behind, content with their lot and grateful for what they had together. They had brought new life to a cracked remnant of something old and departed, making it their own and giving it new purpose as a place to live and play and love and work. And now that would be washed away by a new torrent, this one of flesh and horns and hooves, driven by greed, powered by arrogance. Should such a thing be allowed? Could it be ignored?

Melodious Flight did not know. But he had only one night to find the answer. And whichever choice he made, he knew it would linger with him for the rest of his days, a new note in the melody that was his soul.

The sun was setting when Melodious Flight made his way into the village again. Work was ceasing for the day, the farming winding down as the light fled, cook fires rising instead and carrying the tantalizing smells of stew and bread and rice to him. Men glanced up, saw him, noted his hat and his staff, spied the butterflies upon his fingers, and gave him space, not shunning him but not intruding either. Women looked as well, their gazes lingering on his lean frame, his strong chin, his dark eyes shadowed beneath the hat's brim, but they did not approach either.

The children, however, knew no such boundaries. Laughing and screaming and shouting they descended upon him like a cloud of insects intent on devouring him whole, but instead of consuming they adhered, clinging to his hands, his sleeves, the hem of his worn tunic, even his staff. They ringed him and danced about him in a spontaneous paean all their own, their steps untimed and unplanned but full of the natural rhythm of youth and enthusiasm.

Melodious Flight felt a smile tug at his mouth as the music of their feet and their voices washed over him. He gently detached hands from his staff, raised it to his lips, and began to play. The song that burst forth wove between those little feet and those chubby hands, mingling with their cries and squeals, adding depth and harmony to their exultations, crafting a tapestry upon which their glee could be displayed. He lost himself in the melody, his feet unconsciously moving with theirs, and together they danced through the small village, from one end to the other and back and then around, slowing at last near its center. The children fell about him then, looking up at this tall stranger with awe and delight, begging for another song until their parents gently tugged them away.

A motion to one side brought Melodious Flight back to himself. He turned and found a man standing there, older than most of the others, his hair more white than gray, more gray than black, his features seamed deep with dirt and care, but with mirth as well. The man bowed, and Melodious Flight dipped his own head in return, far more willing to give this old farmer such a mark of respect than he had the puffed-up lord he had addressed earlier. The man's hands were cupped around a covered pot, its rough earthen form blending with his own weathered skin in the dusk shadows, and he held it forth in mute offering.

Melodious Flight's stomach rumbled its assent even as he shifted his staff to one hand and reached forth the other to accept, his butterflies hovering along the pot's bottom edge and shivering slightly from the warmth they felt within. Satisfied, the old man bowed once more and backed away, turning back to a circle of friends and family who were watching closely the Wandering Star that had landed in their midst.

Melodious Flight settled the staff into the crook if his arm and lifted the lid off the pot. The smells he had noted earlier rose to him again, wafting over him full force from the simple meal within, and his eyes crinkled with delight. Allowing his legs to fold under him, he settled to the ground right where he stood, the staff resting before him, the pot nestled in his lap as he drew chopsticks from his belt. Then he dipped into his satchel and from it produced a green-tinted bottle, the glass gleaming even in the dimness. The cork he tugged loose with his teeth, and he took a deep swallow, then sought out the old farmer once more. The bottle was raised in clear offer, and the man was not slow to accept, stepping forward with surprising speed to snag it. He, too, enjoyed a long swallow, and beamed with delight as he wiped his mouth with the back of one calloused hand and held the bottle out to be returned. But Melodious Flight shook his head and waved a hand, the wings fluttering outward to encompass the whole village, and a sigh of pleasure rose from those gathered.

The food was simple but filling, well-cooked and well-seasoned and fresh. The bottle returned to him twice, and each time he sent it on its way again after a swallow, to greater cries of happiness from those about to receive it. By the time he had finished his food the bottle was empty and the sun had fled, leaving twinkling stars and a cobalt sky in its place.

Melodious Flight rose to his feet, the empty pot covered once more and resting still upon the ground, and nodded to the old man and the others who remained. The children had already been taken off to bed, or were asleep in their parents' arms as he approached one of the cook fires that still flickered. A space was made for him there, and the villagers watched without a word as from the pouch at his belt Melodious Flight drew a small bundle. They said nothing as he unrolled it, revealing several wide ribbons of silk, and they stirred but did not interrupt as he began, slowly and carefully, to wrap each finger in turn, hiding his beautiful butterflies from view.

He had made his choice. A Wandering Star could not interfere. So he would still his wings, cloak himself in silk and shadow. And then he would do what must be done. He would do what he knew in his heart to be right.

The Jade-Encrusted Noble had tossed him a coin, as one might throw scraps to a dog. These people had honored him with their food and the warmth of their fire, commodities they could ill afford to give away yet did not hesitate to offer. There were payments, and then there were treasures. He would not allow such a treasure as this to be destroyed for one man's greed. He would not have been able to forgive himself for walking away.

It was hours later when they came. The fires had long since burned out, and the villagers were abed. Many had settled as if to keep him company on his vigil, but Melodious Flight had waved them off, his fingers strangely plain without their customary friends. He had not explained what was happening, but the old man had nodded and led the way, rising and bowing before turning to one of the huts spaced out across the worn-smooth ground, and soon enough the others had followed suit, leaving Melodious Flight alone with the cool night air.

The silence was broken by the sound of men riding horses, and his sharp ears picked out another sound as well—the crackle of torches as they sizzled against the dark.

He rose and met them twenty paces beyond the first hut. His staff was nestled across his arms, his hands before him, the silk wrappings like cocoons from which he hoped his butterflies would rise anew come the dawn.

The men slowed to a walk and then a stumbling halt when the torchlight caught him there. After a second one nudged his horse forward a pace and called down, "You're that Wandering Star was in earlier. What're you doing here? You'd best move out a' the way." It was the rough man named Tsang.

Melodious Flight's mouth and fingers found his staff, his hands settling along it, and he played for a second, though his motions felt clumsy through the silk and the music itself seemed sad and muted. Nonetheless it served to couch his words:

> *water quenches fire*   *music staunches flame*
> *melody stands guard*   *wisdom dictates flight*

The men stared. Then one of them, hidden safely behind his friends, let loose a burst of laughter. Hoots and hollers and guffaws followed.

"You're telling us we should skedaddle?" Tsang asked, arms resting across his saddlehorn, the torch held negligently in one, a coil of braided rope in the other. His eyes gleamed red with fire. "Or, what, you'll 'quench' us?" He laughed, a crude sound more like a snort, though even as he threw his head back his eyes never left Melodious Flight. "I know you think you're bad an' all, with those little moths on your hands, but there's twelve a' us and just the one a' you." He grinned, revealing tobacco-stained teeth. "I think it's you ought to run, with that little flute a' yours. Afore we light it and insert it where it don't belong."

The crude threat brought hails of fresh merriment from the assembled men, but Melodious Flight did reply except to shift his grip upon his staff. He merely waited. He knew it was too much to hope that they would be reasonable, but he felt it only fair to present the option.

Finally Tsang shook his head. He spat, the gobbet of spit and tobacco juice landing just shy of Melodious Flight's feet and flowing toward him in a narrow rivulet that appeared black in the night. "Fine, then," the thug snarled. "Let's do this, boys. An' if Mister Music gets in your way—burn him down with all the rest of 'em!"

With that threat still hanging in the air Tsang kicked his horse into motion. It startled, and leaped forward, straight toward Melodious Flight, who still had not moved. He stood poised and still as the steed charged, hands loose but firm upon the staff—

—and just as the horse's head neared his own he twisted to one side, pivoting to let that long skull glide past, and delivered it a sharp rap upon the nose with the side of his staff.

Startled, the horse flung its head to the side and bucked. Tsang went flying, his ungainly form sailing over Melodious Flight's head, a yelp emerging from his chapped lips as he arced up and then back down, crashing to the ground with a resounding thunk mingled with the sharp crack of breaking bones. Miraculously he missed not only the huts but the stone rings of their cook fires, and it was only hard-packed mud he impacted, but that was enough to leave Tsang groaning and barely conscious.

For a second, no one else moved. They stared at their leader, huddled there in a shattered heap, and at Melodious Flight, who had resumed his earlier stance and faced them once more.

Then one of the men—perhaps the same who had been earlier emboldened by his anonymity—shouted, "He took down the boss! Get 'em!"

The night exploded into violence and motion.

Horses rushed toward him in a tumult, but Melodious Flight raised his staff before him and began to twirl it in both hands, its ends spinning around in a fearsome arc that cracked horse and human alike, the hard wood leaving men reeling and horses panicked. Torches were knocked from hands, guns sent spinning off into the night, whips and ropes fell underfoot and were trampled. It was madness, and in the middle of it he stood, swaying as if drunk, his loose limbs and relaxed stance allowing him to duck beneath blows and glide aside from hooves and teeth to remain unscathed.

After that initial rush the remaining men fell back, more wary now, and surveyed the scene. Tsang had brought eleven with him, he'd boasted, but only five were still ahorse, and of those two were rubbing their heads and wincing. The other three eyed Melodious Flight carefully, watching that staff as it spun, and he could see the thoughts in their heads, the decisions they were weighing. Should they still attempt it, with their numbers reduced so severely? Or should they back away now, leaving Tsang to shoulder the blame?

He saw the jaw of one stiffen, the brow of another lower, and knew with a grim certainty the choice they had made. He also guessed that these men, who had not been foolish enough to plunge forward headlong at the first, had now learned far better than to close with him. They would attack from where they sat, safe beyond his reach, and strike him down.

But he had already made his decision for that night. He was committed. Holding back now would be folly, and would risk his choice having been for naught.

So he attacked.

Sliding forward at a sudden run, his wrapped feet soundless against the mud, Melodious Flight gracefully bridged the distance while the men were still reaching for their guns. His staff shot out, its end slamming into one man's forehead with an impact that sent him reeling back and off his horse, the gun falling from his grip to strike the ground a moment after he hit without even a groan.

By then Melodious Flight was already in among the horses, and he twirled his staff high above his own head, spinning it in one hand so that it struck two other men in the temples and knocked them to the floor of the riverbed as well.

The other two men had drawn their guns by now, but they could not see him clearly to shoot, as he was shielded by the bodies of their friends' horses. He used that confusion to his advantage, ducking behind one horse and then leaping up and forward to straddle another. His feet found the stirrups and he stood, perched above the saddle, his staff striking down one of the last two men from that new vantage. The other was on his opposite side, and had enough time to stare in surprise and raise his pistol but not aim it before a well-placed tap took him down as well.

And then all was silent save the grumbling of the horses, and here and there the moans and whimpers of the men.

Melodious Flight steadied the horse he was astride, calming it with a gentle hand along its heaving neck and a low, reassuring hum. Once it quieted he dismounted and moved among the other steeds, settling them as well. After that he saw to the men. Two were dead, their necks bent askew from falling badly. The rest had bruises and breaks of their own, but they would survive and mend with time. The ropes he retrieved bound them securely, and then Melodious Flight ground-tied the horses, returned to the cook-fire, and stirred it alight, the sparks rising up with the night breeze to flutter about him like the butterflies he already yearned to recover.

It was with thoughts of them that he fell into a light but untroubled sleep.

When the dawn stretched forth its wavering rays the next morn, that illumination found Melodious Flight standing by the prayer gates to the Jade-Encrusted Noble's manse. A servant spied him there and went running within, to return a moment later with the slender man called Nimble. That one took one look at Melodious Flight, not failing to notice the silk about his hands and fingers, and motioned for him to follow into the house. Melodious Flight did, with a touch more unease than had accompanied him before.

They found the master of the house pacing in the same room as before. His robes had been set aside for riding clothes, fitted pants and tall boots and a snug high-collared jacket, jade shining from each. A handsome pistol hung at his side, a sword at the other, both of them with hilts carved of the green stone. When he saw Melodious Flight his glower became a fearsome scowl.

"You," he snarled, the world launched like an arrow across the room. "Tsang and his boys haven't returned. Did you have something to do with this?"

Melodious Flight only bowed. "You're a Wandering Star!" the Jade-Encrusted Noble reminded him, though from his lips the noble clan name sounded almost an epithet. "You can't interfere!"

Melodious Flight played upon his flute, and then explained amid the echoes:

> *warmth and compassion   all given from nought*
> *payment beyond price   safety fairly bought*

"They hired you to protect them, those villagers?" The accusation emerged through a sneer. "With what, mud and rice? But that's not a message, is it? That's not what you do!"

Nimble was there beside him then, and whispered in the lord's ear. Melodious Flight saw the man's eyes widen as he stared, apparently seeing the silk wrappings for the first time. It was clear the slender man knew what they betokened, and now his master wondered at the wisdom of granting him entry.

To allay those fears, and hopefully find a solution to what Melodious Flight knew could be an ongoing feud, he loosed his music again:

> *rhythm soothes the beast   guide the maddened flight*
> *to thread the needle   for a price comes speed*

The Jade-Encrusted Noble studied him, those cold eyes narrowed in calculation, one hand stroking the oiled and beaded hair of his pointed beard. "So you would offer to see my cattle safely past the village?" he asked, and Melodious Flight nodded. "For a price." Another nod.

They stood thus, the lord considering, the Wandering Star waiting and still, the henchman watching. Finally, the master posed the question to his man, "What do you think, Nimble?"

The man called Nimble studied Melodious Flight, and smiled, though the expression had little mirth to it as it touched his thin lips. "I think he could have killed us both within an eyeblink, had he wanted. Or walked away and left you to lose your fortune when your cattle didn't reach the market in time. But he didn't."

The Noble nodded. "Fine. You get my cattle past that village, and I won't hold any of this against them. Nor will I take the riverbed route again—by the time the next season's drive rolls around, the bridge will be restored, and that route's faster, anyway." He paced closer, glaring at Melodious Flight from a distance of only a few feet. "Is that acceptable to you?"

Melodious Flight smiled, and bowed.

"Good." He thought he detected grudging respect in the voice of the cattle baron. "Then name your price. I want my cattle on the move before the sun's any further in the sky."

A short time later, Melodious Flight found himself once again before the village, though now his shadow stretched long behind him as the sun began to rise in earnest. Tsang and his men were stirring, most of them, but the villagers had dragged them off to the far side, up against the riverbank. Their horses were tethered there as well, and one farmer led away the horse Melodious Flight had ridden here, bringing it toward its fellows while he unlimbered his staff once more.

Within minutes the sound of rushing reached them all. But this thundering was not water, and an instant later a cloud of dust came into view from around the bend. As it drew closer, Melodious Flight raised the staff to his lips.

There were no words this time, nor did he need them. And children did not dance around him—they had been taken up out of the riverbed, and were huddled under trees just beyond, with their mothers. Only the men of the village remained, clustered behind him, ready to fight or to flee if necessary, but prepared to face what came. Melodious Flight could feel their determination like a wave of warmth at his back, and he fed that into his music as well, focus and passion and courage and determination and, above all, the unwillingness to be moved for another's pleasure. The song that soared forth was fierce and bold, its melody strong and sharp but not bitter nor wholly somber, its rich rhythm smooth and steady and unyielding.

The cows were visible by then, their heads and hooves surfacing from the cloud at random intervals, as if they were swimming in a sea of dust, and Melodious Flight could see the whites of their eyes as they ran, caught up in the momentum of the herd, wild and crazed and uncaring.

But their large ears twitched as the music reached them. They snorted and bellowed over its rhythm, but Melodious Flight played on, and his song would not be denied.

As the first cow came within a dozen horse-lengths of the village, it shied away from that melody. It twisted to the side, and then it was running abreast of the village, passing it to the side, through the wagon-wide path they had left between the outermost hut and the far riverbank.

The next cow followed its lead. And the next. And those after that. Soon the entire herd was passing through that narrow gap, slowing only enough to shove through before picking up speed again on the far side.

They continued flowing past throughout the day, and Melodious Flight played the entire time. When at last the final cows had charged on by, he lowered his staff. Swaying on his feet, he might have fallen if the old farmer had not reappeared and lent a shoulder for support. Another man was there at his other side, and together they helped Melodious Flight sit. A third brought hot tea, while the other men went to retrieve their wives and children from the bank. A ragged cheer went up when they all saw that the danger had passed, and Melodious Flight allowed himself to smile.

After the tea had soothed his sore lips and jaw, and his hands had stopped shaking from the strain, he began to unwrap his bandages. First on one hand, then the other, his butterflies soared once more, their colorful wings catching the late afternoon light.

And a single drop of jade glittered in his ear, a match for those set in the bridle of the horse tethered off to the side.

His wings freed once more, Melodious Flight lifted the staff again. This song was filled with joy, his and that of the village around him, and the children soon picked up the tune, dancing and singing and laughing. Their parents joined in after a moment, and the dusk was filled with their merriment.

Melodious Flight knew that he would be departing in the morning. But for now he embraced the melody, and committed it to memory. It would reside within him for the rest of his days, and at times when the way was long and hard he would revisit it, and remember the time he had stilled his wings—and brought forth joy and safety to lift them into flight once more.

in stillness, music   *the heart hears truly*
silk settled on wings   *new paths must be found*

Aaron Rosenberg is an award-winning, bestselling novelist, children's book author, and game designer. He's written original fiction, tie-in novels, young adult novels, children's books, roleplaying games, short stories, webcomics, essays, and educational books. He has ranged from mystery to speculative fiction to drama to comedy, always with the same intent—to tell a good story. You can visit him online at gryphonrose.com or follow him on Twitter @gryphonrose.

RIDING THE THUNDERBIRD
by Chuck Wendig

Sometimes, the thunderbirds just run.

Nobody really knows why. The herd will suddenly spook—the bull's head pops up like a whistle-pig at the hole and next thing everybody knows, the entire court is running one way. Then they turn on a silver bit, first going north, then headed east, or south, and then soon back north again.

A ballet of thick-necked, strong-willed birds. The ground grumbling and shuddering like the floorboards of a train depot as the steam engine thunders past.

Casey, age 12 ("and a half," she'll have you know), stands on a butte, staring down at the thunderbirds running. Kicking up wild plumes of dust. Knocking loose scree that slides and skitters down the sandstone edge.

A man stands behind her. She doesn't know it. His shadow faces the other way—apropos, given his name. As the girl stands there looking over the lip, dust-caked red hair wound up in a braided coil, the man makes sure to scuff the ground with a silver-toed boot. To announce his presence.

She wheels. Draws the only weapon she has: a straight razor with a crabshell handle polished to a milky gleam.

"Don't drop it, now," he says. His voice is low, wet, throaty. He lifts the bowler cap, takes it off, tucks it under his arm. She sees his eyes are like black marbles seated in sunburned flesh nicked and marked with the furrows of crow's feet. He holds his midsection, the flat of his hand tucked between the buttons the way a gentleman might comport himself.

But he doesn't look like any gentleman Casey's ever seen.

No. This one looks like a ball of tangled dirty brush blown in off the Sevenfork Road.

"Don't you tell me what to do," she says—she spits it, really, *ptoo*-ing those words at him the way another man might hawk up a loogey and launch it in your eye. Just the same, her voice shakes and trembles.

"Fair enough."

"My homestead ain't but a quarter-click from here."

"I know that. I went by there first."

"You lookin' for my Daddy?"

"Naw." A glint of something in his eye.

"You can't be lookin' for my Mommy because she tucked her tail between her womanly parts and hit the road eleven of my twelve years back."

"I believe that." And by the look on his face, he truly does.

"So whaddyou want then?"

"I just... " Those dark marble eyes search the horizon. Wine-stained fingers rise and see the sun as it sets. Darkness comes, means it's time for the Wolf and the Rabbit to play.

"You just what? Say what you feel or be on your way." The razor trembles in her hand.

"I figure I could teach you to ride one of those thunderbirds."

"You're mule-kicked."

"Ain't no such thing."

"You're thunderbird-kicked, then."

He laughs, but somehow it isn't a happy sound. "Thunderbird kicks you, you'll find your head broken into two pieces, like a blue-knot gourd clubbed with a claw hammer. Ain't that either, little girl. I've ridden the thunderbirds."

"Oh yeah? How?"

It's then he takes another step toward her. His hand slips out of his jacket, and she sees his palm is flaked with red. Blood. Dry, now, but blood just the same.

"Look," he says, pointing down. "It's all about the bull-bird. That fat-necked sumbitch runs the roost and all the other squawkers take a lesson from him." He grunts, adjusts his footing. "You rule that bird, you rule the rest."

Down in the valley, the bull is plainly seen leading the running court. Sounds like an earthquake.

The girls eyes the man, though, instead of the birds.

"Eyes on them, not on me," he says.

"I'll cut you," she says. "I don't trust you. I don't know you."

"You know me."

"I swear I do not, stop playing games."

"They call me Shadow-Faces-The-Other-Way."

The girl is silent. Her mouth opens. Eyes blink.

She knows. Knows who he is. And knows it's true.

"I…" Her eyes dart, look for a way out—a way to run. She even looks over the butte's edge, down into the scrub and the scrape and it looks for a moment like she's thinking of going that way, but Shadow places a hand—a gentle hand, as gentle as a petal from a phial-cactus alighting upon her—on her shoulder and shakes his head.

"I'm not here to hurt you."

"You hurt a lot of people."

"People that deserved it. People that did wrong by me. By others."

"You're a murderer."

"I'm a hero."

The air is still between them. It's just dust and fading sunlight and the tumble of thunderbirds.

Something passes between them then. If not an understanding, then something close.

Casey finds her words past a croak and stammers: "The, uh, the bull-bird. You say you need to ride the bull-bird first."

"Mm, naw," he says, sucking air between his teeth. "That's not it. Never try to ride the bull-bird. Too rough a beast, too headstrong. That bastard will throw you so far you'll wake up in the Dreaming Desert. No, you just have to dominate the bull. Embarrass him a little."

"Embarrass him."

"Yep. Lasso him. Force him to the ground. Pluck a few of his tail-feathers or rub dirt in his beak-holes. An act that shows your mastery. Then you let him go."

"I don't get it."

"The others in the herd. That buys you a kind of respect among them. They start to see you as a bull-bird, too. Then all it takes to ride one is to—"

A sound like thunder—real thunder, close thunder, not the long protracted rumble of the birds running—splits the air, and suddenly Shadow staggers backward, boots kicking out from under him, falling flat on his back. The girl drops her razor, runs over to him.

A hole in his chest pumps red—a black dark bubbler of blood. Shadow licks blood from his teeth.

"Guess I had less time than I thought," he says.

"You're shot."

He chuckles. "You have a profound mastery over the obvious."

"You're shot!"

"Hey. *Hey.*" He grabs her hand hard. Casey winces. He moves her hand to his hip, pulls back his coat, reveals a seven-shooter—a Waoping Silver-Thrower with bamboo grip. "Take it."

"What! My Daddy... he wouldn't want me having a gun."

The man gnaws on the inside of his cheek. Blood trickles from the side of his mouth. "I'm sure he would, darling. I'm sure he would."

Time seems to warp and distort as the sun sets and the moons rise.

With a clumsy fumble he draws the gun from the holster, puts it in her hand.

It's shiny. And cold. And heavy with threat—or maybe promise?

He helps her with the weapon. Tucks it into the back hem of her pants.

"Go," he says, easing her back.

"Wait—"

"*Go.*" A harder shove. She lands on her butt.

Just as another man ascends the butte.

Or, at least, she assumes it's a man. The long leather cloak. The porcelain mask with an owl's face painted upon it. The long rifle with brass oculus.

One of the Marshals.

"Stand back, child," the Marshal says, voice processed through some kind of music box—it tinkles and tinks and behind the words are a strange discordant melody.

The Marshall raises the rifle to its shoulder.

"Casey—" Shadow-Faces-The-Other-Way starts to say, lifting his head.

But his word is cut off by the loud bark of the rifle.

His head thumbs back against the hard rock. Blood crawls between sandstone grooves.

"Why?" Casey asks the Marshal.

But the masked figure doesn't answer. Instead it just slings the rifle over the padded shoulder, pulls the cloak tighter, and once more descends down the sloping side of the butte.

The thunderbirds run. Booming and crashing.

Casey feels the gun, *his* gun, at her back. The Waoping. A gun said to be made in the heart of a Fury Engine by Master Waoping, the Gunsmith of the Malachite Steppe.

It strikes her, then –

He knew my name.

But she never told him.

He knew my name.

She draws the gun. With quivering thumb, pops the cylinder. Sees seven rounds tucked in their place. Casey moves to the edge of the butte, sees the Marshal descending toward—his? her?—men, a cabal of armed soldiers below.

No, you have to dominate the bull.

Embarrass him a little.

Shadow lies dead behind her.

The gun feels proper in her grip.

She cocks the Waoping.

Run, Thunderbirds. *Run.*

Chuck Wendig is equal parts novelist, screenwriter, and game designer. He is the author of the novels DOUBLE DEAD, BLACKBIRDS, and MOCKINGBIRD. In addition, he's got a metric boatload of writing-related e-books available, including the popular 500 WAYS TO BE A BETTER WRITER. He currently lives in the wilds of Pennsyltucky with wife, dog, and newborn progeny.

PURITY OF PURPOSE
By Gareth-Michael Skarka

The old Master leaned heavily on his staff as he surveyed the group of students seated before him on the hard clay of the courtyard. A dozen or so, each of whom had braved the hard climb through some of the roughest terrain in the Eagle's Claws to reach the remote hermitage. Getting here was test enough, yet today, as with every day since their arrival, the old Master continued to test them.

"Answer me this: What are the Unsurpassed Weapons?"

The students hesitated, unsure of how to proceed. The question was simple enough — a recitation of a lesson given by the Master days earlier. His questions were never that easy, however.

The silence of the nervous students was broken by the sound of one rising to his feet. The old Master recalled that this one was from the Thousand Mesas, many days to the south. The Master did not recall his name. He never bothered to learn their names until the second year.

The student stood until he was sure the Master's attention was upon him. He answered, clearly and confidently, in a strong Castalan accent that confirmed the Master's recollection of his origins: "Master, the Unsurpassed Weapons are The Pistol and The Sword."

"Correct," said the Master, "and why are they called so?"

Smiles broke out among the less disciplined of the gathered class. This is what they had feared, the old man's trap.

The standing student paused momentarily before answering. "Purity of purpose, Master."

A slight twitch at the corner of the mouth and a reflexively raised eyebrow where the only evidence of the shocked surprise on the face of the old Master. *This one bears watching,* he thought.

"Correct. The Unsurpassed Weapons represent the pinnacle of the form, due to purity of purpose. Every other weapon is an adapted tool. A spear or a rifle is used for hunting. An axe for the felling of trees. A hammer for driving nails. A knife for everything from cutting rope to whittling to carving a steak. The Pistol and The Sword, though… they were built for a single use. They have no other purpose, but to take a life."

"What are the greatest among the Unsurpassed Weapons, Master?" A question shouted from one of the seated students — a slight boy from somewhere in the Periphery, if the Master recalled correctly. The standing student glared at his classmate momentarily, for the breach in protocol — a student should stand before speaking, and then only speak when prompted. He quickly regained his composure, returning his attention to the Master, who directed him to sit.

"There are many. Weapons built by legendary smiths and wielded by heroes and villains alike. You've all doubtless read the dime novels."

A few chuckles fluttered through the class like butterflies.

"Judge Wellam's Thrice Repeating Sword, The Lone Gun, Green Harmony, The Maiden's Sixgun… all fine weapons, and each rightfully famous. To my mind, however, the pinnacle of the Unsurpassed Weapons would have to be Wind and Fire."

The old Master sat down on a stool under the only shade tree in the courtyard, and wiped his brow with a sleeve. "A matched pair of long-barrel pistols, build over a century ago by a man who was looking to kill a god, or so the tales go. The finest ironwork you've ever seen. Carved into each handle, in the old speech, the names of each gun — Wind and Fire. Those handles have been worn smooth by the hands of many men over the years — some good, some evil, all terrible. Always worn in a reverse rig, high on the belt line, to be drawn cross-handed — and so that the grips, with the names emblazoned, can be seen clearly. Red tassels, like you put on a sword, are hung from the bottoms of the grips to draw the eye. Almost like the guns want their names to be seen, as if to say *'Stand down, for we have killed better men than you.'"*

The old man fell silent for a moment.

"Dismissed. Get to the kitchens and get the meal ready." The students rose, and dutifully filed out, but the old Master saw that the one from the Thousand Mesas stood for a moment, regarding him, before joining his classmates.

The cool night air of the mountains brought an unwelcome ache to the old Master's bones as he finished his evening pipe. Knocking the spent tobacco from the bowl, he slowly made his way through the darkened hallways of the hermitage, back to his chamber.

He was not surprised to find the student from the Thousand Mesas there, standing at his writing desk in the middle of the room. On the desk was the burlap bag from the bottom of the steamer trunk which had served as the old man's dresser since he had carried it up the mountain decades ago.

"Your name?" The Master asked, as he walked, bent with age, towards the desk.

"Navi Herroah," he said.

"And what brings you to my chamber this evening, Herroah-si?" The Master said, in the young man's native Castalan.

Herroah pulled the guns out of the bag. The metal glimmered with an oiled sheen, even after all these years. The worn grips with the carved sigils protruded from the ancient leather of the holster rig, and the tassels seemed black in the moonlight, rather than the vibrant red that was seared into the old man's memory. Even lying there on the table, the pistols seemed like living things, coiled and ready to strike… predatory and heavy with menace.

The old man shook his head sadly. "You didn't come here for instruction. I should've known that. You already knew too much."

Herroah's lip curled in an arrogant sneer at the old man's acknowledgement of his skill.

...which was all the distraction that the Master needed.

With blinding speed, the old man kicked the desk, shattering it in twain. As the desk exploded upward, the guns flew into the air, along with papers, an ink pot and pen, and the other contents of the desk, like blown leaves in the autumn.

Herroah's training took over after only a moment's pause from the shock of the sudden action of the old man he had thought feeble. He drove forward, hands curled into the claws of the Ascendent Eagle style, looking to tear the throat from the old man. His speed was impressive, and his fingers dug deep.

The Master's jacket tore away in Herroah's hand. For no sooner had the Master landed the kick, he had begun his leap. The Thousand Mesa's Ascendent Eagle style, rather than tearing out his throat, only managed to grasp cloth as the old man flipped into the air over Herroah's head.

When he landed behind the young man, the old Master had Wind and Fire in his hands.

Herroah spun to relaunch his attack, only to be cut down in an instant as the two pistols roared their disapproval in the confined space of the Master's chamber. His body hit the floor before the last of the papers had finished drifting to the ground.

The old man looked down at the smoking guns in his hands, the worn grips which fit so perfectly against his palms. They had delivered the final lesson to Herroah.

Sometimes, it's not just weapons which have purity of purpose.

Gareth-Michael Skarka is the creator of Far West -- a writer, game designer, consultant, graphic designer and veteran of over twenty years in the entertainment business. For the past eight years, he's been at the forefront of the growth of the ePublishing industry, appearing in articles on the subject ranging from the Washington Post to the South China Morning Post, and online via dozens of sites, including CNNMoney, ABCNews.com and the Nintendo Wii News Channel.

The married father of three lives in the old frontier (in Lawrence, Kansas), but works in the new one.

PAPER LOTUS
by Tessa Gratton

The sky was the color of azurite when she came to the top of the mesa with only her horse, her sword, and a bag of bones.

It was the crack of gunfire that pulled her here, off the cactus trail. Just one lone echo like a thread tied to her ribs, drawing her up and up until she could see. This side of the mesa sloped just shallow enough she could charge down, over crumbling earth, to the man standing trapped at the edge of a precipice. He barely held his ground against a band of four men with rifles. From this distance he was only a slim figure in a gray coat that must once have been black. A revolver hung loose in his left hand.

Rabbit unsheathed her brother's sword before kicking her horse into a wild gallop.

The band whirled toward the noise, but all they saw was a swirl of dust and the glint of metal as her sword slashed.

Verity saw her come and his fingers clenched tight around his gun. He raised it, finally, as she screamed down the hill, and Casen and his men scrambled to face her. But he never fired on them. The barrel remained on the girl-demon as she twisted off her saddle and cut his enemies down, nearly too quick for even him to follow. The pattern of her sword dance was strange but brutal, as if the curve of steel pushed forward and the girl was the mindless weapon.

She stood before him, four bodies splayed behind her like unfurled petals. Her horse chomped on a clump of sage grass, unconcerned by the violence. The girl lowered the curved sword, nearly to the dust, and stepped nearer to his gun. Improving his shot for him.

Her docile horse was packed with gear. Could take him the whole way to Mudscrap. All he need do was pull the trigger.

But the girl stared down his barrel. Once she might have been lovely, but the hard sun had turned soft skin raw and red, and her long black hair hung in strings down her back.

Verity thought, *she needs a hat.* Then, *Why doesn't she run?*

Rabbit panted through her open mouth while the man took such slow, deep breaths he might suck up the entire air of the desert, and leave nothing left for her. She looked along the barrel of his revolver, up his trembling arm, and to his dark eyes. They were tight with pain. He'd shoot her soon, or put it down.

Her whole body shook, too, from the song her brother's saber sang. A month ago she'd have attacked. Swung the saber through this man's throat to defend herself. But for twenty-eight long days, all her fear had been gone.

The man uncocked the gun and asked, "Damn you, why didn't you run?"

"I'd rather take your bullet in my heart than my back," she said.

When he holstered the revolver beneath his coat, the dark material pushed aside to reveal a spreading gash of red melting into his vest. The smell tickled Rabbit's nose, and the man put a surprised hand against himself. Blood dripped onto his pants. A frown tugged at his suddenly pale lips, and he fell to his knees.

Rabbit caught him, leaving her brother's saber shining against the orange dirt.

He opened his eyes to the stars.

Maiden's blessings, he hadn't expected to wake up at all. The crackle of fire made Verity turn his face toward the warmth. The girl crouched near, poking at the burning logs. He smelled meat, but it only nauseated him. If the Maiden was kind tonight, this girl would have alcohol – though for once he wanted to pour it into his wound instead of down his throat. His entire middle ached, and he shifted to touch the gunshot wound. Pain gripped him hard and sweat broke out over his face and down his spine. *Damn that Casen, damn him.* The bastard had to have known Verity was coming this way. He guessed Tome the Mirror sold him out, and prayed he'd have a chance to spread the word.

The girl said, "I slowed the bleeding, but the bullet's not going anyplace."

Verity breathed through his teeth. Smoke drifted over him, obscuring the night sky. It smelled sticky and sweet as if she'd been burning honey. As he relaxed, the pain didn't diminish so much as he helped it settle into a quieter thrum deep in his bones. When he could, Verity studied the girl. But she was older than he'd thought. A young woman despite her skinny ass. The trousers hung loose on her hips and the jacket was made for a man with wider shoulders. Its cuffs kept slipping over her wrists. Not the great warrior she'd seemed when she came galloping off the mesa, but something about her making him uncomfortable. He wasn't used to discomfort.

"Who are you?" he asked, his voice more raspy and weak than he liked.

She brought him a skin of water. "Can you sit?"

Verity wouldn't begin to say otherwise now that she'd asked, and clapped down on a groan as she pushed his shoulders up and moved him against her saddle. She lifted the skin to his mouth and he drank until the girl touched his cheek, smearing away his tear of pain. Pride forced him to push away the water. "What's your name, girl?"

"My brother called me Rabbit."

"After the moon?"

"The twitching, fearful little animal." She smiled, and her teeth glinted rather like the curved metal of the sword she'd carried. "Will you give me yours?"

"Verity. Verity Longleg of Restless City."

"That's so far away," the girl said sadly.

"You must be... far from home, as well." It took all his strength to focus on her dark eyes. Her lashes fluttered as she looked down, and her only answer was a quiet hum. He continued, "Why did you kill Casen? Did you know him?" Verity would not've been surprised to hear the bastard had more enemies than himself.

"No. I killed him for you." With that, she quickly moved back to her fire, leaving the water skin slumped beside him.

Verity lifted it up to drink again while Rabbit took up a bag the size and shape of a whiskey bottle. He longed for a pull of alcohol. But instead of a bottle, she took out a skull.

It's gaping black eye sockets looked right at Verity.

The water froze in his stomach.

Rabbit reverently set the skull down, facing the fire. Against the curve of bone were painted characters Verity could only just read: *brother* and *wolf* and *life* and *sorrow*.

She unfolded a leather envelope and pulled out a thin sheet of yellow paper. Her fingers moved quickly as she folded the paper into a delicate flower. Verity's heart pounded hard, filling his head with a roar, as Rabbit lifted up the paper flower to her mouth. She breathed onto it, and then gently tucked it into the fire.

He passed out before he could ask for liquor.

The dawn painted pink shadows across their small camp, and Rabbit woke to the cry of a vulture. Overhead, a trio of them circled, heads cast down over the side of the precipice where she'd dragged and thrown the four dead men.

She was alone but for the man Verity, whose snores were the harsh, wet sounds of death. Even her horse had gone: before sunset last night she'd removed the saddle and ropes, knowing this, here, was where her quest ended. Only a single slip of paper remained.

A hollow in her stomach reminded her she should have been afraid in so isolated a place: but nothing had frightened her since her brother's death. Where there had been fear, now there was nothing.

Kneeling beside Verity, she took a deep breath. The bandage wrapping his middle was soaked through again. This morning he still smelled like blood, but there hidden under it was the sweetness she'd waited all night for. The fragrance of death.

Satisfied, Rabbit made the last of her grandmother's tea. She sat again to wait, with her legs crossed and the tea cupped in her palms. The steam cleared her head, bringing with it the memory of kneeling across the hearth from grandmother for her brother's death tea ceremony, when grandmother had reached a gnarled hand to Rabbit. *You'll have twenty-nine nights to send your message, little rabbit.* The number of nights her brother's spirit would wait to gather the prayers and riches his family would send before moving into his next life. The number of paper lotuses she had to burn in her fire.

If she'd had any fear, Rabbit would have been afraid yesterday that she'd never succeed. After twenty-eight days wandering, eyes and heart hunting, with her brother's skull tucked against her thigh.

Rabbit leaned over Verity to skim her dirty fingers against the tattoo curling up his wrist.

She'd found the messenger she needed.

The girl's face leaned too near when Verity dragged open his eyes. He felt as though his flesh was melting slowly off his bones and into the desert rock. Evening sunlight burned his lips, and he finally asked for the gods' own nectar.

But she only had water. After helping him angle up against the discarded saddle, she gave him a sip. He worked his throat and heavy tongue, then said, "Why are you still here?"

"I need you to carry a message for me."

Verity laughed. It choked up from his stomach, wracking him with pain. Sweat streaked down his temples and he gasped as the mesa spun beneath him.

The girl put her cool hand to his forehead, smoothing hair back. She picked up his hat and fanned his face with it. But nothing helped. The fire in his side reached out spider-legs and clutched around him, forcing his breath to be shallow. "I'm no good... for... that anymore," he managed.

"You're perfect," she murmured, pressing close to him. She smelled like fire and smoke, and he glanced at the gentle smile on her lips. Her eyes were dark. Peaceful. Verity thought, *Maiden's blessings*, again, and wondered if he was more dead than he felt. And why it still hurt so much.

"Where... would you have me... go?" he said, more out of habit than anything else.

"Farther than ever before, Verity," she breathed.

He curled his fingers into a loose fist, making his tattoos fly. "You found me... too late."

"Just in time!" Putting both hands on his face, she leaned near enough so he could only see her face, filling his vision. "My brother died without me, Verity. We were supposed to die as we did all things: together. He's waiting, I know. Waiting for one more night, and he cannot go without me."

"You want... me to find him and ask... ask your brother to wait for you?" Verity wanted to laugh again, but she was serious. She was mad. "It doesn't work... like that." He could only whisper.

"I know where he'll be. At the gates between the Horse and Ox, waiting for his sister and his sword." The girl bent away to grasp the hilt of that curved sword, scraping the tip against the red dirt.

Verity didn't know much, but he did know the Ecclesiarchy wouldn't approve of this girl's plan to circumvent the order of the heavens. He grimaced, but Rabbit put her lips to his ear and whispered, "Die as you have lived, wanderer."

Rabbit took her time folding the last slip of her grandmother's paper. Each edge she flattened until it was crisp, each point she ran against her nails until they were sharp. When finished, the lotus perched in the enter of her palm as delicately as a hummingbird.

She knew Verity watched her, knew he struggled to breath. Blood flecked the corner of his mouth, and he wiped it on the back of his hand. Red streaked across his tattoos, caught and turned to fire in the setting sunlight. Rabbit stood with the lotus and her brother's sword. Its song tingled against the pads of her fingers, slipping through her palm and up around her wrist like a gauntlet. She remembered her brother at her back, their energy wrapping around and around them. His sword striking like a serpent, her sword flying to protect.

As the first stars unveiled themselves behind her, Rabbit removed her brother's coat. She unbuttoned her shirt, and she straddled Verity's lap. She held up the paper lotus. "Will you take my message to heaven, Verity of Restless City?"

He put one hand on her face, leaving a smear of blood behind. "You're mad. But... that's... never stopped me... before."

"Open your mouth," she said with a smile. When he obeyed, Rabbit placed the lotus onto his tongue.

She kissed him then. His lips were soft, but she tasted sour old breath and sweat, all the red dirt of the desert, and sharp, copper blood. It was like kissing death itself.

And Rabbit was not afraid.

Verity coughed, shaking as pain wracked at him. As he calmed himself, Rabbit put the flared tip of her brother's sword against her belly. She took Verity's hand and held it against the warm leather grip. "We'll angle it up to my heart," she whispered, leaning in against the point. It slipped into her skin and she gasped.

"Rabbit," Verity said, shock giving him energy. He tried to tug the sword away, but her small hand was strong, and he was dying. Her smile was beatific as she rolled her narrow dark eyes up to the stars.

"Take my message with you," she whispered again, and pushed forward against him with a cry of pain and delight. She hugged him and her blood poured onto his lap, overwhelming the sticky smell of his own death. Her arms circled his neck and she whispered again, "Verity, take me to my brother."

One thing Verity Longleg of Restless City never expected was to meet his death with a strange, lifeless girl pressed against him.

For starting, he'd never imagined dying without a good handle of liquor. Sometimes it was a fine, filtered whiskey, sometimes beer. Usually in his dreams, a milky rice wine.

At least the stars were gorgeous and flickering up there, lighting all the paths one could wander. At least Casen was dead, too. At least he wasn't in a bed someplace. This, here, the flat mesas, the red dirt, the firelight and diamond-tossed sky; this was –

This was –

Wind came up through the precipice, sounding like a song. Like a great low lament.

The last thing he did before he died was swallow the flower grown wet and heavy on his tongue.

Tessa Gratton wanted to be a dinosaur wrangler or a wizard when she was a kid. These days, she writes about magic and monsters instead. The author of BLOOD MAGIC and THE BLOOD KEEPER from Random House Children's Books, and the forthcoming series "Songs of New Asgard," Tessa is also strangely addicted to posting free short stories online. Visit her at http://tessagratton.com

IN THE NAME OF THE EMPIRE
by Eddy Webb

Detective Salia Madweather looked at the man sitting in the cell and shook her head. "I have to admit, it isn't often that I'm asked to clear the *sheriff* of a murder charge."

The sheriff's office was cramped, only big enough to hold a few cells and a couple of scarred desks with mismatched chairs. The whole place stank of old sweat and booze. In one of the cells sat Sheriff Alaric Norna, a tall man with the kind of thick muscle that comes from hard work instead of vanity. His long black hair fell into his eyes as he stared at the ground in front of him. His deputy, Charda Freeder, was much thinner, his hands fidgeting over the straps of his gun belt as he stared at Salia with wide eyes.

She waited for a moment. When she didn't get a comment from either of the lawmen, she opened a heavy leather bag with the Twin Eagle emblem on the side and pulled out a chunky pair of goggles with a large light affixed to the top, like a miner's helmet. "Well, if I'm going to take your case, I'll need to start collecting evidence," she said as she settled the goggles over her eyes.

"What's that?" Freeder said, his hands still dancing. Salia sincerely hoped he didn't end up shooting himself before the interview was over. "Some kind of fancy device from back East to detect lies or somethin'?"

Salia turned to face the deputy, her eyes hidden by the dark lenses. "Don't be daft. There isn't some kind of magical device that allows you to tell if someone's lying just by looking at them."

"Oh," he said. Salia could tell that he was somehow disappointed.

She turned back to the sheriff. "It's a device to take photographs of people just by looking at them. Smile, Sheriff."

The man in the cell didn't move as the flash powder fell to the floor with a brief whiff of sweetness, like burning sugar.

"So how'd you get put in jail?" she asked as she took the goggles back off.

For the first time, Norna looked up at her. "The Magistrate was murdered. His agent claims I did it." He went back to looking at the floor.

Salia turned to the deputy and stuck her thumb at the sheriff. "He's a real talker, isn't he?"

Freeder finally stopped fidgeting. "Beggin' your pardon, ma'am, but he ain't exactly hired for his speakin' skills."

"True enough. However, I would appreciate an explanation for how an agent to the Magistrate has the authority to put the sheriff of a town outside the Periphery in prison as a murder suspect."

"Oh, Agent Jarl didn't put him in that cell, ma'am. The sheriff did that himself."

She stared at Freeder for a moment. "Now why would he do something like that?"

Norna spoke up. "Honor," he said.

"That's not an answer. What in the Many Hells does honor have to do with it?"

Freeder stepped between her and the cell, his voice low. "Sheriff Norno feels that he is all of the justice left here in Pardifall. If the Magistrate's dead and he's accused of murder, it ain't right for him to ignore that charge and go walkin' around. It looks bad on the town, you see."

Salia sighed and opened her bag again, this time pulling out a small notebook and a pencil that had seen better days. "Perhaps you gentlemen had best start at the beginning."

The deputy looked to Norna, who simply nodded. Freeder then cleared his throat and looked back at the detective. "It happened last night, ma'am...."

"'Detective,' please. Or 'Salia,' if you don't feel the need to follow the customs."

"What? Oh, right. Sorry, Detective. Anyhow, last night Sheriff Norna went to the Imperial Magistrate's office. Seems Magistrate Taliwar had something important to tell the sheriff. But when he got in, he found the Magistrate dead at his desk."

"Dead how, exactly? Be precise, please."

"Shot in the head," Norna said.

She glanced at the sheriff. "That would do it. You gave up your guns, of course."

Norna nodded. Freeder reached over to his desk, picking up the two gun belts lying on top of a well-maintained sword and scabbard. "All the bullets present and accounted for, ma'a... Detective."

She pulled a pair of thin silk gloves out of her pocket and slid them onto her hands. She then carefully took the belts and put them into her bag before returning to her notebook. "If you obviously didn't fire the bullet, why do you need to be here?"

Freeder started pacing back and forth, answering for the sheriff. "Once Alaric found the body and called for folks to come get me, the Magistrate's agent came in and started yellin' and screamin'."

"And this is Agent Jarl?"

"Yes, Detective. Sorsen Jarl. He works for the Magistrate, doin' leg work, research, askin' questions, and what have you." He stopped pacing, and went back to fidgeting. "Anyhow, Jarl came in and said that the Magistrate told him that if anythin' were to happen to him, Jarl was to make sure that no one covered up the deed. Jarl said the sheriff was the only one that evenin' with an appointment with the Magistrate, so he must of shot the man himself. Sheriff Norna said he didn't do nothin' of the kind, but Jarl called for a Marshal to investigate regardless."

Salia tapped her notebook with the pencil, thinking. "And so in order that the Empire didn't end up holding the whole town responsible for the Magistrate's death, the Sheriff here agrees to put himself in custody for the immediate future."

"That's right."

"And you called Twin Eagle Security to clear the good sheriff's name before the Marshal gets here."

"Exactly."

"Any idea how long that will be, Deputy Freeder?"

"Tomorrow. Maybe the day after."

"Maiden's Tits." Salia snapped the notebook shut. "Well, that doesn't give me much time, then, does it? The rate's thirty dollars a day, plus expenses. Where's the corpse?"

"Doc has him. I'll take you there." Freeder walked over to the door and started to open it for her, but caught her gaze. He seemed to change his mind, and walked ahead of her through the door.

The main street of Pardifall was just hard-packed dirt littered with horse droppings and wheel tracks. The buildings on either side were low and sturdy, but only the occasional sign or splash of paint made it possible to distinguish between them. As Salia walked out of the door, a light wind kicked up a cloud of dust, and it took a moment before she saw the crowd of men standing menacingly around the Sheriff's office.

"There she is!" A strong voice bellowed from the back of the crowd, coming from a tall, stout man. Salia glanced over the quality of his hat, the fashionable cut of his jacket, and the crisp look of his tie. *A rich man,* she thought.

Freeder put his hands up towards the crowd. "That's enough of that, Tobas. This lady's just here to help."

"That's a damned lie! She's here to help the Empire take our town away from us!" The crowd murmured, sympathetic to the man's arguments.

Salia put her hat on her head, and spoke to Freeder as she casually changed her stance to a defensive one. "Who's this Tobas?"

Freeder kept his eyes on the crowd, talking out of the side of his mouth to Salia. "Tobas Laers."

"Laers? As in Osten Laers, the grocer baron?"

"Tobas ain't no grocer, Detective. But he's influential in this town, that's for…"

A bottle exploded as it hit the wall behind Salia's head. Freeder suddenly had his pistol in his hand and waved it at the crowd. "The man who threw that better step up, or there'll be trouble."

Another bottle flew. Salia heard a sickening *crack*, and Freeder slumped to the ground. She took a step towards him, but by then three men from the crowd were walking up to her, menacingly.

"Three against one. Not quite fair odds, gentlemen. Maybe I should tie one hand behind my back to make you feel better."

A thick-necked, bald man chuckled and swung a heavy fist at her head. Salia ducked the blow and kicked out at his knee. She felt a satisfying *crunch* and he went down screaming. She turned to the second man, who had a thick moustache and a pistol in his hand. *A civilian model, of a small caliber*, she noticed. Salia kicked high in the air before pushing off the ground to launch herself at Moustache. She knocked him to the ground as the heel of her boot smashed into his shoulder hard enough to snap his collarbone. Moustache whimpered as she rolled to her feet behind him.

As she was standing up, a third man with a long scar on his face lunged at her. She just caught the gleam of his heavy knife in the corner of her eye as he stabbed at her back. She leaned back and grabbed the knife-wielder's arm, twisting his wrist. He swore and dropped the weapon, just as the bald man with the big fists swung them down on her head. She just managed to pull back further, dragging Scar with her, but the heavy fists landed on her arms, forcing her to break the hold on Scar. She whipped around and slammed her open palm into Baldy's face, shattering his nose and dropping him to the ground.

Scar used the distraction to scramble forward and scoop up his blade. Once Baldy fell, he lunged forward and knocked Salia to the ground, putting the knife to her throat. She barely had time to put her arms up, holding the blade to where the edge barely touched her skin. Scar leaned hard on her, and she felt the muscles in her arm strain against his weight.

"I'm gonna cut your throat, you Imperial bitch," he said. His breath smelled of whiskey and shit, and Salia gagged as she eased her right hand off of his wrist. He tried to lunge forward again, pressing his advantage, but she quickly jerked her hand hard to the right, and a pistol on a heavy spring shot out of her jacket sleeve. She snatched the grip of the small gun and slammed the barrel hard into Scar's cheekbone. The blade and the breath both disappeared as he rolled off of her.

Salia slowly stood up, pointing the pistol at the men as she went to check on Freeder. He was unconscious, but his pulse was strong. The rest of crowd was gone, including Tobas. She gritted her teeth and walked back to Scar.

"I have a question in our mutual interest," she said, gently putting the barrel of the pistol against his forehead. "Where would a lady such as myself find the town doctor?"

Dr. Dauna adjusted her glasses and looked Salia up and down. "You seem to have damaged our deputy," she said, her voice clipped and sharp with irritation.

Salia helped Freeder, now conscious but still wobbly on his feet, into the doctor's office. He slumped into a chair, holding a bloody hand to his head. "Wasn't me, doctor," the detective said. "It was the three men lying in various states of injury near his office."

"Are they in serious danger?"

"Not as long as they keep away from me, they aren't."

The doctor slipped on some magnifying glasses and started looking over Freeder's wound as she talked. "And I take it you are responsible for their current condition, Miss...?"

"Detective. Detective Salia Madweather." She took off her hat and set it on the desk, keeping her leather bag in her hand.

"The Twin Eagle woman. I had heard you were in town." She looked up from Freeder and slipped off the glasses. "It's just a cut, deputy. A few stitches, and you'll be fine."

"I got a headache a league wide, doc," Freeder said with a slight slur to his words.

"Take a sip of poppy. You'll feel better." She turned and looked at Salia again. "I take it you're here to see the Magistrate?"

"Just the dead one."

The doctor frowned at the witticism. "Well, until my other new patients come in, I have a few moments to spare. Please come with me, and keep your comments strictly relevant, if you please."

Salia smirked. "I like you already, doctor."

The doctor turned and opened a door to a back room. Tendrils of cold slid out from the open door, and Salia could just make out huge blocks of melting ice inside. Then the smell slapped her in the face, making Salia's eyes water. She coughed involuntarily and dug in her bag for a silk mask before tying it over her nose and mouth.

Dauna watched the detective carefully. "I haven't seen a mask quite like that one. I commend you on your preparations."

Salia pulled her photographic goggles out of the bag as well and put them on before setting the bag down at her feet. "I'm surprised you hadn't seen them before. They must have come into use just after you left the Empire."

"How did you...?"

The detective put her hands up in a placating gesture. "Relax, doctor. I've already got a sense of how much this town doesn't like the Empire, so it's not like I'll be telling everyone. Your accent is worn down over the years, but it's still there. Besides, I don't expect there are all that many medical colleges outside the Periphery."

The doctor stared at Salia for a moment before answering. "Pardifall was a place to escape the Empire, at least for a while. But not all of us begrudged having some more law in town."

Salia nodded and pointed at the corpse. "So let's live up to that. Tell me his story."

Both women looked down at Taliwar's body. He was a heavy-set man, with black and gray hair carefully groomed into the queue common to Imperial Magistrates. Most of him was modestly covered with a thin sheet. The precise hole in his head seemed small, almost like an afterthought.

"Magistrate Taliwar was shot in the forehead. The bullet exited in the rear of the skull." Despite the smell and the cold, Dauna's voice was becoming more animated. "Notice the area of the initial wound."

Salia leaned over and looked where the doctor pointed. "No powder burns."

"Correct. So he was shot at a distance at least."

"Which rules out a suicide." Salia toyed with the goggles, and the room was flooded with light and the smell of burning sugar.

Dauna started to protest, but the detective rolled the Magistrate's head to the side to look at the exit wound. "A bullet this small probably didn't come from the sheriff's gun."

"You are likely correct." Her lips pursed together in a thin line as flash powder fell again. She turned and opened a small wooden chest sitting in one corner, pulling out a bundle of clothing. "You may find these of more interest." Dauna carefully put the clothing on the edge of the table. "All of the Magistrate's personal effects."

Salia carefully looked through the clothes. She found a gun hidden in the bundle – a small caliber pistol, similar to the one her attacker with the broken collarbone had carried. "Does everyone in Pardifall carry a pistol?" she asked.

"Not everyone, but many do. It's not uncommon or even illegal to have them on your person, but generally civilians only carry them if they're worried something will happen."

"So he was expecting something bad to happen. And yet the bullet wound is clean in the center of his head. He didn't move or duck – he was surprised. Why would he be prepared to shoot someone if he needed to, and yet be surprised when it happened?"

The doctor leaned over and pulled the sheet over Taliwar's face. "You'll have to ask Sheriff Norna about that. Agent Jarl seems to think he's the one who killed him."

Salia tapped on the edge of the table, deep in thought. "Yes, I really should meet this Agent Jarl."

The Thrice-Blessed Watering Hole Saloon was busy when Salia walked in. Round tables were scattered all over, with grizzled men and worn-out women hunched over tin mugs or cards. A low murmur filled the room, and the familiar odor of stale beer and sawdust filled her nose as the door swung closed behind her. The whole place didn't suddenly become quiet when she walked in – that kind of thing only happened in bit novels – but she got her share of curious stares as she made her way to the bar. "A pint of the regular, and some information," she said, putting her bag and a couple of bits on the bar.

The bartender gave her a quick glance before reaching for a clean mug. "The first will cost you two bits. The other depends on what you want."

"I'm looking for Agent Jarl. Do you know where I can find him?"

The bartender nodded to a tall man standing at the end of the bar before setting down the mug, scooping up the bits, and moving to other customers.

The man had smooth skin and a strong jaw, and his body held a casual grace. This was clearly a man who was used to physical activity, but not a laborer. Salia tried to assess him dispassionately, but she kept noticing how handsome he was. The man looked her over carefully as she grabbed her bag and walked up to him. "Who are you?" he asked, friendly but suspicious.

"I'm Salia Madweather, Twin Eagle Security Agency, looking into the murder of Magistrate Taliwar." She held out her hand – sideways, to be shaken, not palm down.

"Sorsen Jarl, at your service." He turned her hand and kissed the air over the top of it, just as if they were in some Imperial salon.

"Looks *and* manners. You'll be the death of me, Agent Jarl." Salia let her lips pull into a lazy smile that has gotten her out of as much trouble as it's put her into. "But neither are as good to me as answers, so if you don't mind I'd like to focus on business before moving on to pleasure."

"Of course, Miss Madweather."

"Detective, please. Or Salia if you think we can be friends." She tried the smile again, and this time Jarl copied it.

"Of course... Salia. What would you like to know?"

She pulled her notebook and pencil out of the bag. "Why are you so sure that the sheriff was the murderer?"

His smile dropped into a soft scowl, and Salia noticed that this was just as attractive on him. "That man has done nothing but badger the Magistrate for months. They were always fighting. Personally, I suspect he resents the Empire's attempts to bring some civilized law into this town, instead of his own level of casual thuggery that passes as justice."

She started tapping her notebook with her pencil. "I'm not sure 'thuggery' is the right word, Agent Jarl...."

"Sorsen, please." That smile again.

She returned it. "Agent Jarl," she said, putting particular emphasis on the title, which caused his smile to fade, "a man that puts himself in a jail cell while protesting his innocence knowing full well that he'll likely be killed by an Imperial Marshal doesn't strike me as a man that normally plays fast and loose with the law. And he certainly doesn't strike me as someone likely to murder an Imperial Magistrate."

Jarl waved his hand dismissively. "How can I possibly know what these yokels think? I'm surprised they managed to live this long, to be honest." He seemed oblivious to the stares he was attracting as he continued. "But that man had guns on him, and the Magistrate died of a bullet wound. They had fought before about the Empire's laws. He was alone with the Magistrate. That means he had the means, the motive, and the opportunity."

Salia looked Jarl over, much more clinically this time. "That's a nice sidearm you have, Agent Jarl. It's not a military model – it's one usually bought by civilians looking for a little more protection."

He glanced down at the gun on his hip with a start, as if he had forgotten all about it. "I... well, of course. There must be dozens of people who carry these in Pardifall alone."

"It's also a smaller caliber of weapon compared to the one the sheriff carries."

He stared at Salia for a moment in silence. "You aren't seriously looking into the sheriff's *innocence*, are you?"

"Deputy Freeder is my client. You'll have to ask him as to my intentions. I'm not at liberty to say."

Jarl stepped close to Salia, his face inches away from hers, causing her to back up against the bar. "You don't want to be on the wrong side of me, *Detective*. I have a duty to the Empire, and I will do whatever it takes to carry that duty out."

"Including keeping me from looking at the Magistrate's office?" she asked, playing for time as the wheels turned in her head.

"*Especially* that. There are important Imperial secrets kept there, and you are just a private investigator." He paused to look her over again, and his temper mellowed. "Although I'm sure I would enjoy a woman such as you trying to change my mind."

Salia nudged Jarl's stomach with her notebook, causing him to instinctively take a step back. She used the moment to grab her bag and slip past him.

"Unfortunately, my obligation is to my client, and to the honor of Twin Eagle." At the door she turned to look at Jarl once more. "And I would hate to have to ruin you before I had a chance to properly appreciate your many... assets. Sorsen."

She flashed the smile one more time, and pushed open the saloon door. It wasn't until she was on the street that she regretted not having her beer.

The Twin Eagle badge got Salia into Magistrate Taliwar's luxurious office, but not into his records.

"Sorry, ma'am, but Agent Jarl left specific instructions that the Magistrate's office and possessions are not to be disturbed until the Marshall arrives."

Salia leaned over the clerk's dark, well-organized desk and stared hard at the pale bureaucrat. "Look, Mr...."

"Penkins. Josah Penkins."

"... Penkins. I'm here at the request of Deputy Freeder to investigate the Magistrate's murder, on behalf of the Twin Eagle Security Agency. I would like to look at the Magistrate's records, and I would like you to give me access to them." She paused and reached into her jacket pocket. "I can show you the badge again if you like."

"And I've told you, Agent Jarl..."

"... is irrelevant."

Salia and Penkins both turned to look at the new voice. Tobas Laers waddled into the office, guiding his ponderous bulk with an ornate walking stick. "The Empire holds no more power over us, and its tedious bureaucracy will be swept away in the enlightened new age of Pardifall."

The detective stood up and put her hands in her pockets, conveniently pushing her long jacket away from her pistols and sword. "Mr. Laers. I'm surprised to hear a scion of your house so dismissive of the Empire."

"I am not beholden to my father's outmoded views. I care only for business, and this town will thrive and grow under new management."

She looked out of the corner of her eye, and noticed that Penkins had slid under the desk for cover. "I don't much give a damn about your political opinions, Mr. Laers. I'm just here to investigate a murder."

He spread his hands expansively. "To what ends? To give the Marshal more evidence to hang our beloved sheriff? Even if, for some reason, you are inclined to find the sheriff innocent, how does this benefit us... or you?" He tried to look hard at Salia, but his watery eyes and florid face just made him look like he was about to burst. "I can easily double your fee and let you walk away from this dreadful situation, Miss Madweather."

She tried to keep her face neutral, but a small snarl slipped out. "*Detective* Madweather."

"I am only trying to..."

"Maiden's Tits, will you shut up and *listen*, you overbearing ass? I am a detective of the Twin Eagle Security Agency. I don't work for the Empire. I don't work for you. I work for the honor of my clan, and at the behest of my client. Right now, that means I work for Deputy Freeder. So if you're done trying to intimidate me, Mr. Laers, I'd like to get back to intimidating Mr. Penkins here so I can continue my investigation." She turned to look back at the clerk's empty chair, pointedly turning her back on Tobas.

The grocer gave a dry chuckle, as it if were something he wasn't used to doing. "Bravo. Well played, Miss Madweather. But I have heard that you have been talking to Agent Jarl, and I suspect your interests are far more... complex... than you make it out to be." Tobas consulted a silver pocketwatch. "Why don't you come to my home tomorrow morning, and I'll explain the whole nasty affair to you?"

Salia frowned. "Why not tell me now?"

"It is getting late, and I do have other appointments to keep. But tomorrow, I will reveal everything I know."

"Fine. I'll be there at 8 bells."

"I look forward to it, Detective." He turned and waddled out of the room.

Salia watched him leave before turning back to the clerk. "You can come out now," she said, trying to keep the smile from her face.

Penkins slid out from under the desk and back into his seat with as much grace that he could manage. "What a deplorable man," he said. "I suppose I should thank you for your assistance."

"I suppose you should. The best form of appreciation, though, would be to show me what brought him to this office. I'm sure it wasn't just to talk to me."

"As I previously explained to Mr. Laers, an open investigation by a Magistrate is a very sensitive issue."

"Investigation?"

The clerk continued as if he hadn't heard her. "The Empire frowns heavily on such secret documents being shared with just anyone. Even Agent Jarl himself hasn't seen the papers yet."

"But you wouldn't be sharing them with just anyone," she said. "You'd be sharing them with me. And we're a long way from the Empire." She smiled a little at him. "Besides, I'm much nicer than Mr. Laers."

Penkins glanced at the door. Sweat stood up on his brow. "I couldn't possibly let you take them from the building, ma'am..."

She picked up her bag and set it heavily on his desk. "Who said anything about taking them?"

Salia sipped at a chipped mug of hot galao, her elbows on the sheriff's desk. The Castalan drink kept her exhausted mind working as she tried to spell out the details. Freeder sat on the edge of his desk across from her, his head wrapped up in a new silk bandage, while Norna sat in his cell watching her. He tried to look unimpressed (*that damned Far Western honor*, she thought), but Salia noticed a gleam of hope in the sheriff's eyes. She set the mug down and continued.

"The Magistrate's documents were all too clear. Past all of the Imperial speech and flowery legal details, it's all pretty simple. Pardifall is sitting on top of an untapped jade deposit worth millions."

Freeder whistled softly. Norna frowned – the first real show of emotion she'd seen from him. "So Jarl and the Magistrate were trying to get it for the Empire?"

Salia shook her head. "That doesn't add up, though. If they were in it together, why would Jarl kill the Magistrate?"

Norna got up and started pacing his cell. "To keep all the glory for himself. He kills the Magistrate, frames me, tries to keep the records under lock and key, and hands the whole town over to the Empire."

"It's possible, but why did the Magistrate ask for you in private?"

"Maybe he got cold feet?" Freeder said. "Could be he wanted the Sheriff to arrest Jarl?"

"That doesn't work either," Salia said. "The Empire doesn't need a local Sheriff to handle their disputes. If the Magistrate really felt he had something on Jarl, he'd call in a Marshal. If he didn't, why not just take care of it himself?" She tapped her pencil on the photographs of Taliwar's reports. "No, there's something in here that we're missing. Taliwar was pretty vague in some of his notes, but the phrase 'Old Lion' kept popping up. Any idea what that that refers to?"

Norna shrugged, and Freeder shook his head before wincing and touching his bandage. Salia sighed and dropped her pencil on the desk. "My brain is squeezed dry. Maybe this meeting with Tobas in the morning will shake something loose."

"Why does he want to meet with you anyhow?" Norna asked. "The Laers family never struck me as being particularly keen on helping the law, whether it was public, private, or Imperial."

"I don't know, but he was awfully keen on something in that office...." Her eye glanced down at the photographs again, and suddenly she slapped her hand on the table. "Of course! It's been staring me in the face the whole time!"

Freeder stood up and looked over her shoulder. "What? What is it?"

She leaned back, smiling triumphantly. "Gentlemen, I know who killed Magistrate Taliwar."

The next morning was dark with storm clouds, and a slow patter of rain fell from the sky. A few drops fell from the brim of Salia's hat as she looked over at Freeder.

"You don't have to do this, you know."

His face was firm. "Yes, I do."

"I know you're worried about Norna, but this is the kind of thing Twin Eagle gets paid for. You're my client."

He turned to look at her. "No, Detective. I'm the deputy."

She looked at his face for a moment. His jaw was firm, and his eyes were clear, despite the bandage tucked under his hat. Just for a moment, Salia thought he looked very young. "So you are. Let's go in."

The Laers house was large, as big as two or three buildings put together. A couple of men with rifles and swords tried to take their weapons at the front gate, but Freeder showed them his badge, and they both made their way inside unmolested. As they walked up to the front door, Salia noticed a large carriage sitting outside. The black vehicle had the Emperor's logo prominently displayed on the side, and a well-dressed driver stood ramrod straight beside it while the light rain soaked into his uniform.

A uniform of the Imperial Army.

"Maiden's Tits. I bet you a million talons that the Marshal's here. Probably hopped an Army airship to get here faster."

Freeder stared at the carriage, and Salia noticed his hands shaking a little. "Why is he here at the house?"

She adjusted her grip on the bag. "Because he's with Jarl, and Jarl has business with Tobas poking around at the Magistrate's office."

A butler that was probably old when the Secession Wars were just a fistfight led them to an opulent library. Deep red wallpaper peeked out around heavy shelves covered in books that were probably bought to be impressive and never once read. Seated in an overstuffed chair was Tobas Laers, a drink in his hand and Scar and Baldy standing behind him. Baldy's nose was heavily taped up, but she could still see the purple bruising under his eyes. Scar snarled at Salia, and she simply tipped her hat at him.

Pacing the floor behind a matching chair was Jarl, whose dark grimace seemed to light up for a moment upon Salia's entrance. A third chair sat facing a large stone fireplace, making a nice triangle for easy conversation. Cigars and bottles of aged agave wine sat on little tables by the chairs.

At the fireplace was a tall, strong man in a simple uniform of black. His face was covered with a matching silk mask painted with very realistic looking burn scars that almost looked like the Imperial crest. Salia recognized him – Marshal Brand.

She took off her hat, and bowed respectfully to Brand. "A surprise and an honor to see you here, Marshal. I hope that this town's humble problems do not distract you from more pressing duties."

Jarl stopped and looked at Salia, waving a hand dismissively at the Marshal. "He is here at my request, as befits an acting Magistrate of the Empire, to arrest and sentence that murderous Sheriff."

Salia's body stiffened at Jarl's casual treatment of Brand. "You might want to put that pretty little hand of yours back in your pocket, Agent Jarl. He's here at your request, but he isn't your minion, and I'd hate to have you... damaged." She smirked at him before turning to Tobas. "But I'm more interested in why they're here in your house, Mr. Laers. I had the impression that you weren't a fan of the Empire."

Tobas's lips twisted up. Salia got the impression that he was trying to smile, but it came out as a sneer. "I invited Agent Jarl here to discuss the imposition he has on the Magistrate's papers. I was... unaware of the Marshal's presence, but now that he is here, I am happy to cooperate in any way that I can to see that justice is done."

"Well ain't that kind of you," Freeder spat, but Salia put her hand up and shook her head.

"What my client means is that he appreciates anything you can do to help this investigation," Salia said, her eyes still locked on Tobas.

The merchant nodded. "I hope that since these gentlemen are finished with my time, we can move on to our own business?"

"Actually, if you don't mind, Mr. Laers, I'd like them to stay. I think they'll be quite interested in what I have to say to you."

Tobas's smile turned into a more sincere-looking frown. "I would really rather we talked in private. These are sensitive matters, and not for the ears of others."

Salia carefully took the chair between Tobas and Jarl, and crossed her legs – not only to give off a casual air, but to give her better access to the pouch on her belt. "I disagree, Mr. Laers. I think the attempted murder of a member of the Twin Eagle clan is something the Empire would be moderately interested in."

The room fell silent. Scar and Baldy moved slightly, eyes locked on Salia, hands like claws over their sword hilts. She looked past them, smirking at Tobas. She knew that Freeder was carefully freeing his pistol while all the attention was on her.

Jarl was the first to break the silence. "This is a serious accusation, Detective. I do hope you have some evidence."

"Of course she doesn't!" Tobas burst out. "She's lying! Arrest that woman and take her from my house immediately!"

Salia slowly reached into her jacket. Out of the corner of her eye, she saw the two guards grab their swords, but she only pulled out a small stack of photographs, which she handed to Jarl. As she did, she glanced at the Marshal, who looked as still as a statue, never moving.

"The reason why he intends to kill me, Agent Jarl, is that he believes I know the real reason that Magistrate Taliwar was killed. It just so happens that I do."

Jarl took the photographs but kept his eyes on Salia. "Then please tell us, Detective, why the Sheriff shot the illustrious Magistrate, and what it has to do with Mr. Laers here."

She shifted in her seat to look at the Marshal, and she used the motion to pull a small pellet out of her pouch. "The motive is quite simple. There is a jade deposit under this town that is worth a fortune. The Magistrate knew of this, which is why he was killed."

"The Sheriff killed Magistrate Taliwar because of a jade deposit?"

Salia smiled at Jarl. "Oh, did I imply that the Sheriff killed him? I'm sorry, I forgot to mention. Mr. Laers here shot him."

She heard Tobas bark something at his guards, who lunged forward.

She squeezed the pellet in her hand, breaking the thin membrane inside, before throwing it at Scar. The two chemicals inside combined into a fast-acting acid, which hissed and popped as it splashed on his face. He screamed and dropped his blade while she ducked down to avoid Baldy's sword. The blade slammed into the back of the chair, trapping it, and Freeder clapped the barrel of his pistol on his forehead.

The room became still again except for Scar's screaming. Salia took the moment to stand up and dust herself off before looking at Baldy. "Drop the sword and get your friend to the doctor, or he won't have a face left." Baldy hesitated, but Freeder nudged him with his gun, and the guard dropped his sword to carry Scar out of the room.

Tobas gripped the arms of his chair with white knuckles, quivering in fury. "How... *dare* you! You...."

Salia stepped forward. "Tobas Laers, your father, Osten Laers, found out about the jade under this town. I don't know whether you came out here to secure a mine or were already here when he found out, but it doesn't matter. Either way, you were told to acquire the rights to that deposit, no matter what. That meant making sure the Magistrate didn't know what was under the land you were going to try and buy up. But you got his attention somehow, and he looked into it, and found out about the plan. And he took notes, although because he was afraid of who might see them, he only referenced the plan as being driven by 'Old Lion' -- O.L.   Osten Laers -- your father."

Jarl flipped through the photographs. "These are...."

"... photographs of the papers in his office, yes." She glanced at Jarl. "As handsome as you are, I couldn't be sure you weren't the one who had the Magistrate killed, and I thought you locked up the papers to hide the motive for your crime. But then the clerk mentioned that even *you* hadn't seen them yet, which dropped the number of suspects down to one. So I..." She shot a quick glance at the Marshal. "... *convinced* the clerk to give me a look at the papers. He quickly saw it was in the Empire's best interest to let me take a few copies."

She turned back to Tobas. "But you knew that there was no way the

Empire would let House Laers just walk away with controlling interest in such a fortune. So you tried to play on the suffering of these folk, manipulate the fear and resentments of the Secession Wars, and tried to get them to turn against the Empire. It would have been bloody. Folks would have died. If they broke away, House Laers could come in and buy up all the land for cheap under the guise of helping them to rebuild.

"But the Magistrate wasn't a fool. He knew what would happen. So he planned to tell the Sheriff. Maybe he planned to share the mine with Pardifall, or maybe he was going to bribe Norna to stay silent, but no matter what the locals would have known what they were sitting on. They would have had bargaining power."

Salia jabbed a finger at Tobas. "So you killed the Magistrate, and framed Norna. You would have started a massacre, just to make more money."

Tobas's face grew paler during the course of the story. Once she finished, Freeder stepped towards him, pistol still out. "Tobas Laers, I arrest you for...."

Marshal Brand's hand blurred, and a loud crack filled the room as Tobas's brains splatted against the wall.

Freeder spun around while Salia's small pistol shot out of her sleeve. Jarl dropped to the floor as Salia yelled out "Drop the gun, Marshal!"

Brand calmly holstered the pistol. His eyes behind the mask bored into her like two slivers of black jade. "I have judged Tobas Laers, and executed him in the name of the Empire." His voice was deep and calm, like a river with hidden currents that would drag you under. "Magistrate Jarl will rebuild the Empire's presence in Pardifall now, and make sure the mine is given to the Emperor. My duty is completed."

He turned and walked out of the house, and everyone watched him go.

In that moment, Salia understood why people out West hated the Empire.

Eddy Webb (with a "y," thank you) is a writer, podcaster, game designer, and transmedia developer. In his career he has written for a number of role-playing games, as well as for two MMOs, and he's won a few awards along the way. He lives a sitcom life with his wife, his roommate, a supervillain cat, and two pug dogs. An anthology of his fiction and essays, "Slices of Fate," will be coming out from FR Press soon.

ERRANT EAGLES
by Will Hindmarch

Delicate things, airships. The things work only if everyone on board behaves themselves. Get someone on board who ain't got no respect for fellow travelers or the delicacy of flight and the whole thing can fall in a hurry.

The *Maiden's Breath* looked something like a riverboat on its back, slung from its gasbag on hand-woven cables, the sky-ship's white planks and shining brass bright in the afternoon sun. Angled black smokestacks splayed out below like the legs of a newborn foal. Trails of coal smoke smeared the air behind it. In place of paddles, wide props, looking like lovely petals, pushed her through the sky.

She was no soaring ship. She cruised above the plains so low that some small-town temple towers might have scratched her paint. No temples loomed in sight on that wide prairie, though—she sailed over wild grasses and subtle hills, her passengers bound for Prosperity in the west. Her faint altitude was meant to give her passengers a close look at the open range below, at the bucolic charm of its windswept fields of grain and the roaming courts of flightless thunderbirds.

That shallow flight also had Redhand wondering if he could survive a leap from the airship's starboard railing. The sunlit prairie rushed by below. Passengers cried out in panic.

The ship was on fire pretty fierce by then and Redhand thought it might provide him the cover he needed to get free. Redhand hoped Hollowaigh would reel from his pistol-whipping in the parlor long enough for Redhand to vanish in the chaos of the accidental kerosene fire. Maybe Hallowaigh, who said he was aboard on a case, on behalf of the Twin Eagle Security Agency, would stop to put out the fire started when he threw Redhand into a kerosene lamp. Maybe Hollowaigh, who thought so little of pulling his pistol in the crowded airborne parlor, would think twice about making a foolhardy leap that would surely break a leg or two.

Redhand's dreadlocks whipped about his head in the smoke and wind as he thought on the leap himself—thought too long.

Hollowaigh got two fistfuls of Redhand's coat and pulled him clear of the railing, swung him about, and pushed him through flimsy flapping shutter-doors into the ship's game room. Hollowaigh was no big man but he knew how to move. Redhand crashed into a card table, which flipped off its mountings beneath him. Clay chips went flying. The room was already clear of gamblers and gamesters—they'd fled the choking smoke.

Redhand felt the heat of the spreading fire on his face, on his palms; heard Hollowaigh stomping across the wooden floor behind him. Redhand rolled. Ivory game tiles skidded away as he threw himself to his feet, coming face to face with Hollowaigh.

Hollowaigh drew a six-gun from his hip, the oiled holster stamped with twin eagles.

Redhand drew Hollowaigh's other six-gun from the oiled holster on the detective's other hip.

As Hollowaigh raised his gun, Redhand knocked it aside with the gun in his hand, grabbed Hollowaigh's pistol in his free left hand and jammed his thumb between the pistol's cylinder and frame. Then Redhand backhanded Hollowaigh with a fistful of iron.

Hollowaigh reacted less than Redhand hoped. As floorboards crackled and split in the widening fire, the two of them roved, unsteady, trying to get their feet, trying to push the other about. When Hollowaigh finally got a foot planted, he thumbed the hammer in his gun-hand. The cylinder slipped out from under Redhand's thumb.

Hollowaigh put his barrel to Redhand's belly. Redhand slipped his ring finger between hammer and cylinder as the hammer fell. Redhand cussed as his finger broke. The gun didn't go off.

Redhand hit Hollowaigh with his stolen pistol again, yanked Hollowaigh's six-gun from his grip, then shouldered the man against a shuttered window. Slats creaked. For a second, Redhand had both guns. Hollowaigh reached for one and Redhand held the piece straight out behind himself, out of reach, with practiced speed.

Hollowaigh put his knee into Redhand's groin. Redhand doubled over, his right-hand gun tucked in his gut, and flicked Hollowaigh's gun into the fire with his bloody left hand. Hollowaigh groped for the remaining gun. Got it in hand. Redhand put all his weight against Hollowaigh. Shutter slats snapped.

The whole room rolled. Hollowaigh went from being pressed against a wall to pinned underneath Redhand as cable moorings outside broke free from burning boards and the airship's hull sagged and dangled partway free of the gas-filled bag above.

The shutters now underneath Hollowaigh gave way. He fell shoulders-first through the window and tumbled against the starboard railing now below him. Redhand caught himself with a palm on either side of the broken window, as if he was doing push-ups over the gap.

Hollowaigh still had the gun. He shifted it in his hand, palmed the grip, took aim.

Redhand pushed off the sideways wall, rolling along it as Hollowaigh's shot splintered the window frame. Tables and chairs piled up where the floor met the wall, rolled into place by the tumbled hull. Redhand stood on the wall, scaled the furniture heap as flames lapped around him, and leapt for the ceiling made by the far wall. He got his hand on a wall sconce and swung on it. Blackened wallpaper curled away in sheets as the glue beneath it melted and ran. Ashen paper swirled in the air like leaves amid the blowing cinders.

The airship lurched as more cables broke free. Redhand got his hands on the doorframe opposite the one he'd been thrown through a minute before and hung from it. He winced at the weight on his broken fingertip. His eyes poured out water against the smoke.

Hollowaigh, still sprawled on the railing below, caught sight of Redhand hanging above and fired again. The bullet cut the air near Redhand's head.

Redhand pulled himself up through the doorway and rolled across the wall of the tumbled room above—the ship's rear bar.

More shots rang out in the game room as the pistol Redhand threw aside cooked in the fire, its ammo exploding and Hollowaigh firing back at the noise.

Redhand scrambled for the bar, which ran from floor to ceiling now, and heard Hollowaigh clamboring up through the game room below. Redhand swung on a brass fixture, slipped behind the bar, and hoped his instincts were good.

They were. He tossed his dreads out of his face and yanked a twin-barreled breech-loader out of its sheath within the bar. Tucking it into his loose leather belt, wiping tears from his eyes, he scaled the inside of the bar like a ladder until the wood spit out yellow splinters when one of Hollowaigh's rounds punched through it.

A peek around the bar revealed Hollowaigh on his belly, with one leg up through the door in the floor, squinting against the smoke billowing up around him. No way Hollowaigh could make a decent shot like that. Redhand kept climbing. Above him was a window that led to the port-side walkway of the airship—but Redhand would have to come out from behind the bar to get through it. Behind the bar was a door leading back to some modest storeroom and office, a corkboard dangling wild on a loose hook in the wall.

Another shot from Hollowaigh, another wound to the bar. Then Hollowaigh was groaning and dashing toward the bar, glasses rolling about around his feet.

Redhand drew his hand-cannon with his left hand, his broken ring finger jutting out, put his arm around the bar and fired one barrel blind, aiming down. The shot went wide. Hollowaigh ducked instinctively, tripped on a brass sconce curling from the hot floor, and tumbled into the bar.

Something gave way in the rear of the airship. The back of the room sagged and Redhand found the bar angling above him. Hanging from his good hand, he wrapped one leg around the edge of the bar and pushed off with the other to slide down the stretch of polished wood and brass like a pole.

Hollowaigh fired a panic shot. Redhand slammed into him feet first.

Hollowaigh stumbled back against what was now the wall and immediately pushed off of it.

Redhand moved to fire his last barrel from the hip. Hollowaigh straightened his arm, gun pointed at Redhand's chest.

The room tumbled upward as the hull banged against the prairie below. Fingers of fire flashed through the walls and floor, spitting cinders into the room. Broken pint glasses and teacups arced through the air.

Redhand grabbed the bar with his good hand as the room flopped. Hollowaigh went backward, squeezed a shot into the mirror behind the bar, and was buried as the barroom tables and chairs came tumbling down the sloping room in the flailing hull.

The walls shivered and split as the sinking airship gouged the prairie, the hull snagging on the earth in a plume of smoke and dirt.

The house that Redhand built for his wife, Abigail Marsdan, stood on the side of a modest hill crowned by a great oak tree. It was two stories of yellow boards capped with three gabled roofs. Wildflowers swayed when the wind came across the hillside. They were bright white even in the night, seemingly shining in the glow of the Rushing Rabbit's quick course across the starry sky.

Half the house was burned out, leaving it blackened and hollowed like a rotten tooth. A dozen townsfolk stood around the place with lanterns and torches and wet buckets drawn up from the crick at the base of the hill. Each one with a lantern was a bright collar and a fire-lit face hovering in the night; each one without was a dark shape against the backdrop of wildflowers and stars. Somewhere in the dark and the long grass, Redhand's dog was running, barking.

The folk made way for a new pair of shapes coming up the hillside. A horse complained below. One of the new shapes lit the lantern it held and the pale light revealed a ginger-bearded face and high, arched brows beneath a simple hat—Hollowaigh.

The other new shape stood backlit by the lantern. It had the crisp collar and tailored shoulders of wealth and smelled like citrus and cigars. It drew a wad of bright silk from its breast pocket, unfolded a handkerchief, and held it to over its mouth. The other hand held out a brassy badge so it caught the lantern light. The badge was a palm-sized shield emblazoned with twin eagles.

The townspeople looked to each other, nodding. One of them, an older man, pointed up at the house. A younger man gestured for the newcomers to follow him.

"I know the way," said the voice behind the handkerchief. He strode through the crowd, up the hill, the firelight revealing the shiny paisley pattern on his cuffs and lapels.

As he passed, someone whispered to someone else, "That's her brother. That's Jang Marsdan."

The dog came to the edge of the lantern light and ran sideways, barking at the crowd.

"Somebody shut that thing up before I shoot it," Hollowaigh said. Someone separated from the crowd, snagged the dog by the collar, tried to calm it down.

The rest followed the newcomers to the foot of the front-porch steps.

Hollowaigh kept going, stopped where the front door hung open, the top of the jamb streaked with smoke. He looked back at his partner.

There, with Hollowaigh's lantern in front of him, Marsdan's fine red coat and silver buttons were plain to see. One hand held the handkerchief over his mouth. The other held the coat back, away from a bright silver revolver, as though he contemplated shooting the house itself.

"Should I?" Hollowaigh asked.

Marsdan shook his head and came forward. He tucked his handkerchief in a pocket and took the lantern from Hollowaigh. He stepped carefully across the threshold into the house.

A woman lay on her stomach in the front hall amid a dusting of broken glass and a smear of blood, as though she'd been dragged away from the front door. Her hair splayed out on the floorboards and in her blood.

Hollowaigh edged around his partner and stepped closer to the body. Marsdan gestured. Hollowaigh crouched down and moved the woman's hair aside, revealing a pale face with slender, open eyes and a delicate mouth. Her bottom lip was gashed and bloody. Hollowaigh looked back and up at Marsdan.

Marsdan set the lantern on the floor. His hand was shaking.

Hollowaigh opened his mouth to speak, shut it again. Almost touched a spot where a bullet had torn through the woman's dress, then withdrew his hand.

The wind sighed through the back of the house, wide open to night where the fire had eaten half of it away. The dog barked outside.

"Where is he?" asked Marsdan.

Hollowaigh shook his head.

"Where is he?" Marsdan asked again, over his shoulder.

"Redhand?" asked one townsperson.

"He rode," said another. "He rode off."

Hollowaigh stood, drew his six-gun, and stomped back out the front door. The crowd made way. Hollowaigh dropped off the porch, took two steps, pulled back the hammer and aimed his gun at Redhand's dog.

The fellow holding its collar jumped back. The dog stood its ground, growling between barks.

121

One townsperson took off his hat. "It's not what you think," he said.

Hollowaigh turned his head to look at him.

The townsperson looked from Hollowaigh to Marsdan, who emerged from the house and stepped slowly over to stand between Hollowaigh and the townsperson. "What do we think?" Marsdan asked the townsperson.

"It wasn't Redhand. Redhand rode off to find the bastard," the townsperson said. "To get him."

Marsdan raised his eyebrows. A silent question. His eyes were wet.

"Broadhorn was in town today," another townsperson said. "Asked about Redhand."

"Did one of you speak to Broadhorn?" Marsdan asked. In the dark, for most men, the tell would've been all but impossible to read—the townspeople shifting and glancing at each other. Then they all looked away from the man who mentioned Broadhorn. "You?"

The man gave a reluctant nod.

Marsdan drew his bright revolver. Its grip was silver. Rushing Rabbit's light made it shine. "You told Broadhorn about this place?"

The man made a noise, a few babbled, defensive vowels.

Marsdan shot him. Barely moved his arm to do it.

Hollowaigh shot the dog.

The *Maiden's Breath* left a long gash in the green prairie, her hull dashed to pieces here, laid out in odd segments of burned floorboards and shivered timbers there. Half of a wagon-wheel chandelier jutted from the topsoil. The corner of a stateroom lay in the grass like a rough canoe with wallpapered innards. Broken bottles and tin cups lay scattered like coins in a dry fountain.

The ship's gasbag dragged the fore section of the wreck onward across the grass before the hull snagged on some patch of rugged ground. The bent timbers of the ship's open belly looked like a ribcage of splintered bone with a balloon tied to its spine.

The majority of the vessel's passengers and crew took refuge in that forward-most part of the ship, and good thing, for the rear of the ship had torn free when the massive propeller ground into the dirt and the fire burned the frame out beneath the boilers. The back of the ship fell out, crewmen and engines with it, leaving a trail of dry flotsam in the fields.

Redhand stood on the remains of the polished wood-and-brass bar where it angled out of the grass and dirt and shielded his eyes with his good hand. The bulk of the *Maiden's Breath* seemed to be tethered to its gasbag, now, by a single tenacious chain. It would be easy to spot, should anyone come looking. And they would come looking. Hollowaigh had made it clear, before the guns came out, that his cohorts were close behind him. "I only came aboard to make sure you didn't try to vanish through some trickery," he smiled through his orange beard, before the parlor had caught fire, "in case you still thought of yourself as some kind of Ranger."

Now Hollowaigh's body lay broken amid snapped barroom furniture and the barbed wire of a simple fence the ship had torn as it crossed the fields.

Redhand stepped off the bar and walked through the grass toward Hollowaigh's body. Along the way, he pretended not to notice the other figure limping out of a patch of wreckage across the way, thin hair and thin jacket blowing about it in the wind. Redhand crouched down next to the body and went through the its coat pockets with his injured left hand. His right hand went to the pommel of the shotgun in his belt and waited there.

The limping figure took its time. Its wavering path took it out of Redhand's peripheral vision, then brought it back in. As it came forward, it raised and waved a tentative hand. Redhand looked over at the figure but gave it no other signal.

It was some passenger out of the Periphery, by the looks of it.

His tweed jacket was torn at one shoulder, frayed like a rope, and his oiled hair now roamed about his head in the wind. A red tie was still knotted around his neck, its loose end flapping around like a pinned snake. He was at least a head shorter than Redhand. As he came closer, Redhand could see the abrasions on the man's white skin.

The man waved again. "Hello?" he asked.

Redhand raised and lowered his head in acknowledgement.

"Is he alive?"

Redhand shook his head.

The man stopped. "Oh," he said.

Redhand waved him over. The man approached, got close. Redhand was on him in a flash, had the man by a wrist and spun him around into a pressure hold. The man winced and gasped. "Iron?" Redhand asked him.

"What?"

"Iron!"

The man grimaced and pointed inside his jacket. "It—it's just—"

Redhand reached inside the man's jacket with his bloody hand and pulled out a shiny little single-shot squeeze pistol with a fat barrel and no grip. He frowned at it, let go of the man. "Sorry for the trouble," Redhand said. "Can't be too careful."

The man rubbed his wrist. "That's what *I* thought."

Redhand clicked open the pistol with his thumb, like a smoker with a favorite match case, for his thumbnail under the edge of the sole round inside and flicked it out into his right hand. Then he tossed the gun back to its owner, who caught it with both hands.

"Thank you, I guess," he said, waggling the empty pistol.

Redhand grunted and crouched down next to Hollowaigh's body again.

"Did you... know him?" asked the other passenger.

Redhand pried out Hollowaigh's brass shield in its wallet and tossed it into the grass. "I did, once." Redhand checked Hollowaigh's boot, found an empty holster for a drop pistol that must've fallen out in the crash. He grunted again.

"I'm Walner," the man in tweed said.

"Walner," Redhand said in an introductory manner. "Did you know this man?"

Walner shook his head. Redhand believed him. He walked over to a heap of smashed luggage and dug out a box of cigars and a wide coolie hat with one modest break in it. He donned it and tied its chinstrap with casual grace.

Walner went over toward Hollowaigh's badge, bent down, picked it up. It bore the raised emblem of the Twin Eagle Security Agency, scuffed and worn. Walner turned back toward Redhand and found him standing and aiming the short shotgun in an outstretched arm.

Walner made a questioning sound.

Redhand looked at the sun, back at Walner. "We're not far outside of Kalsi now. Less than a league, I reckon. There's a creek west or southwest of us a bit." Redhand paused. He didn't mention the rail line to the east that ran south out of Kalsi.

Walner looked around. "All... all right."

Redhand tilted his head, looked down the length of shotgun at Walner, then straightened his head again. "I ran ahead. I ran to the river."

Walner looked confused. "I—"

"When they ask, you tell 'em. I ran southwest, toward the river. You saw me."

"Of course. Yes. Of course. Should I—"

"You head toward the balloon, meet up with any others. Wait for rescue."

"For rescue."

Redhand nodded once, lowered the shotgun. "Might need this, all the same," he said and tossed Walner the round for his single-shot pistol. Walner looked at it in his palm. When he looked back up, Redhand was headed east across the green prairie on foot, into the deepening dusk.

At his trial a year before, Redhand testified that he found Broadhorn in a town on the outer edge of the Periphery, waiting casually on a platform for a train headed west. Broadhorn smiled when he saw Redhand, said something. Redhand couldn't remember what.

The trial was held in an unfinished new courthouse made of unvarnished boards. The place smelled like paste and pine and a box of nails. The roof leaked over the gallery, so people wore their hats and bonnets inside. Folk from all over came to the trial, in part to see if Redhand would be punished, in part to see if his rumored past would come out—was he really once trained by a Ranger to be one of their outlawed order?

For the Imperial prosecutors, the question of Redhand's training was as important as determining the truth about his revenge killing of Broadhorn. Redhand was evasive on one count and frank, if laconic, on the other.

In his capacity as a shootist in his small frontier town, Redhand confronted the bandit and murderer Broadhorn one chilly day at the beginning of spring. Broadhorn was huge, sunburned pink, and bald as a stone except for a beard as long as his forearm, often split by a wide and lopsided smile. Redhand came at him with a six-gun and a wanted poster with Broadhorn's name and likeness on it.

No one disputed this part of the tale.

Redhand told Broadhorn, "I'm here to bring you in 'fore you do anything wicked in my town."

Broadhorn smiled and, real slow, drew his long-barreled rust-colored revolver from its holster. "I won't ever go back to no jails," Broadhorn said, smiling.

Redhand, jollier in those days, grinned back. "Want to wager it?"

Before the next hour chimed in the saloon's grandfather clock, Broadhorn's gun was in pieces, Redhand had put a bullet through the hulk's fat leg, and Broadhorn was chained to a well.

"You're gonna wish you'd killed me," Broadhorn said.

No one disputed this part of the tale.

"Why didn't you kill him then?" the Imperial prosecutor asked at Redhand's trial. "You knew it was wrong?"

Redhand was steady. "I wasn't a lawman or an executioner. I figured he'd hang for what he'd done before if the Magistrates deemed it so. More killing wouldn't untie the knots he'd made before."

By summer, Broadhorn had busted out of Imperial custody and left a pair of broken necks in his wake. He beat autumn to town, found Redhand's home, found Abigail Marsdan, and shot her dead. The house he burned out of spite.

No one disputes this part of the tale.

Redhand rode after Broadhorn, found him on that train platform. The prosecution had a witness: a postman from the nearby mail shack. That postman said Redhand and Broadhorn had fought on the platform as the train approached, that Redhand dodged Broadhorn's practiced gunfire using the techniques of the infamous Ranger gun style, that Redhand dove and rolled and fired only one shot—the shot that killed Broadhorn.

When Redhand himself was asked what happened, he said, "I shot him down."

"Have you been trained in the so-called Eight Compass Way of the outlawed Knights of the Far West?" Most folk just called them Rangers.

Redhand looked far away. "I took the shot I should have taken before."

"You killed him?"

"Yessir, I did."

"Then what did you do?"

"Then I waited for the law to show up."

The judge didn't contemplate long. Redhand nodded when his sentence came down. "One year," said the judge, "and one day." He put Redhand in a barred wagon bound for labor outside Drywater. Redhand left town in chains before dawn.

Abigail's brother stood on the boardwalk outside the saloon with his partner, Hollowaigh, and watched the wagon and its orange lanterns recede into the night. He wore his fine red coat with the black paisley cuffs. He smoked a slender cigar and, once, dabbed his handkerchief to each eye. "One year," he said.

Hollowaigh looked at his partner's profile, shadows moving on his face from a sputtering kerosene lamp in the saloon window. "Not long enough."

Marsdan barely shook his head, turned to face Hollowaigh, leaned in, mouth to ear. "He didn't do what needed doing until too late. Abigail died because of *him*." Hollowaigh and Marsdan looked at each other. "Can't forgive that,"

Marsdan said. "I won't."

In that dark, the prairie ended where the stars began.

The earth was a band of utter black against the deep heavens. Rushing Rabbit had already completed its first run across the sky, chased by the shadowed gap in the stars that marked the position of Night Wolf, and without Rabbit's light the fields Redhand trod were all but impossible to make out.

This was no tilled field. Unseen grasses with wheat-like caps scratched at his hands. Unnoticed stones tripped him up. This was wild grassland, the overgrown range of roving thunderbirds or absent goats.

It was presumably part of the homestead ahead—an angular shape on the horizon, solid lines against the waving grass, punctuated by a few square lights the color of sunlit bourbon. Redhand headed for it, thumbing his broken finger. He hoped for a barn, for rest out of the wind without having to bother anyone... especially anyone who could report his heading.

As he drew near the house, Redhand caught sight of shapes in the grasses—human shapes—eerily still, with big shoulders and broad heads shaped like the conical sedge hat Redhand wore. He closed on one of them and saw by the light from the house that the figure's streaked green patina had the rugged texture of dark rust, like an engine left to the weather. These rusted drudges hadn't done any work in years.

They stood in a semicircle around the north-facing front of the house, now, like totemic guardians. Each one was locked in a subtle bow, facing away from the house.

Beyond the house was a ramshackle barn disintegrating in slow motion, over years, and so ragged that Redhand could see the night sky right through it.

When he smelled the first whiff of burnt tobacco, he took cover behind a drudge.

"If you're here to steal," a man's voice said from the porch, "there ain't much for you." Redhand heard a rocking chair creak and coast as someone got to their feet. "I'll give you a bullet or two for free, though."

Redhand scanned the night, dashed to another drudge, heard no sign that the homesteader heard him move. Looking back at the house, Redhand saw a slender figure, no hat, holding a long arm, probably an old Loyal Falcon—a large caliber revolving rifle popular west of the Periphery for a generation.

"If you're passing through," the voice said, "you're welcome to move on or to come on up here, so long as I can see your hands."

Redhand drummed his fingers on the shotgun in his belt. He glanced at Night Wolf, then toward the eastern sky. His stomach shifted, complained. "I don't want to be no trouble," he said, finally, to the house.

"Then keep moving," said the voice.

"Could use a clean bandage and a drink, though," Redhand said, stepping out from behind the drudge with his palms in plain view.

The figure pointed his rifle in Redhand's direction. Redhand felt confident the first shot, from the hip, in the dark, would miss. If it came to that. "What's your drink, stranger?"

"Tea?"

The voice made a scoffing sound. "I've got whiskey."

Redhand stepped further into the light, his hands out at his sides, low enough to draw if it came to that. He could make out a halo of silver hair around the figure's head. "Even better," Redhand said.

The barred wagon meant to carry Redhand south through the scrub to his penance never made it to Drywater. Seeing an armored stage with a few gunmen as escort attracted bad attention. Bandits—some of them shooting from the top of towering red stones—picked off the driver, a horse, and one of the escorts as the wagon passed by.

The guards ran to the base of the stones for cover. The bandits ran to the wagon for its treasure. Two of them defended the wagon while the third smashed the padlock with a miner's pick.

The wagon door swung open. Redhand looked up through his dreads, made eye contact with the lock-breaker from his spot near the door.

"There ain't nothing here!" the bandit cried. "It's a damned prison wagon!"

"Maiden's tits!" another bandit yelled back, firing at the guards.

"You!" The first bandit drew his pistol and pointed it at Redhand's face. "You worth anyth—"

Redhand grabbed the bandit's pistol in both manacled hands, ducked his head to one side, and yanked the gun away. The bandit dropped his pick and backed away from the wagon. A guard's bullet took him down.

The other two bandits ran off into the scrub and boulders, covered by their hidden riflemen.

After a long wait in the heat, to give the riflemen time to withdraw, the guards rushed back to the wagon. One of them came around the back of the wagon, far enough back for a good shot, his pistol pointed into the shade of the wagon.

Redhand was sat there, elbows on his knees, with the bandit's gun dismantled on the floor before him. He looked the guard in the eye and made the rest of the ride to his sentence in Drywater on horseback, hands still chained.

When Redhand asked the homesteader for his name, the old man revealed the gap in his teeth with a thin smile. He might have been twice Redhand's age. In an old peasant dialect, rare in the Empire now, he said his name was Modest Hare. Then he dropped the accent altogether and said, "I don't get many Clever Folk out in these parts. That's a name I was given during the war, though, by braver sorts than me."

Redhand nodded at him, unsure if he should smile at that or not. Redhand sipped whiskey from a sturdy cup. The two men sat at Modest Hare's rugged dark-wood kitchen table, crafted from a few stout planks worn smooth and uneven. A moth circled around the lantern on the center plank. The room rapidly fell into tangled shadows beyond the table. Room was packed with half-rusted junk metal leaned against every spare wall, stray wooden shapes stuffed into grain sacks, dusty potatoes piled in a basket.

"What sort of folk do you get out here, then?" Redhand asked.

Hare grinned to himself. "You tell me."

"You live here alone?"

Hare shook his head and shot a dose of whiskey. "My kids," he said. "They're out on the range with our thunderbirds. Gone for weeks, sometimes."

Redhand tilted his head. "This land yours?"

Hare nodded slowly. "It is. Long time, now. Seems longer. We still get rustlers out here—"

"And vagabonds," Redhand smiled.

"—and vagabonds," Hare agreed. "Worse than the wolves, Gods-damned rustlers. With the court on the move, at least the rustlers don't always know where to look. It ain't perfect but it beats leaving the thunderbirds out to be stolen at a thief's whim." Hare poured more whiskey, sipped at it. "Leaves me alone here a bit, though." He looked either out the window into the nighttime or at his own reflection in it. Rushing Rabbit had just started its second run across the sky.

Redhand smoothed the gauze wrapped around his splinted ring and middle fingers, bound together for support. "I couldn't do it," Redhand said. When Hare looked at him, he added, "this house, all alone."

Hare shrugged, got up, went to the cabinet where the bottle of whiskey was waiting.

"Learn to do it, like anything." He came back to the table, set down the bottle and nodded towards Redhand. "What *do* you do, then?"

Redhand swirled his saki. "Some days it's hard to say."

"I'm not joking with you, stranger," Hare said. His Loyal Falcon leaned against the cupboard nearby. Redhand's shotgun was tucked politely in the umbrella bucket by the front door. "Who's in my house right now?"

Redhand looked at him, said nothing.

"Thief?" Hare looked at him. They both sat real still. "Killer?"

Redhand finally said, "I've done a stretch."

"Paid your debt?"

"Far as the Empire is concerned. Not to my satisfaction." Redhand closed his eyes, took a breath, opened them again. "Maybe can't."

Hare waited. When Redhand didn't say anything else, Hare sipped his drink and said, "I'll tell you this, then, Clever one: I don't always live here alone. My youngest rode off to tell folk in Kalsi about the crash."

Redhand nodded. "Saw that, did you."

"Saw that. Now, should I send you on your way now or come

132

morning?"

Redhand shrugged. "What do you want me to—"

"Tell me what sort of man's in my house," Hare insisted.

"I'm no fugitive," Redhand said. "But there's a man in Kalsi, son of a Steam Baron, who's been looking for me since I finished my time."

"Lawman? Marshal?"

"Twin Eagle. This ain't business, though. Can't close the case."

"So you're running."

Redhand nodded, finished his whiskey.

"Can't keep running," Hare said. "Got to turn around, sooner or later, and fight."

"There's a whole lot of frontier out there. A continent wide enough to keep running until I die."

"Sounds like you'd rather run or die, then. Keep your problems on your heels, 'stead of putting them to an end."

Redhand moved his head side to side in a way that said that was a little bit true.

"Now's my time to run. I figure I'll know when it's time to stop."

Hare swallowed some whiskey. "You can't run toward nothing. You can't 'get away.' There ain't nothing there. You got to head toward something, got to have some place to be going to so you'll know when you've gotten there. Otherwise there's no way to know when to stop." Hare moved his head to get into Redhand's eyeline. "Right?"

Redhand nodded at him.

"Your past is always behind you," Hare said, starting to slur his words a bit. "Can't be anywhere else."

Redhand watched him. Hare was showing his sleepiness in his eyes.

"You can stay here a few hours. Come morning—"

"I'll be gone with the moons," Redhand said.

Hare had a serious look on his face. "Good, then." He took his rifle with him to bed. It wasn't until he awoke that he discovered it was empty. The six cartridges stood all lined up on the kitchen table. Redhand and his shotgun were gone.

The fire had gone out and Walner was shivering in his sleep at the wreck of the *Maiden's Breath*. He heard voices around him but wasn't shaken out of his sleep until he heard the horses. The riders were already talking with the airship crew when Walner reached the gathering crowd.

Five riders, all men, sat on their horses in a cluster at the edge of the prairie's black scar. As Walner approached, the leader of the riders dismounted and doffed his tall hat and goggles. He wore a red jacket with big black cuffs.

His hair, oiled in place, was as shiny and black as those cuffs. His holstered pistol seemed to be solid silver, like the buttons on his coat. He held up a brass badge stamped with the emblem of the Twin Eagles.

He squinted in the early morning light. The wind came across the prairie at his back. As Walner drew near, he heard the man speak. "This isn't a rescue," the man said to the crowd. "That comes later. I'm just here in search of my partner and the man he was after."

Walner stopped walking. Put his hands in his coat pockets, against the wind. In one pocket he found his squeeze gun, loaded. In the other, Hollowaigh's badge.

"Kalsi is sending coaches and wagons to retrieve you all," the man said.

Walner leaned over to another stranded passenger. "Who's this?"

"Twin Eagles," the passenger said. "Looking for the bastards who brought the ship down."

"Have *any* of you," the Twin Eagle in the red coat asked, "seen these men?"

"I have," Walner said, loud. "We were wrecked together back that way." Walner pointed.

The Twin Eagle walked through the crowd to face Walner. "You and who? Who did you see?"

"Both of them," Walner said. The Twin Eagle described Hollowaigh and Redhand. Walner nodded the whole time. "Your man," Walner said, slowly drawing his hand from his pocket, "left this behind. He—I'm sorry—he died in the wreck." He held out Hollowaigh's badge.

The Twin Eagle took it, regarded it for a long moment, pocketed it himself. "And the other one?"

Walner looked over his shoulder to the west, then back to the Twin Eagle. "Ran off," Walner said. "Southwest. Toward the river."

The rail line, where Redhand found it, ran through the wide plain between two shallow hills, from horizon to horizon. The clouds above formed a vast bear's paw with long, thin claws. The grasses below rippled in the wind. No train in sight.

Redhand headed to the tracks, then followed them south, away from Kalsi. Leagues south, the rail line forked north off the line that ran west to Prosperity, where the airship was once bound. If he could reach the fork, he could try to hop a train bound for Kalsi or Prosperity and be all the harder to track.

Without thinking about it, he cracked open the breech on the shotgun and checked the ammo inside. One empty shell, one loaded.

The prairie rolled gently down into rippling lands, all green beneath the bold blue sky. Grasshoppers leapt from the fields ahead of the posse. Marsdan and his men were an hour into their ride toward the river, stopping to scout the horizon with rifle scopes, when Marsdan cussed aloud.

Sailkirk, the youngest and fastest of the riders, heard him. He was a straw-haired teen with big, round eyes and last-year's fashions. "What is it?"

Marsdan frowned, shook his head. "This isn't right," he said. He stood up in his saddle and looked back east. "Hollowaigh," he said. "This is wrong."

Sailkirk furrowed his brow. "I don't—"

"Send them on to the river," Marsdan said, pointing at the other three riders. "Just in case. Then you come back and meet me back at the wreck."

"What are we—?"

"A hunch!" Marsdan yelled, spurring his horse and riding back toward the wreck.

Sailkirk rode up on Marsdan not long after and found him pouring over the dirt a few yards from Hollowaigh's body. Broken timbers jutted from the ground all around. A footlocker stood almost upright nearby.

Marsdan had his goggles on, his hat off, and was measuring the depth of a footprint in the dirt when Sailkirk dismounted and walked up to him. Sailkirk knew better than to talk to him while he worked.

Marsdan stood up, walked away from his hat, and crouched again. Another print. "As the Celestial Court sees me," Marsdan said, "I'm a plumb fool."

Sailkirk waited for it.

Marsdan stood up and pointed east. "The bastard's on foot, headed east toward the rail line," he said as he walked past Sailkirk to the horses. "Let's go."

Sailkirk sprung into action, smiling. "That man, the passenger, he lied to us?" Sailkirk was up on his horse in a flash.

Marsdan fit his hat on his head and looked into the east, the sun shining off his lenses. "One thing at a time."

Redhand hoped for a train bound south out of Kalsi even as he headed away from the town. He walked south, toward the fork, checking over his shoulder, sometimes walking backwards so he could see steam on the horizon.

He listened to the wind in the grasses. He looked at the traces he left in his wake and wished he had the time or the knack to cover his trail. Somewhere nearby, a game bird sang.

He passed young oaks and jutting boulders. He followed the tracks across a short wooden bridge across a shallow and dry gully. He watched the sun drift across the sky and wondered if a train would ever come.

Marsdan and Sankirk leaned forward in their saddles, their horses charging across the wild grasses. They leapt a short fence and tore across the property surrounding a peeling wooden homestead, its yard choked with rusted automata. Marsdan caught the glint of the sun off a spyglass or scope on the house's porch as they rode by.

Redhand thought about the proper distance from the tracks to lie down and sleep, if it came to that, so that he could see approaching trains early but not be seen by pursuers. Maybe it was folly to try and make it all the way to the fork, he thought. He finally sat down to rest on a slight embankment facing the tracks and tipped his coolie hat back on his head. He'd take whatever train came, he decided. A train was a moving target. No better way to catch one than to wait where he knew one would appear.

Then he saw steam on the horizon to the north. It was a train headed south out of Kalsi.

Redhand got to his feet but stayed low in the grass. He needed to jump onto a rear car without being seen and he would hardly have time to close on the train on foot. He needed to be close.

He saw the white steam billow. He watched the black engine grow closer in the glaring sun. He noticed the dust coming up off the prairie to the west, rising in the wake of at least one rider. Someone was coming.

Marsdan and Sankirk rode on toward the train. They could make out Redhand as a gray shape and sedge hat in the grasses near the tracks. Marsdan and Sankirk exchanged looks from horseback. Marsdan signaled for Sankirk to press on.

Redhand, meanwhile, dashed across the tracks just in front of the train, put it between him and his pursuers.

"Go!" Marsdan yelled over wind and hooves. "He'll board the train!"

Sankirk pulled ahead. The train was a dozen mixed cars, with passengers and a bar up front and cargo in the back. It rattled and whined as it charged across the plain.

Sankirk closed on the train and came up beside its middle, keeping pace. He adjusted the scoped rifle in his saddle loop, so he wouldn't snag it on his leg. He unsnapped the holster for his six-gun, then looked back at Marsdan, who was still approaching the train. Finally, Sankirk leaned out, put all his weight in one stirrup, grabbed hold of a railing on the side of a passenger car, and swung off his horse onto the car steps. Feet steady on the train, he stepped into the hollow at the rear of the car and drew his six-gun.

Something moved on the roof of the car. Sankirk spun around to follow the sound, found himself facing out the open doorway of the train car.

It was Redhand. Sankirk watched as he leapt from the roof of the train onto Sankirk's riderless horse and spurred it away from the train.

Sankirk fanned his six-gun, squeezing off round and after round as Redhand rode off, putting distance between himself and the train.

Redhand leaned forward, down low on the horse's back, and looked behind himself at the receding train—and at Marsdan's red coat snapping in the wind from the back of his pursuing horse. Then he saw the blood. Redhand's horse was bleeding from its flank where one of Sankirk's rounds hit home.

He turned west, uphill and away from the train, toward the flat prairie above. The horse slowed a fraction with every step. Marsdan drew closer.

Redhand moved his shotgun from the front of his belt to the back, then slid Sankirk's rifle out of its sheath and levered a round into position. Marsdan drew closer.

Redhand swiveled on his horse, tossed one leg over, and rode sidesaddle with the rifle in hand. Marsden galloped hard, riding through the white smoke of an aimless pistol shot.

Redhand crested the hill ahead of Marsdan and took a deep breath. Just as his horse cleared the hill, Redhand dropped from horseback and rolled into the grass, catching his knee on a hidden stone and coming to a stop in a half-kneel. He put the rifle to his shoulder in a flash.

Marsdan crested the hill and rode by at full speed.

Redhand lined up his shot and pulled the trigger. Marsdan toppled from his horse as coat-stuffing and blood flew into the air from a wound in his shoulder. Redhand levered another round into place and started his run toward Marsdan.

Marsdan was faster than Redhand imagined, back on his feet in mere moments and running a half-circle around Redhand, firing his silver six-gun once, twice, thrice.

Redhand dove to one side, rolled back the way he'd come, got to one knee and fired too wide. Marsdan rushed him, then dropped into the grass again. Good timing—Redhand wasted another round shooting where the Twin Eagle no longer was.

Marsdan was quick and cunning enough to rush and weave around a rifle in an open space. Running away would've been asking for a bullet in the back from other riflemen. Redhand wasn't other riflemen. He let

Marsdan crawl around in the grass for a while, knowing both men were creeping toward each other.

Redhand fired off another shot with no hope of landing it, forcing Marsdan to stay down.

Then he worked the lever and heard the dreaded sound of an empty chamber.

Marsdan leapt from the grasses with a pistol in each hand and invoked the name of once-just gods from the Celestial Court, working each pistol with thumb and trigger-finger, back and forth, shot after shot trying to predict Redhand's next move.

Redhand sprang into defensive mode, diving into the grass himself and trying to get within reach of Marsdan. A round split the stock on the rifle. Another put a hole through his hat. A third hit Redhand in the calf. He bled and hissed and then sensed he was close enough to Marsdan. Redhand ditched the rifle and sprang to his feet.

First he put a foot into Marsdan's knee, then pressed off it and swung the other foot across Marsdan's face, knocking him into the grass. Marsdan rolled but Redhand came down heel-first on his left hand, driving one silver gun into the dirt.

Marsdan fired a shot—sending Redhand swerving like a drunk— then got to his feet and took aim.

Redhand drew his shotgun from behind him as he dove under Marsdan's remaining gun, pointed the shotgun upward, and blasted Marsdan's right hand and silver pistol apart. As he came to his feet, Redhand released the breech on the shotgun and snapped it forward, slamming the barrels into Marsdan's nose. Then he kicked the man away and snapped the breech shut with a flick.

Marsdan stumbled back and fell into the long grass again. Redhand picked up Marsdan's bloody silver pistol with two fingers and side-armed it away. Then he left Marsdan there on the ground and limped off to retrieve the Twin Eagle's other pistol. When he came back, Marsdan had a twin-shot pocket pistol in his left hand, held out in front of him more like a talisman than a gun.

"No closer, you bastard," Marsdan said. His oiled hair clung to his forehead in errant strands. "Or I'll shoot you dead."

Redhand stopped. "I believe it," he said. "I made a promise to Abby that I'd settle down. With her. Give up the gun. I failed her at that. And I won't settle down without her. So that leave me this life. Or it leaves me dead by your hand."

Marsdan's breathed out. His whole body trembled with pain but his pistol hardly wavered.

"I deserve to die tired," Redhand said.

"Agreed."

"I swore, once, to tolerate no wickedness." Redhand looked down at Marsdan. Sunlight fell through a crack and a bullet-hole in his coolie hat and lit Redhand's face. "Wicked, though, is what we both are right now, isn't it?"

Redhand put his palm to his back and then showed it to Marsdan. It was dark with blood from a gunshot beneath Redhand's ribs—either Marsdan or Sankirk had got lucky. "You came out here to murder me."

Marsdan blinked sweat out of his eyes.

Redhand cocked Marsdan's silver pistol and aimed it at him. "You'd never forgive me if I let you do that."

"I can't forgive you anyway for what you've done," Marsdan spat. "Cowardice."

"You're leaving me no choice but to shoot you, here, Jang."

"But you won't. You haven't learned anything."

"I learned," Redhand said, "too late." He pulled the trigger on Marsdan's silver pistol, put a bullet in Marsdan's heart.

The wind came across the prairie. The grass swayed, except where Marsdan's body weighed it down.

Redhand climbed aboard Marsdan's horse and ran his hand over the two eagles emblazoned on the saddle. Clouds hustled across the sky. Redhand rode bleeding into the west toward Prosperity.

Will Hindmarch is a writer, graphic designer, and game designer whose work has appeared in The Thackery T. Lambshead Cabinet of Curiosities, McSweeney's Internet Tendency, The Escapist, and Atlanta magazine, among others. He writes fiction, non-fiction, games, screenplays, comics, and more. His hope, in the long run, is to write one of everything.

RAILROAD SPIKES
By Ari Marmell

"I don't get it. I just don't."

The station manager doffed his cap so he might lift a hand to his forehead, wiping away a thin sheen of slurry made up of summer sweat and summer dust. From behind him, across the length of the platform, he heard the clump of boots and the rustling of skirts, the exasperated murmurs of passengers and workers grousing about the unexpected delay. But he had eyes only for the iron wheels before him, and the thick bolts that had been yanked from those wheels and left scattered amidst heaped flakes of rust.

"Robbery, maybe?" he asked softly, trying to wrap his head around it. "Delay you folks so someone could hit you down the line?"

Beside him, the second fellow, dressed in a smart three-piece, frowned beneath a mustache thick as a horse's tail. "Don't track." The Twin Eagles Security man knelt beside the bolts, ignoring what the sand and grit did to his slacks. "Bandits wouldn't want us on our guard. This sabotage is way too obvious. Somebody wanted us delayed, but didn't much care if we knew it. Come to think, I heard tell of something similar happening recently, over near Brogdon." Chewing on his whiskers, he asked, "How long to fix it?"

"Assuming there's no more to the damage than what we see—and accounting for the extra time to make *sure* there's no more than what we see—five, six hours, maybe."

"Huh." The detective rose, brushed the dirt from his knees. "Well, Bilson's workers are gonna have to wait a spell for their payroll, but we'll get it there. Just wish I knew *why* someone'd want to slow us up like this."

As he turned to walk away, the station manager could still only shake his head. "I just don't get it…"

Of course neither of them understood. Neither of them could *see*.

Several miles west of the station, *something* trudged with slow, implacable steps. Dozens upon dozens of short, segmented legs carried what could only be roughly described as a steel caterpillar across the rocky badlands; the clank and clatter could have masked an entire stampede of panicked thunderbirds. Its sides were solid, gleaming in the sharp morning sun. Where the various segments linked to one another, the joins were covered in a mesh of steel rings, covering what would otherwise have been gaping vulnerabilities in the thing's armor. From a squat smokestack up front and numerous smaller portals along the edges billowed thick, greasy fumes. The device, or vehicle, or whatever it was left not only a winding trail of the most peculiar prints, but also a scattered, broken line of cinders and soot.

It finally settled, with impossible grace, over the iron rails that bound each horizon to the other. A shift one way, a minute adjustment the other, and it aligned perfectly with the track. Steam whistled, smoke puffed, gears cranked, and the contraption slowly lowered itself. The legs retracted into the individual segments, revealing narrow wheels behind. The smokestack rose, the chain mesh folded open like curtains.

And that simply, the bizarre vehicle wasn't bizarre at all. Just another train, chugging its way along, riding the rails exactly where, and exactly when, the Bilson payroll delivery should have been.

Just another train. Waiting.

When awareness first returned, it took the form of a gentle rocking of the floor beneath his cheek. A rhythmic sway, almost relaxing in its own right, accompanied by the constant lullaby. *Clack-clack... clack-clack... clack-clack...*

Why, he wondered, *do they always come in pairs?*

The thought, bleary as it was, opened the door for others. Memory returned, and with it, a sharp agony across the top of his skull. Groaning, he pressed his fingers to the mat of bloody hair, and struggled to sit up.

Russ Gandry—or "'Ruddy' Russ Gandry" to his compatriots, to law enforcement, and to the readers of wanted posters everywhere—was the fastest fist in, and the second-in-command of, the infamous Davallo Gang. He had no trouble recalling that. He and over half a dozen of Davallo's best shooters had ridden up alongside the train, whooping and hollering and throwing lead, making sure everyone was nice and cowed before they'd clambered aboard. He'd gone in the very back, just forward of the caboose. No trouble recalling that either.

And then... Flat on his face, with the emperor of all hangovers and the taste of floor lingering on his tongue.

Russ struggled to pry his eyes open, and only then realized that they *were* open. It was just dark as a Marshal's soul in the car.

Dark? Can't be dark. Was just a couple hours past noon when we hit the train. Can't have been out that *long...*

Puzzled, yes, but he wasn't worried. Thanks to that old tinkerer Davallo hired on, Russ and his boys were ready for damn near anything. He reached to his belt, not for a weapon but for a tin tube at his back. The "glow juice" inside—he didn't know what it was properly called, but that's what *he* always called it—had been let to sit in the sun for a full day before being poured into this cylinder, which was mirrored on the inside. That meant he should get at least three hours illumination out of it, easy. He clicked open the aperture and raised the tube high.

"Well." Russ might not have had anyone to talk to, but that didn't stop him talking. "Guess I know why it's dark, at least."

He was, indeed, still in the car—the train's last car, other than the caboose—just as he'd thought. But no, night had not fallen. Rather, the windows that ran along both walls, just below the ceiling, were covered over with what looked, in the dim light, to be steel plates. So too, when he checked, was the door through which he'd entered.

He did not, however, immediately move to examine the barriers that apparently imprisoned him. No, the bulk of his attention was snagged by the ugly contraption hanging from the ceiling just in front of the door (or where the door had been).

It looked very much like a heavy pick-axe, fashioned from a single bar of iron or steel. A careful prod with a finger set in swinging back and forth; it was, as he'd suspected, mounted above very much like a pendulum.

And even the bare light provided by the glow juice was enough for him to spot the darkening stain that ran along the heavy head—not at the end, where the flattened metal would have punched through bone like paper, but along the center.

Now he remembered the last little bit of it. Now he recalled how the train had lurched just as he stepped inside, how he'd stumbled forward, nudged off-balance. The trap—because that's what it *had* to be, a trap—must have caught him at the wrong angle because of it.

He shivered, his skin goose-pimpling and his throat running dry, at the realization that he could have been, *should* have been, lying dead in a puddle of blood and brain.

Who the Hells *booby-traps the door on a train car?! What if it'd been one of the passengers, or the guards?!*

His hands moved of their own accord, acting as they were accustomed to act when the rest of Russ was suddenly afraid. His right hand swiftly passed the glowing tube to his left, and swept the double-six from the holster at his side. Russ glanced down, running the pistol through a quick check to ensure that both cylinders were fully loaded and spinning freely, that both barrels were clear. He wouldn't need his left hand to fire the thing; the rotation of each cylinder triggered a mechanism to cock the hammer of the other. A good thing, too, because he sure as the lowest Hell wasn't letting go of his light!

So, no way back—but that didn't mean no way *out*. Russ held the light before him as far as his arm would stretch, squinting at the far side of the car. It looked to be absolutely empty: No freight, no storage, no passengers, nothing.

"Kinda train *is* this, damn it?!"

Nobody answered, of course.

But at the far end, scarcely visible in the light, he could make out the door. Not a steel slab, but an actual, honest-to-gods wooden door! All right, so he couldn't get out the back. He'd just go on ahead, slip out onto the platform between cars, and get his bearings. Maybe he could see or hear one of the boys, try to get a handle on what was happening.

Russ took a single step and froze once more. He cast his gaze upward, and while he didn't see any more of those pendulum/pick-axes, he *could* see an array of tubes and lengths of metal running, web-like, down the center of the ceiling. No *way* was he walking under *that*! Snickering lowly, congratulating himself on his cleverness, Russ scooted to the left and hugged the wall as he made his way forward.

He'd gotten maybe a third of the way when the floor vanished from beneath his boot.

Russ had trained extensively in multiple combat styles during his soldiering days, and it was Rearing Horse that saved him now. Even as he began to lurch forward he threw his weight back, acting before he was even aware of what had happened. He fell into the rear-leaning stance at the very edge of a precipice that hadn't existed a second before.

Wheezing as he tried to catch his breath and calm his heart, Russ stepped away and knelt, staring in horror. A long stretch of floor had fallen away on hidden hinges; had he plummeted through, as he was clearly meant to, he'd have been chewed like so much tobacco in the wheels directly beneath.

"The *fuck* kinda train is this?!" He was screaming, borderline hysterical now, and he knew it—but that didn't mean he could help it. At least the room was better lit now, than it had been. The sun still shone outside, and while there wasn't near enough room for him to squeeze out over the wheels, there was plenty to let the daylight *in*.

All right, stay away from the walls, then. He moved down the center of the car once more, now in an awkward crouch that was somehow both slow and scurrying, checking his footing and ducking low beneath the contraptions above. And although the wood squeaked and the metal wailed and the wheels screeched, he reached the door without anything further attempting to murder him.

He held the light close to the door handle, but he couldn't see anything harmful about it. Same held true for the hinges. Gingerly, using only two fingers on his left hand, Russ yanked the door open and took a quick step back, his double-six raised.

On the one hand, nothing tried to shatter his skull or crush him to death. That'd be the good news.

The bad was that, though he could indeed step out onto the platform, he wasn't leaving the train.

A net of metal rinks, strung close and tight, covered the entire gap, top and sides, connecting this car to the next. Tiny streams of sunlight filtered through, and if he leaned up against the mesh—risking a nasty pinch as the rings rubbed against one another—he could just barely make out the sight of open plains whipping past. But he certainly wasn't tearing his way through it, and close examination was enough to convince him that he'd just be wasting ammunition to try shooting holes in it.

Russ had exactly two options, far as he could see. He could go back into the room he'd just left and sit, waiting for gods alone knew what, for gods alone knew how long.

Or he could move on into the next car, and maybe the next, until he found *some* way off this gods damned train!

Choking back something between a grunt and a sob, he reached out for the opposite door.

It was in the second car that he found the first body.

An entire thicket of old and rusted spikes rose and fell in waves down the length of the car. Thrust upward and hauled down by the turning of the train's wheels, or so it seemed, they rippled and waved in hypnotic swells along both walls, leaving only a narrow path that snaked and meandered its way from door to door. Fearsome, certainly, but easily navigable by anyone with the slightest agility and sense of balance.

Something that one of Russ's boys had apparently lacked.

"Oh, shit! Mitch…"

The corpse rode the spikes along the left hand side, slowly swaying up and down with the rhythm of the train. Jags of bloody steel punched through ripped clothing and torn flesh, gradually ripping the body apart with their constant tugging. Mitch's eyes and mouth hung wide open; the poor bastard had known what was coming.

Russ gave another moment's thought to retreat, but he still found little point in just holing up and waiting. He steeled himself against the thick miasma of blood and other bodily fluids—he was no stranger to death, having dealt enough of it, but he'd never seen a death quite *this* ugly—and bulled on ahead. Light in one hand, pistol in the other, he carefully took one step at a time, staying between the grinding steel forests while keeping one careful eye on the ceiling above. It'd be just like the madman who designed this place to put another swinging blade or the like in the middle of the only "clear" path.

Still, despite all his caution, he barely escaped it when it finally came.

Without so much as a single moving part to offer warning, a burst of scalding steam erupted from an overhead pipe, aimed with brutal accuracy down the stretch of open floor. Russ allowed himself to fall straight back, beneath the hissing vapors, and even that was enough to redden the skin of his face and neck to match his nickname. His hands slapped out to either side as his back struck the floor, and one of the spikes smacked the double-six from his fist, missing his flesh by little more than the width of his favorite girl's navel.

For long minutes he lay there, listening to the steam whistling overhead, and pondered Mitch's death. The jet of steam, obviously, was intended to startle anyone passing through into leaping aside—and into the path of the spikes. So then why leave the clear path in the first place?

"Hope," he muttered to himself in answer. "So we could see what was coming, and think that just *maybe* we'd escaped it…" Once more he shuddered, this time at the thought of the diseased brain that could have built such things.

Finally, Russ cast carefully about until he'd recovered his pistol and glanced back over his head. Sure enough, the door through which he'd entered was now hidden behind another steel panel. No going back. And since he couldn't exactly brave the *spikes*…

Russ returned the double-six to his holster, raised both arms in front of his face, took a few deep breaths, and rolled to his feet. As swiftly as he could manage without stumbling off course and into the juddering spikes, his face turned toward his feet, he pushed his way through the billowing steam.

He vowed to himself that he wouldn't cry out as the skin on his arms, his hands, and his face begin to burn—even, in spots, to peel away from the glistening flesh beneath in sodden ribbons. He'd almost reached the door before he broke that vow.

A door that, thank all the gods of the Celestial Court, was neither locked nor booby-trapped. Russ collapsed into a tiny ball on the platform between this car and the next, stared out at the passing terrain through the gaps in the chain mesh, and sobbed for long minutes. Tears and snot traced pathways down cheeks and chin, but any humiliation he might normally feel for such craven conduct was well and truly buried by frustration and fear.

But not for *too* long. "Ruddy" Russ Gandry wasn't *nobody's* pansy, gods dammit! Teeth clenched until they ached, he forced himself back under control. From the same leather pouch where he'd kept his tube of glow juice, he removed a small roll of bandages, pre-soaked in some sticky, foul-smelling sludge supposed to keep a wound from festering. He didn't have nearly enough of it, wasn't supposed to have to treat more than the occasional bad gash or bullet graze out in the field, but he could at least wrap the worst of the burns. As for the others? Russ tore strips from the hem and collar of his shirt, now surprisingly clean thanks to the blasts of steam, and bandaged his remaining injuries as best he could. Not much he could do for the burns on his face, though.

Russ stood, groaning in pain, and moved on.

He knew the train couldn't *actually* go on for miles, that he couldn't *actually* have wandered its cars for hours without end, but still he'd have sworn that he had. Each car was worse than the last, the length of the train measuring out a steady descent into the Infernal Judges' most fearsome Hells.

Several of the cars were divided into multiple, claustrophobically narrow passageways, forcing Russ to choose his path and squeeze through with his gut sucked in. Halfway through the walls grew scalding and bear traps waited beneath weakened planks in the floor. The hallway smelled of roast beef; a peculiar mystery that Russ only solved when he rounded a corner and found Werrick caught in a trap and cooked to death against a wall.

Russ didn't even take the time to mourn. He just stripped Werrick's singed duster off the body and used it as extra padding of his own, saving himself from the worst of the burns.

Another contained a veritable maze of spinning, spring-loaded arms that threatened to break bones, to tear skin, to catch limbs in an inhuman grip and never let go. Someone had died here, too, but Russ couldn't even say who; all he had left to judge was a heap of torn, bloody clothes. It took everything he had, all of his training, every duck and doge and leap he could muster, to avoid joining the poor, anonymous soul.

Floor panels rose, threatening to crush him against the ceiling. Gears and spikes shot from walls to rend flesh and bone. Bizarre engines, unlike any he'd ever heard of, sucked the vitality from the air until he very nearly suffocated in a wide open chamber. Static electricity, generated by the wheels, discharged through copper wires dangling from above. At one point, where the designer had apparently gotten bored with "convoluted," a panel dropped open and a series of gun barrels fired at him from multiple angles.

But through it all, thanks to his own skill, to the warnings offered by the bodies of his dead friends, and to no small bit of blessed fortune, he passed—not unscathed, perhaps, but without *severe* hurt.

Until the last.

Not that Russ *knew* it was the last, of course. He'd long since lost track of how far along the train he'd passed, and he certainly had no way of knowing what the vehicle's mad inventor had planned. He knew only that he'd just wended his way through a blizzard of barbed arrows and come to another in the seemingly endless line of doors.

Doors—absolutely none of which had, themselves, been traps or parts of traps. He'd grown accustomed to that, grown careless in his agony and his exhaustion. He'd stopped checking.

It was a lapse he regretted the instant he felt something spongy on the underside of the latch give way beneath his grip.

He tried to pull away, and nearly lost another patch of skin in the process. Two of his fingers came loose before the viscous substance had fully set, but the others—the last two fingers of his left hand— were stuck fast.

"Well. That's obnoxious."

He frowned even as he muttered. It *was* obnoxious, and nothing more. His fingers didn't burn; he wasn't feeling sickly or poisoned. Whatever else you might say about every gizmo and contraption he'd come across, they were all pretty well lethal.

The keening wail of metal on metal made him jump, twisting his arm painfully so he could look behind him. A crescent-shaped blade arced from one wall, reaching to within inches of the other, barely visible as a flicker before it was gone. Steel lightning, flashing across the railroad car. It was at the far end of the room, but each time it emerged from its previously hidden slot, it came a few feet nearer.

Russ stared in horror, his face covered in a fresh sheen of sweat. He had a minute or two, maybe, before that thing would open him up like a sausage. He couldn't duck beneath it, not with his hand stuck to the latch. Couldn't jump over it for the same reason; its distance from the floor had been calculated with a diabolic precision.

He tugged desperately, willing now to sacrifice as much skin as necessary, but the sticky sludge had fused around those two fingers, holding them in a grip so firm that Russ knew he could never yank them free in time.

And with every second, the bloodthirsty scream of the blade drew nearer.

Russ allowed himself a frustrated, furious scream of his own, in answer, before he drew the double-six, placed the barrels against the bottom knuckles of the imprisoned digits, and pulled the trigger.

Again, Russ had woken up on the floor. Agony raced along his arm, a searing, throbbing pain like he'd never known. He must have swooned from the shock, which—thankfully—had laid him out beneath the path of the scything blade. The warm, crimson puddle in which he lay was evidence enough that he hadn't been out for long. Groaning and sobbing, he tore yet another strip from his shirt (not nearly so clean now as it had been) and forced himself to wrap his mangled hand tight. His head swam, and he knew he was on the verge of passing out once more. He bit his lip until it, too, bled, holding himself awake through willpower alone.

Above him, the blade reached the end of its track, retracted once more into the wall, and did not emerge again.

When minutes had passed and the agony in his hand had faded at least a touch—or perhaps he'd just begun to grow numb to it—Russ rose. Now that he knew where to look, it was easy enough to grip the latch without grabbing the gunk smeared over it. His breath hitching in his throat, wondering what sort of nightmare he might encounter next, he pulled upon first the inner door and then (after a thorough examination), the one to the next car.

What he found was more startling than any convoluted death trap.

The chamber was laid out like someone's hotel room. The bed, though narrow, boasted a thick mattress and quilts that were, if far from luxurious, at least without obvious holes or patches. A counter with a basin of (mostly) clean water sat across from it, beside a wardrobe with a number of shirts and pants hanging in neat rows. The room was well lit by the late afternoon sun, pouring in through a barred but broad window. It even had curtains, currently tied open.

In fact, the only peculiar detail of the room at all was the wall above the bed. There, almost two dozen boots of different styles and sizes hung from pegs. Some had spurs; most appeared worn, or torn, or singed.

Russ leaned over the bed, staring, and caught a faceful of an acrid scent. Tanning fluids.

Like he'd smelled before in a leatherworker's, or a taxidermist.

Swallowing, he stepped away, determined not to look *inside* those boots.

"Might as well come on through, son!" It was a pleasant voice, older, almost grandfatherly, shouting from beyond the bedchamber. "I can hear you clompin' around in there!"

Double-six raised and ready to fire, Russ limped across the room and hurled open the final door.

Had it not already been getting on toward evening, and had he not been partly acclimated by the bedroom windows, Russ would have been practically blinded by his sudden exposure to the sun, after so many hours in the gloom. The wind whipping past his face smelled better than a bouquet of roses on prostitute's bedside table. No chain mesh, no bars, no walls, separated him from the open air.

He was standing at the rear of the engine itself, a behemoth of iron and steel and coal-smelling smoke. A narrow corridor to the left led, no doubt, to the boiler room itself, but Russ's eyes—and gun—were trained unerringly up and to the right, at the engineer's compartment.

The fellow inside, peering back down at Russ, looked pretty much the average, everyday engineer. Cap, striped shirt, an old, friendly face liberally strewn with wrinkles and rough white whiskers in equal measure. It was only as he shuffled out onto the steps, beyond the shadows of his tiny box, that Russ could see the single abnormal trait about the man: His left leg, from the knee down, was a framework of brass, exposing the occasional ticking gear within.

"Well, Hells, son," the geezer said, voice raised just enough to be heard above the rushing wind. "I'm impressed. You know, you're only the sixth fella to actually make it all the way through."

"Sixth… What?" Russ shook his head, trying to blink away the dull throbbing throughout his body while keeping the pistol aloft. "How long you been doing this, old man?!"

"Oh, couple years, now. Maybe three?"

"You fuckin' lunatic, I oughta—!" The double-six was quivering, Russ's finger tensing on the trigger.

"Really don't wanna do that, son."

"Yeah? Why's that?"

The engineer smiled and lowered himself—with the occasional grunt and the pop of old joints—to sit on the steps. "You heard of 'Five Dog' Creighton?"

"What?" Russ, still vaguely light-headed, wondered if he'd missed part of the conversation. "What are you—?"

"Have you," the old man repeated, "ever heard of 'Five Dog' Creighton?"

"Course I have! Shit, *everyone's* heard of—"

"You hear about what happened on the Pedroyo line?"

"Uh… Something about Creighton and his boys derailing a train after they robbed it, right? Why are we talking about—"

"I built the engine on that train, son. Supposed to be a new machine, cheaper'n anything House Marghul has on the market, but almost as fast and reliable. Guess Creighton, being a train robber'n all, didn't cotton to that much. After he took my passengers for everything they had, he and his boys beat me bad and left me lying where I couldn't reach the throttle. Nothing I could do to stop us…"

His voice trailed away for an instant. Russ wondered if the man was totally gone, until he blinked, hard, and spoke once more.

"That's where I lost my leg, you see. And I was lucky. Most of the passengers died. My boy, who was helping me out on my test run… Died. Molly, she couldn't live with that. She'd left me before I was even back on my feet. Well, foot." He tapped the brass prosthetic with a fingertip. "Course, a lot of my railroad backers weren't happy 'bout what'd happened. Couldn't do much formally, but a few of 'em slipped me some funding under the table, so I could build myself a *new* train. It ain't as fancy or as comfortable as the last one, but I'd say it's got its charms, right?"

"You got something seriously not right with you, old man. I ain't Five Dog, ain't even ever rode with him! I—"

"I know that, son. But *someday* it will be. And until then… Well, Hells, you're a bandit, boy. Sure you done more than enough bad to deserve this."

Russ's hand steadied, his lips turned up in a sneer. "Well, I survived your traps, you bastard, and now it's your turn to—"

"Traps? Those devices weren't traps, son. Those were just meant to weed out the dross, make sure I'm only left with the strong ones, the ones who *really* wanted to live. The *train*, that's the trap.

"The train, and the air you been breathin' since you climbed aboard."

"What?" Not quite a whisper, not quite a squeak. "What are you talking about? What did you *do*?!"

"Nifty odorless gas of my own devising. Ugliest death you can imagine, son. Like the worst case of Digger's Lung you ever saw. Weeks, maybe months, of coughin' blood and shittin' bile. Open sores, big as gold Talons and angry as Night Wolf's face. No cure, no relief…

"*Except* the gas itself. You take a good couple deep breaths of that, every couple days, it keeps the symptoms from appearin'. Course, nobody but me knows the formula, and I only make a few days' worth at a time. So yeah, son, the train is the trap—'cause you ain't leaving anytime soon. And you'll be wanting to point that gun somewhere else; wouldn't want to shoot me by accident now, would you?"

He was bluffing. He *had* to be bluffing!

Except that Russ had seen enough, in the past hours, to know better. His shoulders sagged and his fingers opened. The double-six fell to the platform with a dull clatter.

"Why?" He heard the begging in his voice, and was ashamed. "Why would you *do* that?"

"You don't think I can manage a train like this by my lonesome, do you?" The engineer struggled to his feet and limped back up into the compartment. "Running the engine, feeding the boiler, maintaining the devices. Gotta have some help. I got myself five assistants. Well, six, now."

Levers clattered and the train lurched. Segmented legs sprouted from the sides and lifted it up off the tracks. Ponderously it swayed to the left and began to march.

"You're in a bad way, son," the old engineer said. "I'll introduce you to the rest of the workers tomorrow, and they can show you where to get started. Why don't you go and get some sleep until then, regain your strength?

"We got us a long, long road ahead."

Ari Marmell would love to tell you all about the various esoteric jobs he held and the wacky adventures he had on the way to becoming an author, since that's what other authors seem to do in these blurbs. Unfortunately, he doesn't actually have any, as the most exciting thing about his professional life, besides his novel writing, is the work he's done for Dungeons & Dragons and other role-playing games. His published fiction includes both The Goblin Corps and Thief's Covenant, from Pyr Books; The Conqueror's Shadow and The Warlord's Legacy, from Spectra (Random House); and tie-in novels for multiple gaming properties. You can find Ari online at http://www.mouseferatu.com and http://twitter.com/mouseferatu.

THE FURY PACT
By Matt Forbeck

Shen's joy at flying through the sky on his father's Fury pack evaporated the moment he spied the smoke from the fire consuming his family's farm from a full league away. He'd been busy putting his father's latest invention through its pace, and the stark beauty of the High Plains rolling out between the unseen towns of Eldaire and Prosperity had entranced him so much that he'd not looked back until the alarm his father had set began pinging. That meant he had depleted half his fuel, and he would need to go straight home.

Shen had once been forced to land the Fury pack more than a mile away from the farm, and he'd waited there for hours before he realized his father wasn't coming to rescue him. He'd considered abandoning the contraption there and going to ask his father for help, but he knew what the man's answer would be. Instead, he hauled the heavy machinery through the tall grass, cutting a path toward his home.

When he'd arrived, he'd expected his father to be angry. Instead, he'd found a hot meal waiting for him, along with a smile and a gentle request that Shen tell the story of his day's adventure. He knew he'd find no such welcome waiting for him today.

Shen raced back to the farm as fast as the Fury pack would carry him. As the black and oily column of smoke that stained the clear blue sky grew closer, his worry grew with it. By the time he could see through the pillar of blackness to the hungry gouts of fire, he hoped he might see his father trying to fight the blaze on his own, or maybe standing safe on the southern rise, mourning his losses.

Shen brought the Fury pack lower as he neared the farm, and he spotted his father face down on the trampled ground next to their little buckboard. The man lay sprawled in the stretch of open turf between their humble house and the barn in which he conducted his experiments, the ones he said might one day revolutionize the Far West. He did not move.

Shen wound his way around what he now saw were twin columns of smoke and brought the Fury pack down near his father with a practiced ease that would have made the man proud. He shrugged the amazing machine off with a haste that would have earned him a scolding and rushed to his father's side.

The man's body felt heavier than Shen had expected, but he managed to roll his father over onto his back. A hole showed through the leather apron his father wore most days when he worked in the barn, and blood had seeped through it and stained his entire chest, both apron and shirt. His eyes gazed open and lifeless at the cloudless sky, no longer aware of the smoke that threatened to clog it.

Shen grabbed his father by his shoulders and hauled him away from the flames, afraid that they would otherwise come to consume his body as well. He didn't know what he would do with the corpse, but he knew that his father deserved better than that.

Shen was soaked in sweat and his face was covered in tears by the time he'd dragged his father to safety. He knelt down next to the man then and, despite the fact he knew better, checked him for signs of life. They were at least a day's ride away from the nearest doctor, and the Fury pack wouldn't support the weight of them both. Even if his father's eyes had flickered open, Shen knew that all he could have expected was to snatch one last moment with him or maybe to hear a few last words.

He could not manage even that.

He was bent weeping over his father's body when the shadow fell across them both. Shen cursed himself. He had known that his father had not set fire to their buildings and shot himself, but his grief had overwhelmed him so that he'd forgotten to ask himself who had.

Shen looked up to see a towering figure silhouetted against the lowering sun. He shaded his eyes with a hand coated with his father's blood to get a better look at the murderer. He wished he hadn't.

The intruder stood taller than any man Shen had ever seen. He wore a large conical hat of bamboo, the kind favored by the people who worked in the rice paddies clustered around the inland sea known as the Shining Mirror. It had been bleached white like his leather coat and the leather riding chaps he wore, and it gleamed as if it had never seen dirt in all its days. Beneath the coat, the man wore a shirt and pants of the deepest crimson. A silver pistol hung from the man's left hip, a gun belt of ebon-colored leather, its gleaming butt facing out toward the world. A silver mask concealed his face.

The mask gave the man the face of a demon with large, angry eyes and wide, fat lips curled into a snarl around fangs glinting with menace. The eyes and lips bore holes through which the man could see and speak but Shen could see nothing inside them but the whites of the man's eyes and the flash of his perfect, sharp teeth as he spoke.

"I am an Imperial Marshal of the August Throne." The man's voice sounded low and raspy, as if he'd once swallowed burning coals. "I came here to offer your father a fair price for his glorious invention."

Shen's gaze shot to where he'd left the Fury pack in the grass. It sat safely away from the flames that continued to devour everything his family had left. Soon nothing would remain but the pack and the clothes that Shen wore.

"What do you want from me?" Shen said. His tears had dried, but his emotions still shook inside him, making him unsteady. "You see what you came for. Take it."

"I am no thief, boy," the Marshal said, "but the Emperor's will shall not be denied."

"What did you offer my father?"

"One hundred gold talons."

161

Shen gasped. He had never known anyone to have such a fortune. Nobles of all sorts would have such riches, he knew, but he had never met any of them.

"And what did you propose to take?"

"His invention. And his name."

Shen stood then, leaving his father's cooling form at his feet. "And you killed him when he refused."

"When he denied my first offer, I was compelled to make another. He denied that to his death."

Even standing, Shen had to crane his neck backward to take in the Marshal's height. His father had told him of such men before, hands of the Emperor, the living god who sat on his distant throne. They acted with impunity, serving as judge, jury, and executioner. They recognized no other authority than that of the Emperor himself, and he was so very far away.

Shen gazed out past the Marshal. On one side, the only home he could remember burned to the ground. On the other, the endless prairie of the High Plains stretched out for untold leagues. Between them stood the Marshal, and Shen knew he would allow no escape that he did not himself dispense.

"I don't understand," Shen said. "What is my father's name to you?"

The Marshal's even rows of teeth flashed behind his silver mask as he laughed. "The name didn't belong only to him, boy, and the people he shared it with want it back."

Shen screwed up his face, confused. The thought that anyone would care about his father had never occurred to him. They had lived out here on this quiet plot of land by themselves for so long that Shen had assumed that no one outside of the Lees — the family that owned the nearest trading post — would even care if they lived or died, and then probably not for weeks.

The Marshal had shattered that illusion.

"Can't a name be shared?"

The Marshal nodded. "Things that can be shared can be sullied.

These people were tired of the stain that your father left on their honor. They petitioned the Emperor to have it cleansed."

The Marshal put his hands on his hips and stood back to stare at the buildings as they became poisonous billows of smoke. "And so I have taken the necessary steps."

Shen rushed the Marshal then, his teeth bared and his hands out before him. He didn't think then about the legends that surrounded the Marshals and their martial prowess. He didn't think about himself for an instant. He could only think of his father, whose blood still stained his hands.

As Shen charged at the Marshal, the man spun and backhanded him to the ground with a single, sharp blow to the eye.

Stars flashed before Shen's injured eye, and the world swirled around like a drunken dog in the other. He fell flat on his rear and remained there, waiting for the earth to stop swimming beneath him. He waited there for the man to draw his gun and place a single pistol in his heart. At least he would die in the same way as his father before him.

But no bullet came. Instead, the Marshal crouched down on his haunches and stared into Shen's eyes. He scratched the unshaven stubble on his exposed skin beneath his mask, and Shen spotted some of his own blood on the wrist of the man's snowy coat. Shen reached up to feel his throbbing eye, and it came away wet, his blood mingling with his father's on his fingers.

"Why haven't you killed me?" Shen asked.

"You are your father's sole heir." The Marshal reached down and grabbed a handful of grass. He tossed into the air behind him, and the wind took it and blew it toward Shen's burning home, where the flames consumed it. "You haven't heard my offer yet."

Shen's eyes widened. "You'll let me live?"

The Marshal stood and dusted off his hands against each other. "And pay you handsomely to boot. In exchange for your father's invention and your name."

"Why?"

"Your uncle in Sedoa, I'm told, wanted you and your father dead. If he'd had his way, I would have been sent to scour every hint of you from the earth. In his infinite mercy, the Emperor instructed me to offer you this deal."

Shen stared at the man for a long while. He couldn't read a thing about the person who stood behind that mask, and he soon gave up trying. He shifted his gaze to the fury pack instead, until he came to a decision, the only one he had left.

"Who am I to stand in the Emperor's way?"

The Marshal laughed and held out his hand to help Shen to his feet. Shen accepted it.

"Your father may have been a great inventor," the Marshal said, "but you have a brighter future ahead of you."

"How's that?" Shen strove to keep the bitterness from his voice.

"You're already far smarter."

Shen grunted, then walked toward the Fury pack. The marshal followed close behind him and watched him pick it up.

"I'll need to show you how to use it," Shen said. "It can be tricky."

The Marshal rested his hand on the butt of his pistol. "Please do," he said. "But you won't be wearing it out of here."

"Of course not." Shen held the pack up high and gestured for the Marshal to step forward. The large man did so and shrugged the pack's straps over his shoulders.

"How does it work?"

"It has a Fury engine in it that draws in the positive and negative Furies from the air around it and pits them against each other until they are so exhausted that natural forces in the area no longer apply. In this case, that's the force of gravity."

"I know what a Fury engine is, boy." An edge of irritation crept into the Marshal's voice. "How do I use the damned thing?"

"Nothing could be simpler." Shen pointed at the pack's controls, which arched out over the shoulder straps on a set of reinforced brass tubes. "The one on the left controls the amount of thrust from the steam engine paired with the pack's Fury engine. You just push the button to release the jet of steam. It comes out here behind you, so be careful not to let your legs drag too far back as you go."

The Marshal snorted at the thought of the machine hurting him, and Shen walked around behind him, checking connections and adjusting straps as he went. The Marshal was much larger than he, and it took a few moments to get everything right.

"And the control on the right?" the marshal asked.

"You swivel that about to control the direction of the steam jet. Again—"

"Keep it away from my legs. Got it."

Shen came around the front of the Marshal and checked the straps to make sure they were tight across the man's chest. "I don't want you coming out of these," he said.

The Marshal grunted at him. Up this close, Shen could smell the man. He wasn't a demon, as his mask implied, just a person of flesh and blood — the man who'd killed his father.

"You haven't asked me about the gold," the Marshal said.

Shen finished up with the final adjustments. "My life is worth more to me than any coins."

The Marshal fished a white leather pouch out of an inside pocket of his jacket, working it out past the Fury pack's straps. It bore flecks of crimson across it, and Shen had no doubt whose blood had stained it. The Marshal took Shen's hand and pressed the heavy pouch into it, the coins clinking against each other inside.

"Don't say the Emperor never gave you anything, boy."

Shen could see the man's smirk behind his mask. He ignored and twisted a dial that sat on the strap on the Marshal's left shoulder. As he did, the Fury engine thrummed to life, and the scent of a lightning strike filled the air.

Shen gave the knob a hard twist then, and it snapped off in his hand.

The Marshal glared down at him. "Take care, boy. That's the

Emperor's property now."

Shen braced himself against the earth beneath his feet and shoved up against the marshal with all his might. Without the force of gravity to hold him to the earth, the Marshal sailed straight up into the air and kept going.

"You can give it to the Jade Emperor," Shen said, "when you see him in the heavens."

The Marshal reached out and grabbed the Fury pack's controls. He pressed the button that let loose the jet of steam, and it shot him higher into the sky. He fiddled with the other control, but all it did was shake him about in the air like a marionette being played with by a child.

"What have you done?" Panic rose in the Marshal's voice. "How do I get down?"

Shen held up the dial that controlled the Fury engine. "The gyroscopes my father implanted in the fury pack keep it upright, so the steam jet can only force you in that direction."

"Then I'll just wait until the weather brings me back to earth." The Marshal snarled at him. "I can be patient boy."

Shen shook his head. "If you don't release the pressure in the steam engine, it will build until it has no choice but to explode."

The Marshal hung there in the air, already higher than the top of any tree. Shen could see him weighing his options. The man went for his pistol then and fired down at Shen.

The Marshal moved almost faster than Shen's eye could follow, but he'd expected the man to do something desperate. The moment the Marshal made his move, Shen sprinted away.

The bullet grazed his thigh, cutting a long furrow through his flesh and knocking him from his feet. Shen tumbled into a painful roll and somersaulted back onto his feet, limping away as fast as he could manage. Other shots rang out, but they went wide and sounded farther and farther away with every pull of the Marshal's trigger.

After the Marshal fired all six shots, Shen risked looking back to see the man spiraling higher and higher into the sky. The recoil from the gunshots had kicked him higher than the eagles that sometimes circled overhead but had now vanished, fleeing from this stranger in their midst.

Shen sat down then and bound his wounded leg and watched as the Marshal struggled against his fate. When, after several minutes filled with pleas and curses raining down from the sky, the Fury pack exploded, Shen did not smile.

He stood on his feet, his leg already stiffening, and weighed the bag of the Emperor's gold in one hand and the Fury engine's knob in the other. Then he set off toward the setting sun, toward the west, where many leagues from here the great city of Sedoa lay sprawled and waiting on the Shining Mirror's other side.

Matt Forbeck has been a full-time creator of award-winning games and fiction since 1989. He has designed collectible card games, roleplaying games, miniatures games, board games, and toys, and has written novels, short fiction, comic books, motion comics, nonfiction, essays, and computer game scripts and stories for companies including Adams Media, Angry Robot, ArenaNet, Atari, Boom! Studios, Del Rey, Games Workshop, IDW, Image Comics, Mattel, Playmates Toys, Simon & Schuster, Tor.com, Ubisoft, Wired.com, Wizards of the Coast, and WizKids. He has fifteen novels published to date, including Guild Wars: Ghosts of Ascalon and the critically acclaimed Amortals and Vegas Knights. His latest work is the Magic: The Gathering comic book. For more about him and his work, visit Forbeck.com.

SEVEN HOLES
by T.S. Luikart

He never sat, at least, not that Kana had seen. He perched, like a
raptor, on the edge of seats. Waiting, watching, always. Even when they
rode and now, while he was working, more than ever. She'd made him
the tea he liked; he thanked her without ever taking his functional eye
from the bed before him or its occupant.

He sipped from the cup occasionally, with his right hand always,
for his left never strayed far from the hilt of the sword leaning against
his leg. The sword she had heard whispers of long before she'd met
him, or ever thought to. It was an Eldaire blade, but travel the West
entire and you'd never see another like it. It was made of peach wood,
lacquered with a mixture of pine resin and his blood. Along the cutting
edges, the blade changed from wood to razored silver, without a trace
of seam to be seen as if the wood itself had sprouted the metal. Seven
holes pierced its length. He said he'd never sharpened it, not once, since
the day he'd been gifted it, more than two decades before by a master
swordsmith grateful for his daughter's life.

Kana believed him.

They were sitting (perching) in a barn loft along the southern edge
of the Mist Sea Valley, near the foot of the Eagles' Claw Mountains.
He was here because they'd summoned him with the promise of a
challenge and a goodly quantity of silver. She was here because her

mentor had saddled him with her for a year. "Good for both of you," Asra-soah had said.

Kana didn't think Eldorah Tolnik thought so.

The one on the bed stirred, groaning, and it was all Kana could do to not recoil. Perhaps his hand tightened, perhaps not, but Tolnik showed no other sign of having heard. Kana had watched six strong men wrestle the figure on the bed to the ground and bind it in rawhide ropes at Tolnik's direction. Kana couldn't think of "it" as a "him", not after she'd seen it punch a man's heart clean out of his chest and tear another's head off.

It still looked very much like a seven year old boy to her though.

It was times like this that she was near convinced he could read her mind.

"He's just a little boy, Kana, nothing more."

She shook her head. "How can that *be*, Tolnik-si? I *saw* the things he did, how can you say he's not possessed by a demon?"

"I told you before girl, there are no such things as demons."

She snapped at him, exasperated. "I do not understand how you can say that, Eldorah Tolnik, with the things I've seen at your side. With what you are!"

"Nevertheless, it is so."

"How?"

For the first time, his gaze shifted away from the figure on the bed and he looked directly at her for a long moment. His face was a study in varied scars, each stranger than the last, but none so grim as the long grey welt that started above his forehead and worked its way down his face, bisecting his right eye, to end up just south of his chin. Eldorah Tolnik had once been a handsome man, but no more.

"A question at last. You Castalan can be so damn formal."

"My pardons."

"Ha! Truth can be a heavier burden then duty, Kana."

"My shoulders are strong, Tolnik-si."

"So too is your mind, according to Asra. Alright, girl, you've certainly earned the right."

He paused, gathering his thoughts and when next he spoke, there was a distinctly formal tone in his voice. "What most folks call 'demons' are the result of a martial Spirit being ignited without the proper training to control it. On the Dust Road, we train for years to channel the Furies within us. Some poor souls unlock their Spirit's strength by accident, usually due to injury, either physical or emotional. Their Spirits, released but undirected, are usually furious and lash out at everyone around them. Eventually, they descend into following the whims of dreams and momentary desires. An unfettered Spirit can corrupt the flesh, twisting it over time. Simple folk, not understanding any of this, see an angry madman with seemingly impossible strength, other unexplainable abilities, along with frightening physical changes, and say they're possessed by a demon."

Kana considered his words for a time. "So what is it that you do?"

"I help their Spirit to go back to sleep for a time, if I can. If not, I end their suffering."

"For a time?"

"Yes. Especially a young one like this, he'll likely walk the Dust Road one day, if he survives. If we can save him, perhaps his family can find a master for him or maybe send him to the Sleepless Scriveners. Once your Spirit has used the power of kung-fu though, there is no way back," he raised a single eyebrow, "less the demon return."

"What if… what if someone already knows kung-fu, but unfetters their Spirit on purpose?"

Tolnik turned from the boy and look directly at her, his glance approving. "How do you think I got the worst of these scars?"

She smiled slowly, but stopped when she saw the look of concern, then anger, pass over his face.

"What it is?"

"Idiots. Final Song take the lot of them."

"What?"

"This is at a delicate point. The boy's Spirit is struggling, a choice will soon be upon him and I both. I cannot leave. There is a mob approaching us. I can feel them."

"Where?"

"The road, not far at all, now."

Kana leapt to her feet, grabbing her long spear up from where she had carefully laid it. She kneeled before him, one fist to the floor. "Tolnik-siah, please allow me to deal with this matter."

He smiled, slightly. "Go, Kana-so. But remember, they're just frightened of what they do not understand."

She nodded once and sped from the loft, barely pausing as she leapt down to the barn floor below. The fields outside the barn were covered in thick green grass, and the sun was still shining, but there was already an evening chill in the air, carried by the wisps of fog that drifted between the trees of a nearby orchard. While it was not yet twilight, Kana could see that the people coming up the road already had torches lit.

She took up a position in the center of the road and planted the butt of her spear in the soil beside her. Closing her eyes, she waited. She heard exclamations and a few muttered curses when they noticed her in the road. The one leading them urged them on, heedless. When they came fifteen paces, she opened her eyes to regard them.

Their leader was squat, flushed, and breathing hard. Kana judged him a farmer, like most of the folks before her.

"We've got no problems with you, girl, but you had best stand aside."

"What will you all do, if I should do so?"

"What must be done."

"My present teacher is already attending to that. It a burden neither he, nor I, wish upon any of you."

"You have any idea how many that thing up there killed?"

She nodded slowly. "Many. Did you lose someone?"

The farmers face twisted from anger to grief. His voice was low. "I set my boy on the pyre this morning."

172

"May the Maiden watch over him." She raised her voice, so the whole crowd could hear her. "I know you are angry, but this is not justice. I cannot stand aside."

Whatever the farmer was about to say changed as he looked past her, his eyes narrowed and he pointed a shaking finger. "This is your doing, Jandel! That monster is yours!"

Kana didn't turn, but she felt the 'possessed' boy's parents coming to stand beside her.

"I know it, Tern. I'm so sorry about your boy, but killing mine won't bring him back."

"It may bring his spirit peace, though!" The crowd, content to listen till now, growled at that and surged forward.

Kana dropped into a martial stance and leveled her spear. She surprised herself at how steady her voice was. "I am sorry, but I cannot permit this. I promise you, I will take *many* of you with me." The end of her spear flickered like a living flame. The mob paused, taken aback by her calm certainty…

And then the top of the barn exploded.

The crowd collapsed to the ground, as wooden shards rained down throughout the clearing. Kana shook her head to clear it as she used her spear to push herself upright. Her ears were ringing with the blast, and she was disoriented, but she finally managed to focus her eyes on something that was moving amidst the wreckage . The indistinct shapes in her vision slowly resolved into Tolnik and the boy, free of his bonds, fighting in the ruins of the barn.

The boy was a blur of motion, dancing back and forth across the shattered barn supports. Tolnik smoothly countered his every move, keeping pace with his blade. Occasionally, he would lunge in and strike the boy, before withdrawing. Kana immediately saw, to her amazement, that with each blow, Tolnik deftly twisted his sword so as not to cut the child, instead striking him along the flat of the blade.

Their fight slowly moved towards Kana and the fallen farmers behind her. Seeing how the tide of battle was flowing, Kana dug her feet into the sod. "All of you, get behind me, quickly!" They didn't need to be told twice.

As they drew closer, Kana could see an eerie radiance dancing about the boy's eyes, his little hands twisted nearly into claws. Sparks spilled down from the holes in Tolnik's blade. She realized he was grinning, teeth clenched. More and more of his blows landed, as the boy appeared to be, ever so slightly, slowing.

Kana caught a woman from running past her. "Mir, please!"

The demon-who-wasn't turned. "Mama?"

Tolnik punched him squarely in the center of his back, two knuckles extended, as the boy began to fall, he hurled his sword into the ground, where it spiked upright, and jabbed two fingers into the side of the boy's neck. The boy fell heavily to the sod.

"MIR!"

The woman rushed forward to collect her son, sobbing. Tolnik stood panting heavily.

"No need for tears, Mam. I think you may have saved your boy's life."

She looked up at him in pure astonishment. Tolnik turned away and looked at Kana. "Well done, apprentice."

She smiled and bowed formally, to a short bark of his laughter.

The mob soon dispersed, embarrassed, and somewhat overawed by the presence of Dust Roaders in their midst. After Mir had fallen into a quiet sleep, the Jandels were lavish in their praise. Tolnik waved them off, saying they'd only gotten their money's worth.

The next day, Tolnik slept in, telling Kana they would head east towards Semberhane sometime after lunch. His rest was interrupted just before noon, though, when a group of farmers, including Master Tern from the night before, slowly approached their small campsite.

The assembly of farmers advanced, no weapons evident. When

Kana walked out to meet them, Tern and several others removed their hats.

"Gentlemen... can I help you?"

"Oh, Miss, I sincerely hope so. We're in for the Hells now, if not."

"What is it?"

"Bross Crysimper and his gang have returned!"

"Who?"

"Crysimper, he and his men have raided our village for years. They've come again and say we don't have enough goods to satisfy them. They're threatening to take women, children. Please, you must help us!"

Tolnik's voice emerged from his blankets.

"Must we?" He stood, shaking off his bedding and stalked across the clearing toward them. Several of the farmers recoiled a bit as Tolnik walked right up to Tern and leaned down to look him square in the eye.

"You were perfectly willing to burn a small boy, but you can't face down a single gang of bandits?"

Tern's eyes were downcast. "I already lost one child. I am truly sorry, I didn't really want to hurt Jandel's boy. But we were afraid the demon would take others and now these bandits..." he trailed off.

Tolnik turned to Kana. "This is not our problem."

She met his gaze levelly. "How is it not? What do we stand for, if not for this?"

"There will always be bandits. *Always*. If we answer every cry for help, we run ourselves ragged." He pointed at the farmers. "They *can* deal with this, they just lack the courage to act."

"Then maybe we should inspire them. You're right Tolnik-siah, we can't be everywhere, or help everyone, but we are here, now."

He sighed. "You want to go play hero, feel free. I'll be certain to tell Asra you died valiantly." He laid back down and made a show of rolling over.

"So be it." Kana quickly gathered her spear. "Lead the way, Mr. Tern."

"Oh thank you, Miss. With your help, I'm certain we have a chance against the Demon."

Tolnik sat bolt upright. "What? What did you say?"

Mr. Tern repeated, hesitantly, "With your help, I…"

"No, no," Tolnik interrupted. "The last bit."

"…the Demon?"

Tolnik stood. "What about 'the Demon'?"

"It's what folks call Crysimper. Bross 'the Demon' Crysimper."

Tolnik looked at Kana for a long moment, than guffawed.

"Somewhere, Immortal Tolis is laughing at me."

She grinned.

"What a pathetic excuse for a village!" Roared Bross 'the Demon' Crysimper. "I've seen outhouses with more class!"

"Hey, Boss…" one of his men motioned to the end of the road. A man stood on the road coming from the West, into the village. At his side, a revolver was holstered. An enormous sheathed sword was balanced across his shoulders.

"Looks like some sport, eh, lads?" Laughter ensued. Crysimper brought his horse about, along with several of his men. As they drew closer to the approaching man, who Crysimper took to be a freeblade, he noticed the sword was mostly made of wood.

"Maybe they are too poor, they can't even afford to hire a warrior with a proper blade." Laughter again. The man lifted his head and Crysimper clearly saw his scarred features. "That tears it, ugly to boot."

Crysimper grinned down at the poor freeblade. "Tell you what, I'm feeling merciful today, just go, really."

The man smiled grimly back. "I'm not."

His first blow split Crysimper's right hand man in half, the backstroke decapitated a horse and sheared through the rider. His punch hurled Crysimper from his horse, slamming him to the ground five paces back.

Crysimper came up gasping. "Who, what?"

An iron grasp seized his throat, choking the wind out of him. "Introductions? Oh very well. Bross Crysimper, Demon, I'm Eldorah Tolnik, Exorcist."

The last the Demon saw was sparks falling, as the wooden blade descended.

T.S. Luikart is an award winning writer and game designer. As the co-developer of Far West, he's spent a great deal of time over the last year or more constructing a very large sandbox for y'all to play in. He is thrilled to see the other writers in this anthology bringing the lands beyond the Last Horizon to life and looks forward to seeing what everyone else will do with them in the years to come.

LOCAL LEGEND
by Jason L Blair

Dunephy swaggered into the bar, a cocky grin plastered on his face and a long satchel strapped across his back. The patrons of Loyal Oak had become used to his bravado, his smarmy way of speaking to folks, and the ladies of the establishment had become accustomed to his roaming eyes and grabby hands. Since he blew into town a week ago, they'd come to know Hano Dunephy well. Of all the colorful names you could apply to the man—rogue, scoundrel, bastard—liar was surprisingly not one of them.

"Red Phoenix is dead," the man said, slinging the satchel off his shoulder. He set it down on the table closest to him. "And this here's proof."

The bar went silent. All eyes turned on him. He untied the golden string holding the satchel fast and unfurled its dark blue cloth. He brought up a wooden sheath, the image of a wiry bird burned into it, and held it above his head.

"Laughing Wind," Dunephy smiled. "The man's signature sword."

He clasped the pommel and drew the length of the sword slowly. He held it up, tip facing downward, for all to see. The distinctive mark of Red Phoenix—three flames—was etched into the steel.

"I came to this town to claim this bounty. I have done so. Now," he looked over the crowd, his smirk widening, "I will be paid."

A lone clapping sound erupted from the back of the bar. Dunephy scanned the crowd, trying to place it. Sheriff Lojin sauntered forth, wearing his own smirk.

"Well, well," the lawman said, adjusting his belt. "Killed the Scourge of the Bulk Line, eh? And this, this weapon, is your proof?"

Dunephy stood proudly by his prize. He pointed at the markings on the blade. "Here. Proof this is the villain's sword. Used to kill twelve widows over a single winter, and their orphan children as well."

"Oh, I know the tale," Lojin said, eying the sword. "And this may well be the famed Laughing Wind. But this is no proof Red Phoenix is dead, or that you killed him."

Dunephy's face turned sour. He brought the sword up in an offensive posture. "You calling me a cheat, sheriff?"

"For the prize on Red Phoenix's head, we're gonna need more than this sword."

"I heard Red Phoenix loved that sword," a voice in the back said. Dunephy's eyes shot through the crowd. Cheen Yergen, one of the local merchants, stood up. "Said he'd never part with it alive."

Dunephy's smile returned. "That's right. Yeah, that's right. Never part with it, not alive. Killed the man myself. But his body is gone. Burned up. But I have this." He sheathed the blade, placing it back onto the wrap.

Cheen stepped forward. "I'll gladly appraise that, sheriff. I'm quite familiar with the legend of Red Phoenix. Seen some of his earlier swords too."

"Even if you prove the authenticity," Lojin countered, "it doesn't prove Dunephy killed Red Phoenix to get it."

"I have no reason to believe Mr. Dunephy would lie about how he came to acquire the sword," Cheen said. "I, for one, am willing to take him at his word should the sword be proven to be of proper origin."

The sheriff considered the merchant's idea. He had known Cheen for a long time and he had no reason not to trust the man's judgement.

"Fine," Lojin said. "You check that sword. If it is what Dunephy says, and you full believe it," he pointed to Cheen, "then we'll pay up."

"Very fair," Cheen nodded to the sheriff. Then, to Dunephy, "Come to my shop. I have my equipment there."

The gunslinger finished wrapping the sword and carried it, one hand clasped around the sheath, out of the bar. He followed Cheen onto the street, eyes open for trouble, and continued on, down the road, to Cheen's Mercantile.

The old man rubbed the head of the cat statue by the shop's door and encouraged Dunephy to do the same.

"One can always use fortunes, yeah?"

Dunephy obliged, rolling his eyes as he did so. He stepped into the shop after Cheen, the soft ting of the door bell rang out over them.

The store smelled heavily of jasmine, thanks to Cheen's wife and her obsession with scented oils, and the place was twice as warm as it was out in the street. Dunephy immediately felt uncomfortable. But if this was how he was going to get his reward, he was willing to suffer through it.

The gunslinger unwrapped the satchel and set the sheathed sword on the front counter.

"Red Phoenix," Cheen said, putting on his merchant's cloak. "Very impressive. How did you do it, huh? Bullet? Sword stroke?"

"One shot," Dunephy said, stabbing a finger toward his left cheek. "Right through the eye."

"Ooh," the merchant winced. "Gruesome. Very gruesome."

"Nothing compared to what that man's done in his lifetime. He deserved worse."

"I suppose that's true," Cheen laughed. "Mercy is for the merciful, eh, Mr. Dunephy?"

The gunslinger nodded. "Sure thing." He unbuttoned his collar and fanned the fabric a bit. Sweat was trickling down his neck. "So how long's this gonna take?"

"Not long," Cheen answered. "Oh, one moment."

The shopkeeper went through a beaded curtain into the back room. Dunephy looked around at the knick-knacks and oddities throughout the shop. Cheen's sold all sorts of household staples, as well as exotics such as sugar and patterned textiles, but it was known for its accents, like the small ivory statues that lined the shelf above the counter. Dunephy counted a dozen intricately carved effigies. Most of them were mythological creatures, stained a variety of bright hues. At the end, a jade-colored dragon scowled at him, a single burst of ruby fire dribbling from its rolled lip.

Cheen reappeared, an examiner's bag in his left hand. He set it on the counter next to the jian and took out a variety of tools.

"You're not going to mess it up, are you?" Dunephy placed his hand over the sword protectively.

Cheen chuckled. "Of course not. I wouldn't dream of harming such an important piece of history." He unsheathed the weapon and placed it gently on its cloth. He secured a loupe into his right eye and turned a crooked smile toward the gunslinger.

"Please, Mr. Dunephy," Cheen pointed at a chair. "Make yourself comfortable. Relax. Would you like some tea?"

Dunephy dragged the chair closer to the counter and sat down. "Yeah, I'll take some tea. Not too sweet."

Cheen called to his wife in his native tongue. She snapped back a long string of harsh-sounding words.

"Ah, the tea will be ready shortly," Cheen assured the man. "Now, let's take a look at this."

The merchant dipped some gauze into clear spirits and rubbed the surface of the sword vigorously. His fingers glided over the instrument delicately, lovingly.

"The craftsmanship," Cheen said, "is very impressive."

"Good," Dunephy said, shifting in the chair. "I plan to sell it when I'm done."

"Sell it?" Cheen looked up, surprised.

"Should get a pretty coin for it, too," the gunslinger said. He looked over some of the bric-a-brac scattered on a small wooden display case. "What with its, y'know, historical value and all. The fact it's a good sword on top of it, well, that's even better. Proper value on top of it."

Cheen fought back a scowl. "Proper value. Hm."

"What's that?" Dunephy said, turning a crystal sphere in his hand.

"Tell me, Mr. Dunephy," the merchant said, wringing the rag over a clay pot. "How did you come by this sword?"

"You losing your beans there?" the gunslinger scoffed. "I just told you."

"Ah, you told me the facts. But this, well, this is a story, Mr. Dunephy. One you will tell a hundred times. Best to practice it. Many will want to hear about the man who killed Red Phoenix."

"Heh," the man grinned. "I suppose you're right." He looked over Cheen who was dutifully drying the steel with a fresh rag. Dunephy had no idea what the merchant was doing but he knew that sword had better not get damaged. "Sure, settle in. I'll spin you a yarn."

Dunephy leaned back and spoke.

I had come to Painted Valley following the Bulk Line, knowing it was a favored target of Red Phoenix and his gang. Folks had been telling me for months how Ol' Red was on the lam—hiding away, they said—but I knew the varmint was biding his time. That's how outlaws operate. They never stop and they never retire, just take a breather now and then. Trust me, I've known more'n a few.

Stakes as published were, anyone able to stop Red Phoenix, stop him dead, would get their prize in this town right here. As it was Painted Valley that put out the call for the scoundrel's head, I decided to stop in and see what folks knew.

The townspeople were surprisingly tight-lipped, as you well know there, Cheen. Something about them here, secretive, but it was one

183

person, Miss Maddy Crane, former courtesan to our Mr. Phoenix and ancillary to the Loyal Oak, who gave me insight into the devil.

"His greed is only matched by his vanity," Maddy said. "He does nothing without the prospect of notoriety."

See, that's the kinda tip a man like me can flip into silver, son. No way a man like that can lay low. And with the Bulk Line on its way one town past, after its gold stop on the rail, I knew Red would be waiting there. A job of that level, with that much reward, guaranteed to make the papers like, he was already itching for it.

I knew then I needed to beat that train. I checked with Phan over at the yard, made sure of my timing with the Bulk Line, and plotted my course.

The Bulk Line was half a day's chug from here and another league to Pale Water. I could wait for it to pass through or I could lie ahead in its destination. I figured this: Red was persona non grata here in this town. He wouldn't come back, not yet. But with a good stretch of trail between here and Pale Water up north, he'd lie in wait somewhere in between.

But, see, this here is where things get sticky. The Iron Dragons have kept mum about the true toll Red Phoenix and his men have taken on them, not only by making the tracks inhospitable but the loss of life as well during robberies previous. Dragons hold secrets like politicians hold liquor but I've gotten both out of either in the past. Learned a few things about our man Red.

'Course I also know better than to step on a Dragon's claws. So I took care to avoid their trailing routes. I stuck to the clusters, moving fast but not making a spectacle of myself.

Said and done, it was a fair easy ride through to Pale Water but I didn't see any good place for Red and his men to shadow, no bottlenecks or overcast passages, so I couldn't say just yet where they might strike.

Traveled the whole run between the two towns and heard from the teller in Pale Water that the Bulk Line was held up by broken trucks.

This was after the gold stop though which meant they were dead on the line, prey in the trap.

I knew my time was limited. I had to get to that train fast. Dragons weren't dummies, the gold would be offloaded, but was there a place they could take it that Red couldn't find them?

I rode hard as I could toward the downed train, not stopping for nothing. Came to a rest atop a bluff overlooking the line. Night had come, and the train slumbered there like a fallen giant. Tracks cold ahead of it. Then five horses came from a cloud of black on the other side. Red and his men.

I hitched toward the rails, going hard as I could, but the old girl took a tumble and went ass over end onto the sand. This pitched me forward and I tumbled as well, coming to a stop against a rock.

The clatter of a tray broke the man's concentration. Hano watched as Cheen's wife set down a tea serving. The merchant himself was staring at the gunslinger intensely, drawn into the story.

Dunephy thanked Mrs. Yergen and took a sip of the olive-tinged water. It tasted like pure sugar. Far too sweet for his tastes, but he did the polite thing.

Cheen's wife went to the door and fussed with something. The merchant cleared his throat, urging Dunephy to continue. Hano took another sip, the final polite third, and set the cup down.

The girl had broke her leg in the fall. Couldn't do nothing for her but mercy. Thankfully the tussle at the train covered the sound.

Red's crew and the Dragons were clashing steel to steel. I ambled toward but my feet had gone all twisty and I could barely set straight. Cursing myself blue, I held back, knowing I couldn't take on the Phoenix in this shape.

But I wasn't going to let them just go. I hid best I could behind the rock I'd landed against, and watched as the dozen or so able men clashed on the field.

The battle was over far quicker than either side would have liked. Red stood victorious, down one man, and the Dragons, down three, retreated.

Most-revered guardians out there won't stand toe-to-toe with Red given the option. Now what does that tell you?

All I could do was sit and watch. Turned my stomach. I saw Red and his men grab some crates, tip off the lids, and plunge handfuls of something into large sacks. Couple of the men walked the far side of the train.

Took no more than a few minutes before the four were off and away. By this time, the sky was pitch.

Chancing my ankle, I strode up to the mess. The fallen lay out like scrying stones, the portent of something awful on the wind. Taking what ammunition I could use from the bodies, I set about following the tracks. Most of the horses had skittered off but one remained.

The conductor was dead, the pitchman too. Splinters from three broken crates scattered the landscape.

I rode hard that night, eyes set on the horizon, knowing Red Phoenix and his men were over the hills, somewhere. The trail was still warm from the hooves that carried them. Their sweat still sizzled on the sand.

But the way soon enough ran cold. I wandered that desert for what seemed like hours, cursing my luck. I was half a tick from heading back when a howl split the distance and snapped my neck toward the north.

That's when I heard the shot. A whimper followed, like a strangled beast. I drew my gun and skulked forth, using the dark to shield me. I left the horse, my ankle healed up alright by then, and went ahead on foot.

I could smell the sulfur on the air. Soon enough, I saw the creature's body. One clean hole through its neck. Shock knocked it out; the pool of blood around it took its life.

I saw the light then, partially hidden by some stone columns. The superstitious remnants of one of the old religions. I crept up, gun up, doing my best not to shake the sand.

Red was hunkered by a campfire, that there weapon you're eying at his side. His men were gone. Now whether he killed 'em, left 'em, or they were just making water, I had no idea.

But Red Phoenix was alone. I aimed my gun and sauntered forth.

He knew I was coming. But I ain't no coward who'd shoot from behind a rock. I wanted him to know who it was what done him in. Hano Dunephy. I wanted my face to be the last thing he ever saw.

He drew on me—and I fired. He fell there, into the campfire. His body went up like nothing. And I couldn't believe my luck. The Scourge of the Bulk Line, feared more than death, taken out by a single bullet.

My bullet.

Dunephy took another sip of his tea, biting through the sweetness and glanced over at the merchant.

"And that was it?" Cheen asked. "That was the end of Red Phoenix."

"Sure and truly," Hano nodded.

"How did you know it was him? So few who have seen him come out alive."

Dunephy shrugged. "His sword, like I said. Famous as anything. What are you—are you getting at something, Cheen?"

"No, no," Cheen said. "You've told a fascinating tale. Indeed." The old man flashed his gapped teeth at the gunslinger. The clapping rang hollow in the still scented air.

"Indeed," another voice said from the back of the shop. Dunephy's hand flew to his gun but Lojin already had his piece drawn and aimed. The sheriff parted the dense beading that separated the front of the shop from the back and strode into the main room. "Drop your iron, boy," the lawman commanded. Dunephy held his weapon level.

"What's this about now?" Dunephy stood slowly, aiming at the sheriff's belly. He knew he'd had to get a second shot off to make it

187

count but a gutshot would buy him the time to do that. He couldn't afford to adjust his aim just then.

The gunslinger dared a glance at Cheen. "This some kinda scheme, merchant? I expected better."

Cheen set the sheathed weapon, Red Phoenix's famed blade, behind the counter and replaced it in his hands with a double-barreled shotgun.

"You slimy sonsabitches," Dunephy spat. "This how it is? I do you a favor and you what? You're gonna kill me?"

"A favor, huh?" Lojin looked over at Cheen and chuckled. "Now, Mr. Dunephy, you did it for the money. Let's not pretend otherwise."

Dunephy's blood was bubbling up in his throat. He tasted copper, hot and red.

"Funny thing," Cheen said as he stepped around the counter. "You say Red Phoenix is dead."

"Deader than shit," Dunephy kept his gun on Lojin but darted his eyes toward the shopkeeper. "Now I ain't leavin' without payment or that sword."

"You say Red Phoenix is dead," Cheen repeated. He spread his arms wide, hands flat toward Dunephy. "Yet here I am."

Dunephy stammered a bit, forcing a smile. "What? What in the fortunes' names are you talking about?"

Cheen walked toward the gunslinger, taking slow careful steps. Dunephy's eyes went swimmy.

"That man you killed was named Hollus Gat," Cheen rocked back the twin hammers. "He was a good man."

"What the hell?" Dunephy staggered. His hand dipped, involuntarily lowering his gun. Lojin took the shot, sending the man's shoulder rocking back.

Cheen approached Dunephy slowly. "When I retired, Mr. Dunephy, and came to this town, I was forced to leave many things behind. My name, for one. And that," he gestured toward Laughing Wind, "was another."

Lojin loaded another round into his gun.

"I passed my name onto Hollus. He took up the mantel. He took up the blade. But it was stolen from him. By a man named Dunephy. Stolen in the middle of the night like a common thief."

Dunephy got to his feet, spots dancing in front of his eyes, and clawed his way along the wall to the door. He tried the handle but it didn't budge. He fumbled at the draw lock but his fingers didn't respond. He could barely see.

"Four men left that train, Mr. Dunephy. You killed one. The three that were left came back. Saw how you had butchered Gat's body. And one of them arrived in town hours before you did."

Cheen turned the gunslinger around.

"You killed a friend of mine, stole my sword, and then came to brag about it in my face, Mr. Dunephy. What kind of man does that? Killing Red Phoenix. Ha!" The merchant shook his head. "A man like you. You really think you could kill a man like me?"

"What's going on?" Dunephy said, his mind ascatter. "I don't--" The gunslinger dropped to the floor. After one last gasp, he went quiet.

Lojin looked down at him for a moment. He touched his boot to the gunslinger's thigh and kicked. The man's leg wobbled back and forth dully.

The sheriff knelt down and checked the man's breathing. It was faint and fading quickly.

Mrs. Yergen brought a shovel from the backroom and yelled at Cheen in her native tongue. Cheen squawked a sharp response.

Lojin watched the two bicker for a moment, finally grabbing the shovel from his friend's hand.

"I'll set it up," the sheriff said. "If we're lucky, he'll still be breathing when we drop him in. Serve him right."

The town was asleep by the time the two men piled the last of the soil atop the shallow grave. Lojin patted it down with the flat of the shovel and ran over the top a few times to smooth it out. While the

189

lawman worked, Cheen rested on a small stone column to catch his breath. Lojin chuckled, knowing he had done twice the work of the shopkeeper. He couldn't imagine what the merchant must have looked like back when he was an outlaw. How such a legend stemmed from someone so frail anymore baffled the man.

"Now you told me," the sheriff said, pitching the shovel intot he ground and leaning against it, "that Hollus Gat was a liar and a cheat."

Cheen wiped the sweat from his neck with a thin cloth. "The dirtiest kind," the man huffed. "Stole my name. And my sword."

"So what in the good graces was all that you told Dunephy?"

The merchant flashed his wide, gapped smile. "It's the fear. You see it in their eyes and it makes," Cheen leaned back a bit. "It makes me feel young again."

"You are peculiar, my friend." A silent pause passed between the two. "We'll have to explain to everyone about Dunephy's disappearance."

"What's to explain?" Cheen shrugged. "I declared the sword a fake, he got angry, we ran him out of town."

"So what about Red Phoenix. Anymore of him out there?"

Cheen slid off the statue and stretched. "Just one."

"Last of the old group, huh?"

The old merchant nodded quietly.

"How you handle it?"

"Just like the others."

"You sure you don't want to take 'em out yourself?"

"Haha, sheriff," Cheen laughed humorlessly. "Were I in my prime."

"We'll have to put another call out then. Find ourselves another would-be hero."

"Yes, yes," Cheen smacked some dirt off his pant legs. "A hero."

"Alright then," Lojin said, pulling the shovel from the dirt. He waved to his friend as he passed. "I'm heading off to sleep. I'll put up the sign in the morning."

Jason L Blair has been a fiction writer, game designer (video and tabletop), scriptwriter, comic book author, graphic designer, book publisher, poet, and amusement park ride operator. He is an IGN Best Story of 2011 Award Nominee and won't shut up about it. You can keep tabs on him at JasonLBlair. com.

(Bumper cars, if you're curious.)

CRIPPLED AVENGERS
By Dave Gross

Despite her predicament, Pei Pei couldn't help but laugh. A few hot drops flecked Pei Pei's cheek, but the wind had shifted the instant Denson spat. A ropey brown strand curled up over the gunslinger's lip like the waxed moustache of a flicker-show villain.

The men laughed too, all except Denson. Like the scavengers they had become, they pounced at the first sign of injury among their own.

Denson wiped his sleeve across his mouth. His glare fell not on his fellows but on the helpless Pei Pei. He limped across the tracks, raising a dusty boot above her head.

"No," said Presteign. His pale blue eyes mirrored the cloudless sky. A word was all it took to stop Denson from kicking the captive. A word from Presteign was like a bullet from any other man. He didn't carry a gun himself. He employed men who carried guns.

Pei Pei knew Presteign didn't stop Denson out of any sense of mercy. He was reminding his men of his authority. No one made a move without his say-so. Pei Pei would suffer in the manner that he alone chose: to have her bound to the tracks, legs across the sun-heated rail, waiting for the train.

Presteign was the real flicker-show villain. Pei Pei had realized that long before Denson came for her. As bad as Denson was, he was still only a hired man.

Denson had left her alone while her grandmother lived. The old woman posed no physical threat, but one glance from her half-lidded eyes could paralyze a man like the sound of a rattlesnake.

Her magic was in her age. Pei Pei's stepfather was already an old man when he married her mother. His own birth must have surprised a woman who surely believed herself beyond childbearing. Before Grandmother came to live with Pei Pei's family in Sevenfork, her other sons and daughters had already succumbed, one by one, to the influenza or plain old age.

In the year she'd lived with them, Grandmother had little to say to Pei Pei. She squinted at her adopted grandchildren, her face an unreadable mass of brown wrinkles that reminded Pei Pei of something from the root cellar. Grandmother never met her son's wife. Pei Pei suspected the only reason she agreed to come live with her youngest son was that his foreign bride had died the year previous.

Even so, Grandmother settled in at Sevenfork only long enough to persuade her son to follow the booming trade opportunities in Sedoa, far away on the western shore of the Shining Mirror. Pei Pei sensed her father was reluctant to leave this last bastion of civilization not out of sentimentality for her late mother—although surely he loved her—but out of fear.

Pei Pei found the wild tales of the Periphery exciting, reading every bit novel she could persuade her brother to smuggle into the house. The stories of mysterious Foxglove ladies, seductive mariachis, and noble Twin Eagle agents fired her imagination.

Grandmother's ceaseless arguments eventually wore down her stepfather's caution, and he agreed to the move. Ever frugal, he arranged for the family to join a wagon train rather than conveying them by train. It was, Pei Pei thought, the last mistake of a weak, miserly man. Pei Pei regretted harboring such an uncharitable thought,

but she couldn't help it. After Presteign's men attacked, neither
her father nor brother had lived to endure the harsh servitude that
followed.

Corralled with the survivors, Pei Pei and her grandmother followed
their captors to the dig, an excavation the size of a town. There was
a barracks for the guards and overseers, although it smelled more like
a saloon. The pen in which they kept the prisoners confined at night
might as well have been a horse paddock, so crude were its amenities.
The various guard stands, storage sheds, and powder shacks were the
little houses in this unhappy community.

In the middle of it all stood a four-story scaffold of timber and
iron. Around it the laborers had already constructed a portion of the
steel skeleton of a giant airship. The bronze-colored hull of a gondola
lay atop the scaffold, awaiting the return of its unrecovered parts.

What Presteign could not recover from the crash site, he shipped in
on the railway he had built for this singular purpose. The tracks wound
through the low mesas to lie beside the central crater. There rested
Presteign's personal quarters in the form of a fabulous train car.

Only after they labored for a week at the dig did Grandmother
begin speaking to Pei Pei. Unlike the men, whose backs burned red
and brown as they dug in the open sun, the women knelt under screens
made from scraps of the airship skins. They were even permitted to
talk, so long as their hands never stopped scraping caked dirt from the
mechanisms salvaged from the crashed airships.

Grandmother only asked questions, so Pei Pei answered them. She
told the old woman about her life before the doomed trip to Sedoa. She
described her dance lessons, both those her stepfather had arranged
and those she had begged from her brother. From Madame Bohvay
she'd learned to dance. From Kong-sang she'd learned to sweep the legs
from beneath an opponent.

Pei Pei surprised herself by telling her grandmother about the time
she had put her brother's lessons to good use. One of Kong-sang's
friends became fresh after he and his friends had offered to walk her

home from the dance studio. When they herded her into a dead-end alley, she drove her erstwhile rapist into the hardpan and crushed his fingers under her heel. One of the others tried to capture her arms. The first kick stopped him in his tracks. The second drove the breath from his lungs and laid him on the ground.

The third man demonstrated his good sense. He turned tail and ran.

Only when her grandmother laughed did Pei Pei realize she would never have told the story if not for their desperate straits. She knew there was scant hope of escape, less of evading Denson's cruel desires. Pei Pei wanted her grandmother to know she would not submit meekly. She liked to think the old woman was proud to hear it.

Less than a day after Grandmother died, the sifting pan still on her dusty lap, Denson came for Pei Pei.

"Come along now," he said. "Else I'll have to exert a little discipline."

Pei Pei had heard that phrase before. Usually it came just before a beating for a man the guards decided was working too slow. When Presteign's men said it to one of the women, it meant she was to follow him to one of the shacks. Those who refused were beaten and dragged inside anyway.

At first she kept her eyes on the ground and shuffled along beside him. As the vise of his grip slackened, she waited until they were farthest away from both the guards at the dig and the guards sitting in the shade of the overseer's shack.

The first kick threw a leg out from under him. The second knocked away his hat and caused a tooth to leap from his mouth. He went down. She didn't count the blows after that. Her eyes were hot with tears for her father, for Kong-sang, and for the old woman she had just begun to love.

By the time they pulled her away, Pei Pei had one of Denson's guns. She was pulling the hammer with both thumbs when the men struck it away.

They dragged just outside of Presteign's car. The men bound her to

196

a chair. They glared at each other until the weakest broke eye contact, removed his hat, and climbed into the car to inform Presteign of the fractured discipline of the site. When the messenger returned, he took a pitying look at Pei Pei.

They turned the chair to make her watch as they spilled a canteen over Denson's face. Sputtering, he emptied the canteen and dropped it on the ground at her feet before limping away. Pei Pei watched the last beads of moisture evaporate from the canteen's mouth.

Hours later, she realized the cruelty of the gesture. Before sundown, she almost wished she had given in to Denson, if only to drink a cup of tepid water. By noon the next day, there was no "almost" about it. When the men loosed her bonds, her limbs were too weak to struggle, her mouth too parched to speak.

As they pulled her along behind the horses, a fat horsefly buzzed around her head, distracting her from thoughts of what they planned for her. In its way, that fly was the last mercy she'd enjoy.

They dragged her to a spot along the tracks. It was barely a mile from the dig, sheltered from sight by a low mesa ringed by withered junipers. Pei Pei knew only that they called the place Devil's Platter. She'd heard the scream of the train engine come from this direction before its monthly delivery of provisions, tools, and fresh slaves.

Pei Pei began struggling when she saw the stain and strands of rope still bound to the spikes on either side of the rail.

Bloor, Presteign's secretary awaited them beside a smoldering iron brazier. He squinted at them through a smeared monocle. His yellow waistcoat made Pei Pei think of a children's book character she had once seen, a porcupine or a hedgehog. Four branding irons jutted from the brazier. Bloor removed one to test the heat. Its point glowed white.

The first call of the steam whistle startled him into dropping the iron brand. Two of Presteign's guards mounted up and rode toward the plume of steam. The huff of the engine grew louder as the train came into view. Presteign's men fired a shot to gain the engineer's attention. A face of sooty whiskers leaned out to peer down the tracks. The man shook his beard until the men pointed their guns at him. The engine picked up steam.

"Listen good, girl," said Bloor. "Chances are the shock'll kill you outright. If not, I'll see that you don't bleed out. Mister Presteign likes to exert a little discipline, but he's merciful."

The man choked, maybe on account of the coal smoke. Pei Pei decided he couldn't swallow that last, ridiculous word.

As the engine came closer, Bloor kept talking. She couldn't understand the rest of what the secretary said. Something about cauterizing the wounds, and that she had a choice. She could crawl back to the camp and beg Denson's forgiveness. Or she could crawl out into the Thousand Mesas desert to die alone. He leaned close to her face and shouted over the engine's whistle. "Maybe that'd be for the best."

It didn't matter. As the train thundered past, Pei Pei couldn't make a decision. All she could do was match the whistle scream for scream.

Night Wolf stalking the hare, belly scraping over the flints. Low mounds of cactus crouching beneath the blurry moons. Thistles forming a new skin as the shredded rags of the old slough away on the stones.

Rushing Rabbit creeping along on forepaws.

Two paws.

Laughter rattling in a dry gullet. The breath gone before the rattling stops. The rattling is not inside. It's nearby.

A dull blow slaps the thigh, another the hip. Rolling, reaching, sharp sting on the palm, the wrist. Fingers closing with unexpected strength. Teeth breaking warm, dry flesh to unleash the hot torrent beneath. Blood thick and wet, softening the dead tongue, the brittle lips. Tongue burning, numbness spreading from the dead stumps, coursing through the remains. Poison. Poison for sure.

The bleeding moons. Sucking the last moisture from the snake's flesh, a desperate reflex that only intensifies the thirst. There must be more to drink, but there is no breaking open the cacti without a machete or the strength to lift a rock.

Crawling out of the thistles. Hands reaching, nails scraping, arms pulling, body dragging. The last of the warmth dies beneath the crust of the earth. The cold air falls still in anticipation. Stars fade and perish in the dawn.

The hunter comes.

Night Wolf struggles to rise but cannot stand tall enough to make a shadow. Rushing Rabbit can only crawl. They are not a wolf and a rabbit. They are a snake full of its own poison.

She is dying, but she does not die. The rising sun warms her blood and the poison in it. She could stop, let it take her, but a cold desire fills her heart. She needs more time. There is one more thing to do.

With every painful reach and grip and pull her thoughts become clearer. Legless and feverish, poisoned and parched, anointed in dust and blood, she creeps toward the west. Every desperate inch is a prayer, but not for salvation.

A shadow falls upon her. Through the desiccated earth she feels the thunder. Her body longs for the rain, but when she falls onto her back, all she sees is empty sky. The shadows are not above her but all around.

Their rounded bodies are shorter than her legless carcass, but so close they look like behemoths. She has seen them before, from a distance. They are reptilian herd beasts, greps.

The stampede shudders through the herd. An instant before the disturbance reaches her, she raises her arms. The gesture reminds her of reaching for her father—her real father, gone so long that all she remembers of his face are his black, black eyes and a missing tooth. How he would scoop her into his arms.

She reaches up again. Something lifts her and drags her along. She smells the reptilian musk and clings tight, looking past the grep's shoulder at the sun. It is as pitiless as Presteign's eye, but it is not the Hunter who stares back at her. It the Maiden, who smiles down a secret.

Pei Pei hugs the grep tighter, nuzzles its neck, and bites.

Each night, the music drew them out, one by one. Pei Pei watched them from the adobe hut in which she first awoke. There the boy had brought water and bathed her face every hour. Every fourth time he visited, a woman accompanied him to check her dressings, feed her a thin broth, and clean her body.

Or what was left of it.

The train had taken off her legs high on the shins. Yet when she awoke she saw that her legs were shorter still. Even the knees were gone.

The horror of the violation drove a hot spike into her heart. Her tears evaporated from the heat of her anger before they could run onto her cheeks. Her rage was too great for words. And so she did not speak, not to the boy who gave her water, nor to the woman who tended her.

They did not seem to mind. They spoke neither to her nor to each other in her presence, although she heard voices speaking Castalan when they left the hut. She heard other voices as well, men, women, and children. She saw none of them until the sawbones visited.

He was a pale man with limp yellow hair and white stubble for a beard, but he spoke to the others in what sounded like perfect Castalan. When he spoke to Pei Pei in that language, she shook her head until he introduced himself simply as Doc.

In Sevenfork, there had never been a need to understand Castalan. Most of what Pei Pei had learned were swears coaxed out of Kong-sang. The thought of her dead brother cracked something that had hardened inside her. For the first time in memory she wept.

Doc did not touch her, but he lay his hand within reach of hers. He was missing two fingers. For a moment she almost took ruined hand, but instead she tried to calm her racing heart while he examined the stumps of her legs. Instead of the seared meat left by Bloor's irons, she saw tidy stitches on either side of her legs. She could feel another line beneath, where the surgeon had folded her skin over like the end of a gift-wrapped present.

He'd had to amputate the stumps, Doc explained, because the flesh had gone sour. The alternative was to let the rot climb up her legs until it took the rest of her as well. He was sorry, he said, but he'd meant only to save her life. His apology sounded like a speech he'd had occasion to practice.

The good news, he told her, was that her fever had passed. He was afraid she'd been poisoned, too, judging from the snake bites he'd found. How she'd survived those he could not explain. In fact, he said, he couldn't understand how she'd survived any of her ordeal—the amputation, the thirst and deprivation, or the trampling of a grep stampede. A groepero from the village found her in the herd's wake. He'd meant to fetch her body for burial and nearly died of shock when he heard her speak.

Pei Pei asked Doc what she'd said.

Just one word, said Doc. "Denson."

When she was alone, Pei Pei listened to the sounds outside. From a distant building she heard a clamor and guessed it came from a smithy. Sometimes she heard a whistle or the clatter of metal plates. Other times she heard the grunts of men laboring. She couldn't imagine what kind of labor it must be, but the rhythmic clack of wood made her drowsy.

Mostly, she slept. That was all for the good, said Doc as he felt her wrist to measure the pulse of her heartbeat. Most healing comes from sleep, he said. When he left, Pei Pei noticed for the first time a pair of wooden blocks resting beside the rattan chair. Affixed to each was a sturdy handle wrapped in thick cotton. They were like no tool she had seen before. She wondered whether Doc, the boy, or the woman had left them.

No one else visited her, but Pei Pei regained enough strength to sit up during the day. Through the window of her room she could see at least four other buildings nearby, as well as a screw-driven well drawn by a scabby burro led by the boy. Pei Pei heard the others call him to other chores. Beto was his name.

Most of the villagers appeared to be farmers, but the brown fields beyond the farther house suggested they eked out a meager existence that way. A few men rode out in the morning. Sometimes they returned with a grep or two. Pei Pei watched Doc slaughter and drain them of blood, which he captured in milk cans. Afterward, two women blanched the carcass before separating the hide and butchering the meat.

The rest of the day was filled with routine work, except for a few hours at midday when everyone retreated to shelter for a rest. It was after sundown that the village truly came to life.

Beto was always the first to arrive. He brought the mariachi's guitar, almost too large for him to carry, and laid it reverently beside the low stone wall ringing the fire pit. Sometimes he led the mariachi to the fire, lit a cigar from the flames, and placed it in the man's mouth. Other times he stood upon the low clay wall and shouted, "Erasmo! Erasmo!" until the man appeared.

At a nod from Erasmo, the boy removed the guitar from its case and settled it across his knees. His fingers were too short to span the fret, but he could manage two strings at a time. Erasmo offered instructions, and the boy formed a few simple chords. When Erasmo was satisfied, he spat out the cigar and whistled the melody to Beto's accompaniment.

The villagers arrived as soon as their chores allowed. The men came first, sharing cigars and passing a jug until the women arrived. Most nights, the other strangers joined them one by one. They were the ones that fascinated Pei Pei.

The Widow always arrived alone, her face veiled beneath a black tasseled hat. She walked with the stately care of a matron arriving at her own centennial. No matter the temperature, she wore spidery black lace from head to toe, except for the ivory colored fan that dangled from her wrist. She never spoke above a murmur, but Pei Pei judged by the smooth skin of her hands that she was not old.

No one dared sit near her, except Invincible Tsau. Whenever the widow arrived, Tsau stood and doffed his well-worn hat. Beneath its brim, something glimmered bright in the firelight. He often spoke too loud, but not in anger. Even though no one else came armed to the fire, he kept a rifle near to hand. It was the most splendid weapon Pei Pei had ever seen. Upon its stock she saw the famous Twin Eagle embossed in nickel.

Usually there was no sign of the Tinker, but those nights when he appeared were the loudest. He stood barely taller than Beto, although his green stovepipe hat gave him almost another foot in height. Beneath the curling brim, yellowed gray tufts of hair curled up in all directions. When he doffed his hat, Pei Pei saw scars on the bald top his misshapen head. When the Tinker spoke, she couldn't understand a word he said. He jabbered and howled, but the others responded as though he'd said sensible words—a few of which did slip from his tongue from time to time. One slug of whisky was all it took to set him capering to the music.

Erasmo soon joined the Tinker. The first time he stood to dance and his serape stirred, Pei Pei realized he too was an amputee. His arms had been severed between the shoulder and elbow. Seeing his injury made Pei Pei's stumps ache.

The mariachi's lack of arms did not diminish his grace. He stamped the ground, turned and stood at perfect attention. His gaze slid over the faces of the audience, his eyes lingering on the women until they giggled and turned away. Then his feet exploded in a complex rhythm while his body barely moved. Slowly his body turned while the patter of his feet outraced Beto's guitar.

The others clapped, cheering the dancers until the first song was done. Then the villagers joined them, dancing and singing around the fire while Pei Pei remained outside the circle of light and laughter.

203

At first she pitied herself, trapped in bed without the legs she used to have. Then she realized she was not alone in. Even before Erasmo, she had seen amputees before. Most were men who clutched bricks on which they walked with their hands. The pitiful things dragged their stumps along the boards, begging for bits or food or a drink of whisky.

Pei Pei finally recognized the blocks for what they were. She could grasp the handles and pull herself along like those crippled men. Nobody had the guts to tell her so, or mabye they had been left there as a cruel joke.

No, that did not seem right. The people who looked in on her had shown her only kindness. Nothing about it seemed pitying, either. Pei Pei thought of how the old Doc had stopped himself from taking her hand but left his nearby there in case she chose to take it.

Much as she longed to sit beside the fire, Pei Pei could not bring herself to crawl. She did not want the others looking at her the way she had looked at those crippled men.

She wondered why no one offered to carry her out. No one even asked whether she wanted to join them. Instead, they left those blocks. Maybe they hadn't wanted to offer her a hand that she might strike away in pride. Instead, they had left one nearby. It was up to her to choose whether to take it.

She threw the sheet off and looked at her ruined body. The absence of legs no longer shocked her, but her thinness did. She feared she would not have the strength to stand after leaving the bed. But she reminded herself she had crawled halfway across Thousand Mesas, or so it felt. In truth she had no idea how far she was from Presteign's dig.

She raised herself up on her hands—there was still some strength in her arms—and pushed her thighs over the side of the bed. Trying to lower herself onto the floor, she slipped and fell hard upon her stumps. The pain dazed her, but the heat that flushed her face was not from despair. It was anger. There was a fury engine inside her, as surely as there was one somewhere beneath the dig.

Pei Pei dragged herself over to the blocks and pulled them down from the chair. She set them on either side of her and gripped them as she might handle the bar at Madame Beauvais' studio. She raised herself up, shifted her weight, and stepped forward with her right hand.

It was easier than she'd feared, but her strength waned. The extra height she gained from the blocks was all she needed to walk without crawling. Even so, with her weight on her arms, every step felt a hundred times harder than it had legs. Every time she moved forward, just a few inches, she reminded herself she had crawled much farther without the blocks.

As she emerged from the hut, no one by the fire noticed her. She hesitated for a moment, afraid of seeing pity or disgust as they turned to see a freak approach. Then she saw Erasmo' gaze lock as he twirled in place. Each time his head whipped around, his eyes found hers. His chin rose as he saw her coming, not in a disdainful gesture but in one that Pei Pei had seen far too rarely.

Erasmo looked at her with admiration.

His approval sped her gait. As her walking block touched the first stone around the fire pit, the Widow turned her head. She did not look directly at Pei Pei—indeed, Pei Pei could not imagine how the woman could see through such a thick veil even in daylight.

Invincible Tsau noticed her next, already smiling as he turned to look at her. He did not offer her a hand, as a gallant should, but with a bow he surrendered his seat for her. Pei Pei struggled to pull herself onto the wall.

As if that motion was their cue, all the people turned their full attention to Pei Pei.

"We are so happy you chose to join us," said the Widow. Her voice was softer than the breeze, warmer than the fire.

"Everyone here has good reason to hate Presteign," said Erasmo. He looked longingly at the cigars that lay beside him, but the boy had long since gone to bed.

Pei Pei took a cigar and placed it between his lips.

"I can guess your offense," the mariachi said to her. "For punching a guard, they let the train take my arms."

Invincible Tsau lit Erasmo's cigar. "I overheard Bloor talking with Presteign."

Not for the first time, the Widow laid a hand on Tsau's arm. The rifleman lowered his voice whenever she reminded him, but invariably his volume rose as he became excited. "They do not care so much about the airship itself but about its weapons. I tried to learn more by asking the other prisoners."

Doc nodded as if to confirm the tale.

"Another prisoner told Denson I was asking questions. Presteign decided I'd heard enough for one lifetime." Tsau cupped his shriveled ears. "Steam whistle on either side, all day long. In my head, the whistle never stopped. I thank the heavens that it did not drive me mad."

"No such luck for the Tinker," said Doc. He indicated the little man lying beside the fire, arms curled around a whisky jug. "He was one of Presteign's men, until he refused to build a collar to shock the prisoners. They put his head in a vice. Funny thing is, they didn't squeeze out all of his wits. He's the one who freed Tsau and the Widow, because the guards considered him harmless."

"Harmless enough," said Doc, stretching his remaining fingers. "Long as you keep him away from the dynamite."

The Tinker made a sound in his sleep and stirred like a dog dreaming of a chase. Doc took the opportunity to retrieve the whisky jug from the little man's arms.

Pei Pei turned to the woman in black. She noticed that the Widow's hat matched the mariachi's cape, although it suited her black lace gown well enough. "What did Presteign take from you?"

"My eyes," she said in a husky whisper.

"How can that be? You walk without a cane," said Pei Pei. "You saw me when I came out of the hut."

"No," said the Widow. She reached beneath her veil as if to remove a necklace. Instead she withdrew a strange apparatus of bone and wire. "I *heard* you. While wearing this device, I could hear you breathing even before you left your bed."

"The Tinker works wonders," said Erasmo.

Pei Pei pointed at Tsau, noticing that he looked at her mouth as she spoke. "You also turned as I approached. If Presteign had you deafened, how did you hear me?"

"I did not hear you," Tsau grinned and tilted his hat back. Pei Pei saw a pair of curving mirrors affixed to the brim. "I *saw* you."

"But how can this Tinker be so clever? He acts like a little child."

"Yes," said Erasmo. "But also sometimes no. He may behave like a child, but he likes to play, too. And he likes to win."

"Just don't let him play with dynamite," grumbled Doc. He tipped the jug over his shoulder and took a swig.

Tsau nodded. "The Tinker saw that I had taken to turning my head all the time, to see behind me what I could no longer hear." His voice grew loud again, and the Widow nudged him. "He said I could use some eyes in the back of my head. When I told him that's exactly what I needed, he came back a few days later with these mirrors for my hat. Now I don't even need to turn my head to know someone's sneaking up on me."

The queer wonder of it all caught Pei Pei's breath. While it was marvelous that the Tinker had helped these other crippled people, it wasn't enough.

"Why has no one told the marshals that Presteign is capturing all these people to use as slaves?"

Doc shook his head. "The marshals work for men like Presteign. They serve the powerful, not the weak."

"But what about the Twin Eagles?" said Pei Pei. She looked at Tsau, who cocked his head. She repeated the question, and he saw what she said.

"First thing I did when I could ride again was report to the

Aagency," he said. "The trouble is that no one can hire the Agency for such a risky operation. Even if all the families of all the people he's kidnapped pooled their money, it wouldn't be enough to persuade the Agency to go up against a man like that. For even suggesting it, I put myself out of a job. All I could get out of them was a new rifle before they cut me loose."

"And yet you came back here," said Pei Pei. "Why?"

"From what we can understand from the Tinker, it won't be much longer before Presteign finishes his operation," said Doc. "Once he can fly off in his airship, he'll have what he came for. He'll have no more use for his prisoners."

"He'll kill them all," said the Widow. "And knowing Presteign, he will do so in the cruelest manner possible."

"Until then, we remain here and hope one day enough of Presteign's prisoners will escape that we can turn them against him," said Doc.

"One day? Hope?" said Pei Pei. "Every one of us is miracle simply because we survived. How many folks will die while we wait for them to escape?"

"What are you saying?" said Doc. Pei Pei sensed mockery in his voice.

"I'm saying—" It was too absurd to consider. Apart from the villagers, they had a blind woman, a deaf gunslinger, an armless mariachi, an insane dwarf, and a legless dancer.

"Go on," said Erasmo.

"Someone must say it," said the Widow. "No one has had the courage to say it."

Pei Pei looked back at Doc. In his eyes was a twinkle, but it wasn't full of mockery as she'd first through. It was a gleam of hope.

"I say we go back to the dig. I say we free everybody."

"And when Presteign and his men try to stop us?"

"We exert a little discipline."

It was Pei Pei's turn to mind the Tinker. Doc was serious about taking turns keeping the odd little man away from the dynamite he'd smuggled out of Presteign's dig.

"The little fellow can do marvelous things with the few scrap parts we've found in the area," said Doc. "And sometimes he needs a little boom powder to make 'em work. But we got to keep track of the powder less he were to leave something dangerous lying around."

They sat just outside the workshop, watching the Tinker through open panels that let a breeze pass through the cluttered interior. The little man smoothed a length of wood with a carpenter's plane. He blew away the curling scraps, measured the thickness with a pair of calipers, and set the wood aside. For a moment he appeared confused. He checked his watched, peered out at the sun, and waddled over to a worktable to inspect a regiment of screws, washers, and bolts organized in ranks by size.

"What is he doing?" Pei Pei whispered.

Doc tongued the wad of tobacco to a new position in his cheek. "Sometimes he forgets what he's doing, moves on to another project, maybe three or four others, before remembering the first one."

"Why don't you remind him?"

"Don't help," said Doc. "Confuses him all the worse, more often than not. Best to let him take his own path, meandering as it may be."

"He seems so gentle. It is hard to imagine he was working for Presteign."

"That gentleness could be why they butted heads. From as much as I can understand of the Tinker's stories, I reckon the weapons on the ship Presteign's after were something special. Some Steam Baron had it built a few years back. Spent half his fortune, but it got the job done. Still, the other Steam Barons had their spies on this fellow. When they heard what he'd made, they tried to buy it from him. When he wouldn't sell, they sent their own ships to steal or destroy it before he could turn it against them." He turned his head and spat. Pei Pei grimaced, remembering the last time a man spat so close to her. Doc paused, noticing her expression. He shook his head and didn't ask about it. "Anyhoo, I get the impression this particular airship was armed with some kind of lighting cannon. Heavenly powerful. Like whatever it was burned down Diamond Spur."

Pei Pei shivered in the afternoon heat. She'd heard the legend of Silas Lash, greatest of all Engineers, one of the Peerless Seven. Whatever the people of Diamond Spur had done to earn his wrath, the city ruins still smoldered thirty years later.

"Then it's even more important we stop Presteign before he can use such a weapon."

Doc nodded, but he stared an unspoken question at Pei Pei.

"What?" she said, irritated by his expression.

"Is that your real reason for rounding up this posse?" he said. "Or is it revenge you have in mind?"

"You think I just want to kill Presteign because of what he did to me?"

"Maybe," said Doc. "But it wasn't his name you said when that groepero picked you up."

Pei Pei bit back her reply. Denson was the name she wanted to spit on the ground.

The Widow walked along one side of the target room, little more than a roof on four posts with a single wall lined with straw dummies. Invincible Tsau pulled a string, ringing a bell above the third target.

The Widow flicked her fan. A steel dart quivered in the ring around the bull's eye.

Pei Pei shook her head. She was no longer surprised to see the Widow strike her target, but the accuracy still astonished her. More than that, her constant poise inspired an unexpected pang of envy. Despite the woman's disfigurement, her husky voice and assured demeanor charmed the men. At first Pei Pei assumed the Widow had accepted Tsau as her courtier. If true, that did nothing to stop the other men from doting on her.

Pei Pei felt ugly as she followed the Widow on her crude "shoes." A few weeks earlier, someone replaced the wooden blocks with bricks. It was a struggle moving them the first few days, but she grew stronger. The trick, she learned, was not gripping the handles too tightly. Instead, she balanced her weight on each palm, fingers loose around the grip.

Sometimes Pei Pei resented the devices the Tinker made for the others. When she asked why the Tinker had given her the marvelous fan as well as the hearing device hidden beneath her veil, the Widow smiled and opened the fan to reveal its colorful face. Painted upon the silk was a scene of imperial courtesans lounging beside a willow-steeped pool.

"This heirloom has been passed down among the women of my order since the time of Chessa By Damn."

"You're a Foxglove woman!" Pei Pei had read countless stories about the mysterious order of female assassins.

The Widow nodded. "I was sent to spy on Presteign. Before I could get close enough, one of his men intercepted my orders. They were encoded, but Bloor deciphered them."

Pei Pei didn't need to hear the rest to know Presteign decided the Widow would read no more messages.

Outside the village, Tsau took aim at a distant cactus. He fired, but Pei Pei saw no impact.

She held herself up on the twin rails of the nearby fence. At the Tinker's direction, Tsau and a couple of the village men had rebuilt them as a pair of parallel bars. Using her hands to walk their length, Pei Pei could build her arm strength while becoming as nimble on her hands as she'd been on her feet.

Erasmo stepped in front of the rifleman and shook his head. "The wind shifted." Tsau stared at him, so he repeated the words.

"Oh," said Tsau, watching Erasmo's mouth. He scooped up a handful of dust and observed how it spilled through his fingers. "There are so many ways to listen," he shouted. "It is harder now for me to understand why some people choose not to hear. The Agency, for instance. They could do something about Presteign, but all they hear is money."

Pei Pei swung beneath one of the bars, folding herself over the next and letting her momentum bring her all the way around to perch atop them.

"What were you doing at Presteign's dig, anyway?" She winced when she realized she was shouting.

"I was searching for a missing family," Tsau yelled back. Erasmo nudged his foot, and Tsau lowered his voice. "Found 'em."

He fired again. A bud the size of a man's ear flew off the cactus.

Erasmo fought the wooden dummy. To Pei Pei, it looked more like a hat rack than a person. Erasmo kicked each of the limbs as quickly as she could have struck them with her fists. She had seen him kick a target a foot above his head without leaping. He hit each limb of the dummy too quickly for her eyes to follow. He repeated the pattern three times before changing the order of his routine.

"You could have been a dancer," said Pei Pei.

"I am a dancer. Both a lover and a fighter, as the young men say." said Erasmo. His smile faded beneath his pencil-thin mustache, which Pei Pei had seen the boy shave for him. She wondered how old Erasmo was. When he smiled, he looked younger. His eyes reflected the mischief she had so often seen in Kong-sang's eyes.

"I meant, how did you come to be at Presteign's camp?" She thrust her hands into the pot of sand. Her fingers bled less than they had the day before. Her skin was hardening.

Erasmo did not pause in his attacks. He struck the dummy with his toe, his heel, either side of his foot. "My brother Blaz went to work for this man Presteign. Hearing of his reputation, my mother sent me to bring him home."

That morning Pei Pei found her stone shoes missing, replaced with bricks of lead. She could barely move them, grunting with each step toward the other wooden dummy. From the floor, she could attack only its lower half. She began the practice that Tsau and Erasmo had taught her.

"He wouldn't go with you?" she asked. The wooden dummy no longer hurt her hands. She struck harder and harder, her arms stronger than they had ever been.

"He was afraid," said Erasmo. "But I insisted. They stopped us before we could get away, but not before I shot a few of their men."

"That's why they took your hands," said Pei Pei. She looked at her own toughened fists and wondered whether it was worse to be armless than legless. "What happened to your brother?"

Erasmo struck his heel to the ground. A triangular blade snapped forth from the toe of his boot. With a single sweep, he severed two arms from the wooden dummy.

"Those aren't legs," said Pei Pei. She complained to cover her excitement. At last the Tinker had built her new legs.

"Rushing Rabbit!" The Tinker hooted, a smile creasing his whiskers. He waved the metal limbs above his head. The legs were steel arcs composed of shorter tubes interlocking like an armadillo's shell. They did not resemble legs at all. Each looked more like a drooping V with a leather cup and straps on one end. At the joint was a cluster of gears and springs leading to a short cylinder just beneath the hip. With those attached to her stumps, she would indeed resemble a rabbit, at least from the waist down.

"How could I even stand on those?"

The Tinker chortled as he cinched her legs into the cups. He pulled the straps tight enough to make her flinch, but she did not complain.

He stood back and waved his hands. "Hop, hop!"

Pei Pei leaned forward, pushing herself off the high stool in the Tinker's workshop.

The weird legs supported her, even though it took time to adjust to the backward-bending joints. She felt taller than she had before losing her legs. She had to duck her head as she stepped through the door.

"Hop, hop!" cried the Tinker. He slapped his thighs, laughing.

Slowly at first, and then with increasing confidence, Pei Pei strode beside the village huts. She loosened the dials on her thighs and grew taller still, the legs expanding as she moved more quickly. In a moment she stood as tall as a stilt-walker.

"Hop hop!"

The day the Tinker strapped new arms on Erasmo, the cripples began training in earnest. While he could not play the guitar with his mechanical hands, whose fingers were more like metal claws, the mariachi could shatter a fresh timber with one blow or crush an iron pipe.

Pei Pei learned to use her rabbit's legs. When she gradually turned the dials on the thighs, she could release the springs until she stood over eight feet tall. Then her stride was yards long, and she could outrun the swiftest of the village horses. With Doc to translate the Tinker's instructions, she learned to tighten the dials just enough to let her weight press down on the springs and return her to her normal height. When she saw the mad engineer slapping his thighs, she did the same. The spring legs threw her high in the air. She struggled to turn, but she crashed onto the roof of a nearby house. If she had been going any faster, she might have leaped all the way over and broken her neck as she hit the ground. Erasmo and Doc ran over to help her down, but the Tinker danced a little jig and cheered, "Hop, hop!"

Every week or so, Tsau borrowed a spyglass from the Tinker's workshop and rode northeast to spy on the dig, returning a few days later. Two months after Pei Pei's arrival in the village, Tsau reported that Presteign's people had begun covering the airship's superstructure.

"How long before the ship can fly?" asked Pei Pei.

The Tinker leaped up growling. Twice he pounced on some imaginary prey and snapped his teeth as it escaped him. Then he paused to consider before spreading the fingers of both hands, then four more fingers. With a grimace, he opened up his thumb for a fifth finger, then bobbed his head dubiously as he raised three more on his other hand, one at a time.

Doc began to explain, but Pei Pei understood the pantomime. "Two weeks," she said, thinking of the time it took Night Wolf to catch up to Rushing Rabbit. "Maybe a little more."

The Tinker whooped approval of her translation.

"Ha!" Tsau pointed at Pei Pei's legs. "Now that he has turned you into the rabbit, you understand his language."

Erasmo passed the spyglass to Pei Pei. She peered through it to see the guard patrolling the perimeter. Like a puppet, his silhouette was stark black against the lights illuminating the airship's belly. He stopped for a second, whipping around as if he'd heard a sound. Whatever he saw caused him to relax, and Pei Pei spied the unmistakable outline of the Widow. The man strode toward her, reaching for her arm. The Widow's fan snapped open to tickle the man beneath the chin. It snapped it shut again and the guard fell to his knees, clutching his throat.

"That's four," said Erasmo. He whistled. "That woman, how formidable she is."

Pei Pei passed the spyglass to Invincible Tsau, slapping it against his shoulder with more force than she'd intended.

"You are also very—"

Pei Pei silenced him by lifting her chin, offended at the suggestion that her pride needed mollifying, but also embarrassed that she had once again let slip her growing jealousy of the Widow. No matter how horribly she had been disfigured, the mystery of the woman's veil preserved her beauty in the men's imagination. Thanks to her new legs, Pei Pei looked like a tall, skinny rabbit.

"Time to move," said Tsau. He lifted his rifle. "I will cover you."

Pei Pei was glad he had remembered to keep his voice low. The rifleman had been anxious both because the Widow had been elected to eliminate the guards and because he was to be last to enter the compound. Once he began firing, the time for surprise was past.

Pei Pei touched Doc on the shoulder. "Get the Tinker to the gondola as soon as we clear a path. He has to stop that thing from using its weapon."

Doc took the Tinker by the arm and nodded.

Pei Pei tightened the dials on her legs. Speed was less important than quiet, at least until they reached the barracks. At their shortest, her mechanical legs barely creaked when she walked.

The inflated airship blotted out the stars over the dig site. Both of the moons had run behind it, both the dark mass of Night Wolf and the misshapen white Rushing Rabbit. From below the light of campfires illuminated the airship's gondola. Blue-white light flickered from its portholes, and through the wide glass canopy Pei Pei saw the shadows of men moving inside the bridge.

They dashed down the slope beside the barracks, pausing to listen for the snores. They jammed wedges beneath the door, knowing they would only slow any response to an alarm. Pei Pei glanced at Erasmo, who nodded. Their next move would trigger that alarm.

They sprinted toward the slave pen, patrolled by armed guards. The nearest one saw them while they were still forty yards away.

He raised his rifle. "Hey!"

The man fell backward. An instant later, Pei Pei heard the crack of Tsau's rifle far behind them. That was more than enough to wake the camp.

Pei Pei dialed out her mechanical legs, darting forward to reach the gate just as the next shots rang out. One stirred the dust at Erasmo's feet. Another tugged his cape to the side, but he kept running.

Shifting her weight, Pei Pei shortened her legs and dialed them tight. She kicked through the stout beam of the pen. A second later, Erasmo arrived and chopped through another span of timbers.

"Get up, all of you," Pei Pei shouted at the prisoners. She pointed to the sound of Tsau's steady rifle shots. "Run this way. Our friends will cover your escape."

After a moment's hesitation, they obeyed. When a frightened man ran to the front, pushing aside a teenage boy, Erasmo snarled at him. "Help the women and children."

The man balked until he saw the steel glint on Erasmo's fist. Then he did as he was told.

Tsau's rifle continued its deadly cadence. Guards from the far side of the pen returned fire. The barracks door burst open to release a mob of groggy men in long underwear. The first fell to Tsau's fire. Another died as they surged back inside for cover.

The last of the prisoners emerged from the pen when a voice called out behind them, "Hold it right there."

Pei Pei turned to see one of the men who'd dragged her to the rails. She didn't know his name, but she'd never forget his face.

"You!" He hesitated a moment after recognizing her. An instant later, his eyes widened further. The tip of his rifled bobbed down as his arms trembled and slackened.

Erasmo lunged forward and grabbed the man's gun, his steel claws crushing the barrel. Still the guard stood dazed.

Erasmo regarded Pei Pei. "So formidable you appear."

Before Pei Pei could object, a shadow emerged from behind the guard. The Widow jabbed another needle dart into the guard's neck. He stiffened and fell flat on the ground.

Erasmo's regard shifted to the Widow as he bowed toward her.

"Presteign is in the airship." She scanned the dig, spotting several places where the guards took cover from Tsau's fire. One group seemed to realize they faced only a lone attacker. They took turns moving one at a time toward the next shelter while the others fired in Tsau's direction.

"Where is the Tinker?" asked the Widow.

He should have reached the scaffold by now, Pei Pei thought. But she saw no sign of the little man or Doc.

"There," said Erasmo, pointing with his metal hand.

Pei Pei saw them running hunched over from the direction of the powder shack. The Tinker carried a bundle under each arm. Doc's eyes were wide with fear as they hustled toward the scaffold.

"That was not the plan," said Erasmo.

"We have to clear the way for them."

As they reached the scaffold, men emerged from the gondola. One of them was Denson. Erasmo called out at the sight of the other one.

"Blaz! Come home with me."

Blaz hesitated.

"You said you killed him," growled Denson. He drew his own pistol and pointed it at Blaz's head. "Do it now."

Blaz drew his gun. He pointed it downward, its muzzle wavering between Erasmo, Pei Pei, and the Widow.

"Shoot him!" howled Denson. He cocked his pistol.

Pei Pei crouched, slapped both of her leg dials, and leaped. She soared past the first three levels of the scaffold, angling to intercept the gunmen on the fourth.

Too late.

Blaz fired twice. Down below, Erasmo threw himself in front of the Widow, shielding her with his body. He fell, and she dropped to her knees beside him, her hands searching for wounds.

Denson tried to turn his gun from Blaz to Pei Pei, but she hit him first. They tumbled together on the platform, long legs tangling beneath her. They remained stretched out to their full extension because she hadn't landed on her feet.

After a moment's wonder at her strange legs, a fierce grin creased Denson's jaws as he recognized his attacker. He pointed his gun at Pei Pei's face. She grabbed his wrist. When he felt her strength, his smile faded. His other hand snaked up and caught her by the throat, squeezing her windpipe shut.

"CAST OFF!" boomed a voice inside the canopy. Even distorted by the mechanism increasing its volume, Pei Pei recognized Presteign's voice.

"Not yet, damn you," grunted Denson.

Pei Pei grabbed his strangling hand but lost control of his gun hand. They struggled for a moment before Denson got his knee up and knocked the breath from her lungs. She faltered. He kicked again, throwing her back to fall on the iron scaffold.

"Stand away from her, Denson!"

Bloor called out from a turret in the airship. He gripped the handles of a cannon, a shining steel sphere with a conical barrel enmeshed by copper wire. He pointed the apparatus at Pei Pei, who smelled the unmistakable odor of a coming storm. Bloor kicked a pedal. A keening whine grew louder and higher as blue-white sparks danced along the coils.

"Wait!" shouted Denson. "Don't leave me down here."

Pei Pei closed her eyes against the flash. She kicked back, scrabbling away from the impact. The blast jerked her legs up, flipping her across the scaffold. She crashed against the rails, dazed and blinded.

When her sight returned she saw the white edges of a hole burned through the upper platform. Her metal legs glowed red, and she felt the searing heat of them even through the leather harness. She grabbed the dials at her hips, but they were too hot to touch. She was trapped by her own legs, floundering on the iron platform.

Above them, the vast airship moved. Its crew had already released the other moorings, but one remained bound to the scaffold.

On the other side of the molten gap, Denson cringed away from the heat. When he spied Pei Pei, he bent to retrieve his fallen pistol.

"RELEASE THAT MOORING, DENSON."

The scaffold listed to the side. Pei Pei grabbed hold of the rail while Denson scrambled for his gun.

Behind her, two men dropped onto the scaffold from a rope ladder hanging from one of the canopy windows. One cried out and fell to a gunshot. Another shot pinged off the scaffold as the second man drew and crouched for cover.

Pei Pei glanced down to see that Tsau had run into the open for a clear shot at the men on the scaffold. He drew a bead on the second man behind her. Before he could fire, a volley of shots rang out from the barracks. The first spoiled his aim. The second struck the mirrored hat from his head. The rest knocked him to the ground.

The gunman near her paused to enjoy a look at Tsau's fate. Pei Pei grabbed his gunbelt, pulling him down even as she pulled herself up, and punched him hard in the throat. The man choked and lost his grip on the pistol. Pei Pei struck it from his hand, then jerked him to the side to throw him over. He tumbled over the railing, his weight sending the scaffold listing to the side as the molten hole parted the upper platform.

"Are you all right?"

Pei Pei nearly lashed out before she recognized Doc's voice. He crawled onto the remains of the platform, pressing both hands to the wobbling platform to keep his balance.

"Where's the Tinker?" she asked.

Doc looked up. Pei Pei saw the rope ladder shake and imagined the little man's round bottom disappearing into the portal a moment earlier.

Another shot, and Doc clutched his belly. She whirled back to see Denson aiming his pistol at her.

Another crackling beam struck inches away from Pei Pei. She

reached for Doc, but he had already fallen away. She watched in horror as his body plunged down, striking a rail on the second level, then hitting the ground near Erasmo and the Widow.

Pei Pei felt the Fury engine in her own heart. She heard the whine of Bloor's lightning cannon and saw Denson raise his gun for another shot. She could not retract her legs, but she could still use her arms. She pushed herself off the platform as Denson fired again. She grasped the iron railing and swung to the level below.

Hand over hand she went, her long legs scraping the platform below her. Denson fired. His shot ricocheted off an iron post a few feet away.

The lightning beam sputtered and blasted its way through the iron above her. It spat chunks of glowing metal to the ground, and thunder shook the scaffold. Denson shouted at Bloor. The snap and hiss continued a second longer. The scaffold bent deeper, a willow bowing to the storm.

"No!" cried Erasmo.

Pei Pei looked down to see him pushing the Widow away, encouraging her to flee before the scaffold fell on them.

She heard the charging whine of the lightning cannon and looked up. Denison climbed up the last mooring line up to the gondola. From the gun turret, Bloor turned the cannon toward her. He didn't leer like the other men. Instead, he clamped his jaw shut in an expression of determination at odds with his comical attire.

A single shot cracked, and the monocle shattered. A red tear oozed out beneath the shattered glass as the man tumbled backward, out of sight.

Even riddled with bullets, Tsau made the perfect shot. His legs lay motionless, but he crawled toward the Widow and Erasmo.

Pei Pei released her grip on the scaffold and fell down beside them. The metal of her legs complained as the shafts drove back into place. She felt the click of the dials on her hips. Looking back up at Denison, she knew she could make the jump. Her legs could carry her all the way up to her revenge.

But to do that she would have to leave the others to die.

She pulled the Widow to her feet. "Help me carry him."

They reached for Erasmo, but he shook his head. "I can move," he said. "Help Tsau."

Pei Pei could not understand how he had survived the gunshots until she saw his metal arm. Imbedded at the wrist and elbow were the flatted slugs from his brother's gun.

They ran until the force of the collapsing scaffold threw them to the ground. Molten fragments rained around them. Pei Pei raised her metal legs to shield Erasmo, who covered her with his steel arms. When the storm ended, they looked up to see Tsau and the Widow sheltering each other.

"We can't leave," said Pei Pei. "Presteign is still up there."

"She is right," said the Widow. "There is no hope of the prisoners' escaping that cannon."

As if the man had heard her words, the airship bobbed free of the scaffold. Pei Pei saw Presteign behind the wide viewport of the bridge. She could no longer hear his voice, but she saw him shouting at Denson, who ran to take over the gun turret. He turned it toward them.

They took shelter behind the barracks, where the confused guards had ceased shooting and began shouting at the airship not to abandon them.

The next blast of the lightning gun silenced their cries as it blew the barracks to flaming splinters. A few survivors ran from the smoldering wreckage, cursing. Presteign wanted no survivors knowing where he had taken the airship with its terrible weapons.

"Run!" cried Erasmo.

Pei Pei could not move. She stared at the rising airship. The distance made the men inside look like toy manikins through the window of a dollhouse, but she saw Presteign recoil at something behind him. He backed toward her until stopped by the viewport glass. A green stovepipe hat bobbed into view. Pei Pei barely glimpsed the Tinker's grin as he weighed a bundle of dynamite in either hand.

The airship explosion left them all blind, deaf, unable to walk or even drag their bodies away from the burning pit that had become Presteign's grave. After what seemed like hours, a few of the bolder prisoners returned for food and water.

Of those who had escaped the dig and come back to release the others, only the cripples survived. Invincible Tsau had lived up to his name. That miracle was some solace, but Pei Pei could not help thinking of the ones they lost.

She might never meet another Engineer clever enough to rebuild such rabbit legs, but that didn't matter. With or without legs, Doc and the Tinker taught her to walk. They were the parents of her second life.

Eventually they gathered most of the prisoners together and led them back to the village. Promises of rewards inspired the groeperos to act as messengers, and within a week the first of the coaches arrived to take the survivors home. A few were wealthy enough to make arrangements for the others, at least after Erasmo had a quiet conversation with those who balked at the idea. One was grateful enough to bestow cash reward on their rescuers. With her share, Pei Pei knew she could start a new life in Sedoa or Sevenfork. Neither of those choices appealed.

"Where will the rest of you go?" she asked the others.

Erasmo carefully plucked the cigar from his mouth and held it in his left hand. The right no longer worked since the bullet had struck the mechanism. "I know I should visit my mother's home," he said. "But I do not have the heart to tell her what became of Blaz."

Invincible Tsau turned back to see that Erasmo was talking. Since losing the mirrored hat, he had taken to glancing over his shoulder regularly. Pei Pei repeated her question.

"I don't expect the Agency wants anything to do with me after this mess," he said.

"The Society would make a place for me," said the Widow. "And yet

I do not think I would find it comfortable."

"Then it's settled," said Pei Pei.

"What do you mean?" asked Erasmo.

"You're coming with me."

"But where?" said Invincible Tsau.

Pei Pei smiled. If Doc and the Tinker were her second parents, these were her brothers and sisters.

"When I fell, you helped me stand," she said, thinking of all the other places that could use a hand from a group of determined cripples. "Now it's time to take a walk."

Dave Gross is the author of about half a dozen fantasy novels, including Black Wolf and Lord of Stormweather for the Forgotten Realms, and Prince of Wolves and Master of Devils for Pathfinder. He lives in Alberta, Canada.

FAR 遠西 WEST

FICTION, GAMES, ART, MOBILE APPLICATIONS, WEBSERIES AND MORE~

START THE JOURNEY AT
INTOTHEFARWEST.COM